THE DARK DEEPS

THE HUNCHBACK
ASSIGNMENTS
2

ARTHUR SLADE

THE DARK DEEPS

THE HUNCHBACK ASSIGNMENTS
2

WENDY
LAMB
BOOKS

All rights reserved. Published in the United States by Wendy Lamb Books,
an imprint of Random House Children's Books, a division of
Random House, Inc., New York. Originally published in Canada
by HarperCollins Publishers Ltd., Toronto.

Wendy Lamb Books and the colophon are trademarks
of Random House, Inc.

Visit us on the Web! www.randomhouse.com/teens
Educators and librarians, for a variety of teaching tools, visit us at
www.randomhouse.com/teachers

Library of Congress Cataloging-in-Publication Data is available upon
request.
ISBN 978-0-385-73785-2 (hc)
ISBN 978-0-385-90695-1 (lib. bdg.)
ISBN 978-0-375-89740-5 (ebook)

The text of this book is set in 11.5-point Transitional 521.
Book design by Vikki Sheatsley

Printed in the United States of America
10 9 8 7 6 5 4 3 2 1
First U.S. Edition

FOR TORI,
with all my love

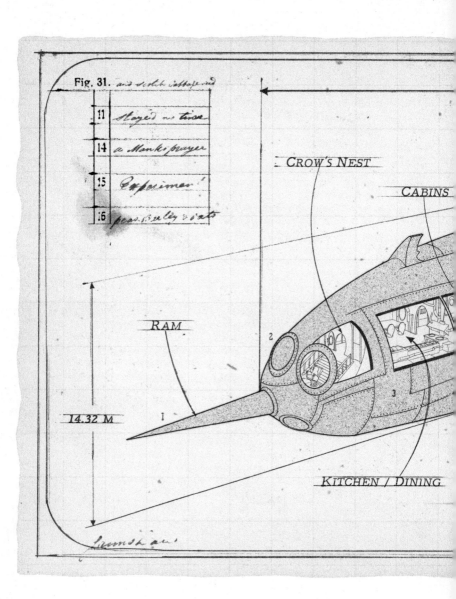

Fig. 31. *and scribble written*

11	*played no tricks*
14	*a Monk's prayer*
15	*Experiment*
16	*peas, Barley & oats*

CROW'S NEST

CABINS

RAM

2

3

14.32 M

I

KITCHEN / DINING

Lumshan

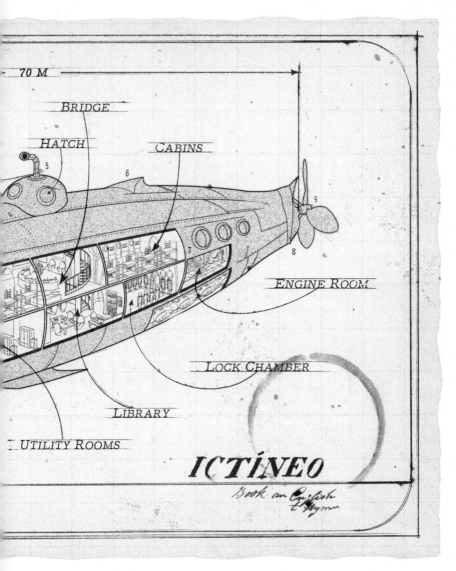

70 M

BRIDGE

HATCH

CABINS

5

6

9

7

8

ENGINE ROOM

LOCK CHAMBER

LIBRARY

UTILITY ROOMS

ICTÍNEO

Book an English

The Yellow Boy

THE BOY HADN'T ALWAYS been yellow. Once he had been lily white, had worn cravats and fancy shoes instead of rags. But that was before he was brought to this island to help the old doctor with his work; before the salt pills, the elixirs, the teaspoons and teaspoons of ingestible compounds, and the horrible injections. It was only after the first year in the employ of the doctor, his eleventh year of life, that the boy understood that he was the subject of a long-term experiment.

The boy often dreamed of his mum and father arriving on a steamship and taking him away from this cruel place. Mum would sing and lull the evil dogs to sleep, their mechanical jaws slowly clanking shut. Father would climb up to the cave, throw the wicked doctor over the cliff, carry the boy to their ship, and steam far, far away.

The boy knew the dream was impossible, since his parents

had drowned in the same shipwreck that had stranded him in this part of the world. The boy had survived because he was small enough to cling to a broken section of the ship's mast and his mum and father had pushed him as far as they could before their bodies weakened. Mum's last words to him were "I love you, dearie," and his father's were "You have a great destiny, Griff, my son." Then the two of them waved goodbye as the boy drifted on.

His "great" destiny was to spend six months surviving on a deserted island, eating berries and other fruit and muttering to himself. He grew thinner as he shivered through the cold nights. His clothes turned to rags and he wore reeds and leaves. And then nothing at all. At least the daylight hours were warm.

Then one day the hounds arrived and pursued him from one end of the island to the other, jaws snapping like traps. Their skulls were made of metal; their eyes reflected fiendish light. They didn't bark or even snarl. They ran with the speed of panthers and the weight of bulls, crashing through brush at his heels and finally cornering him on a rocky cliff. They were soon followed by soldiers in gray, who were just as silent. One grabbed Griff by the hair, dragged him to a steamship. They transported him to a larger island and threw him down at the feet of Dr. Cornelius Hyde. "You asked for a servant," the soldier said. "We have delivered one."

And so that became the boy's role. Hyde rarely spoke to Griff, other than to tell him to fetch powders or scalpels from the shelves or to lug crates of medicines from the docks. Griff learned what he could about the doctor from his rambling and his many rages. Hyde's accent was English. Upper-class. He said he'd been betrayed by "those black-guards at the Society of Science." And Griff had learned that the doctor liked dogs.

The cave was not a pleasant workplace. Chimpanzees trembled in cages. Puppies yipped in boxes. The place reeked of animal excrement. Griff grew used to that, and to sleeping on the straw pallet next to the cages. Slowly his childhood memories of Liverpool, of growing up in a small house that overlooked the bay, were lost to him.

Despite the drudgery, many things captured his fancy. From what he could tell, the island was owned by a man called the Guild Master, who must have been very rich to have his own cannons, steamships, and small army. The soldiers were constructing a massive building at the far end of the island.

What the boy loved most was the airship that returned every few weeks, bringing the red-haired woman with a metal hand. She was thin and very beautiful, and moved with animal grace. She was powerful, he knew by the way she carried herself, and by the way the soldiers saluted her. Her accent was odd; her voice commanded attention, but she sometimes spoke as softly as his mum had. He picked flowers for the woman every time she visited.

"You will grow up to be the greatest man who ever lived," she'd told him during her latest visit. "The good doctor will see to it."

"Yes, this is true," Dr. Hyde said. He was always kinder

when the woman was near. "You shall be the first human to experience a new state, a new form. Now, swallow this sugary treat."

Griff did so. The pill tasted acidic and burned like a hot coal in his stomach. But he didn't wince—he so wanted the woman to see how strong he was.

She gently held his shoulder with her human hand. "One day you'll be so much more than you are now. You must train. You must follow the doctor's advice. And always take your medicines, my dear little Griff."

"I will," he whispered. "For you I will."

That afternoon he watched her stride down to the docks. He didn't return to the cave until her airship had disappeared behind the horizon, even though Dr. Hyde would be angry at his tardiness. Griff wept, knowing it would be weeks before he would see her again.

The medicine burned in his stomach all through the night. In the morning he awoke to find that his skin had turned completely yellow.

He looked at his yellow fingers. Poked at his yellow stomach. "What is my great destiny?" he asked his pillow. "What is it?"

Seven years passed before the answer became clear.

1

Under a Hunter's Moon

The stars saved her life that evening. Colette Chiyoko Brunet was in her cabin aboard the steamship *Vendetta*, seated at a small oak table papered with maps, diagrams, newspaper clippings, and agents' reports. The oil lamp swayed on its chain as each wave struck the ship. In her eighteen years of life she had never had an experience more frustrating than this mission. Even the taunting of her fellow French agents, who called her *la sorcière ainoko*—the half-breed witch—was nothing to what she had undergone this night. They would be snorting derisively now if they knew of her failure.

She glared at the papers: a map with several points ticked off, sailors' accounts of sightings of a sea monster or a giant narwhal, and a pencil drawing of a massive metallic fish with the name *Ictíneo* written below it.

She pressed her fingers against her forehead. What was

the answer? What had been sinking the ships in this quadrant? She wanted to tear the documents to shreds. She had spent two weeks on the *Vendetta,* searching for the "peculiarity" that lurked in the depths. The French government had financed the mission. Ministers believed that the secret of the attacks could unlock some new underwater military weapon for France. Colette had no inkling how they had come to that conclusion. They'd given her a mess of scribbles and madman's tales, nothing more. Did they intend for her to fail?

Calm down. She sat back. Ah, Papa, she thought. Her father had been an artillery captain in the French army and had married her mother, Amaya, during his first visit to Japan. He'd spent his every spare moment training Colette to survive in *un monde sévère,* a harsh world. The analytical lessons and the discipline stuck early, her mind becoming so sharp it cut through most myths and falsifications. Ah, Papa, I am failing tonight.

An overwhelming sadness consumed her when she thought of her father's death in the Boshin War, on Japanese soil. A land that was half hers. She knew he'd be proud of her, of everything she'd done in her short life. She had risen to a prominent position in the world of French secret agents, despite her *ainoko*—half French, half Japanese— blood.

Colette stood. Fresh air and a view of the sky would help her focus. She tied up her black hair, wrapped a long sable coat about herself and opened the metal door to her cabin, then tiptoed past the snuffling and snoring sailors in their bunks. Next to them was a locker of rifles. She gently ran her hand across the stock of the last gun, then climbed the iron stairs.

The November wind chilled and awakened her. The deck was deserted, but there was a light in the bridge and an ember glow from the crow's nest—a cigarette. Colette imagined that the only others who were awake labored in the engine room, feeding coal to the furnaces to keep the steam engines chugging.

She breathed deeply and strode across the deck, grabbed the rope railing, and gazed out over the Atlantic. She smelled the salt water and heard the splashing waves, but the sea was so dark it was as if they were sailing through ink.

On the outside the *Vendetta* looked like a research ship, with the crew dressed as ordinary sailors. Colette knew better. They were marines handpicked from the First Regiment of *L'infanterie de marine*. The rifles were on board in case they had to defend themselves. A ten-pounder gun was hidden under a canvas in the bow of the ship. Hunters had to be prepared to hunt.

She looked to the heavens. Her father had taught her the constellations; she easily picked out *la Grande Ourse*, and was comforted. She relaxed her mind by triangulating her position in the Atlantic. They had spent the past few days zigging and zagging through the same coordinates—her maps had indicated that the "peculiarity" usually appeared here.

Colette leaned against the railing. The darkness reminded her that she was no closer to finding her prey. Tomorrow, the *Vendetta*'s coal stores would be too low for them to sail further and they would have to return to Marseille in failure. Colette would be laughed out of the position she had fought to win. There were always other agents scheming to take her place.

A shattering noise startled her; then she fell hard against the railing, then to the deck, smashing her head. She lay still for a moment, realizing she'd been inches from plunging to a watery death. The Klaxons sounded and she struggled to her feet, but there was something wrong with her legs. No, not her legs—the deck of the *Vendetta* listed sharply toward starboard.

"Helm, hard to starboard!" the captain shouted from the bridge.

My papers! she thought. The deck was at such an angle that she would have to climb toward the stairwell. She took a step, leaning forward; then the ship lurched and she slipped and struck the railing again, jarring her ribs.

"Mademoiselle Brunet, are you hurt?" It was a seaman, one hand on a rope, the other extended toward her. Marlin from Cherbourg. The son of a tailor.

She took his warm hand and stood again. "Did we hit an iceberg?"

"Not at this time of year," he said.

"A naval mine?" She hadn't heard an explosion. "What have we struck?"

"Something struck us," another voice said. She turned to see Chief Petty Officer Fortant, holding his balding head, blood seeping down his left cheek. "The hull has been breached!"

"You're injured!" Colette exclaimed.

"It doesn't matter. We've got to move! We're sinking fast!"

"But I must have my papers!"

"No time!" Fortant replied, pulling her toward the line of lifeboats swinging like pendulums on their davits. "Your papers will go down with the ship."

That gave her some solace; at least no one else would read them. Briefly she thought of the lives lost in retrieving those documents from foreign embassies and enemy agents. Such information always had a price.

The ship made a metallic moaning as it listed further. Sailors leapt into the water from the forecastle. The door on the bridge banged open, revealing the captain holding firmly to the wheel, bellowing orders. What few men were able to climb out of the hold lost their footing on the deck and fell headlong into the water.

Marlin was already lowering a lifeboat.

"Get in!" Fortant shoved Colette into the boat and then he and Marlin tumbled in after her. The boat swung wildly.

"What about the sailors below deck?"

"Faster with that rope, seaman!" Fortant said. The lifeboat slipped closer to the water.

"What about the others?" she demanded, working to keep her voice from cracking.

Fortant shook his head. "There is nothing to be done."

She shuddered to think of the sailors in their cots and the engineers and stokers far below in the engine room. At least a hundred men.

Marlin and Fortant worked the ropes, the pulleys squealing. "We don't want to be near the *Vendetta* when she goes down," Fortant said.

With a lurch they smashed into the side of the ship; to her shame Colette let out a yelp. When they finally hit the water, they were nearly swamped by the splash. The men grabbed oars.

"Row hard, Marlin!" Fortant yelled. "Harder, you dog! She'll suck us down with her."

As their boat rode the waves, Colette looked back at the vast sides of the *Vendetta*, the stern lifting higher and higher, gleaming wet in the moonlight. The roar of wind and waves could not drown out the desperate cries of the sailors in the water. The lifeboat tossed up and down as they rowed away.

"We'll return for the survivors, once the *Vendetta* has sunk," Fortant said. "I've never seen a ship go down so fast." His face glistened with fresh blood.

"Let me row! You're still bleeding," Colette said.

"No! I must do it."

Stupid, bullheaded man! she wanted to shout. She shivered; her feet felt much colder than the rest of her body, though she wore good boots. She reached down to touch her feet, then snapped upright. "We're taking on water!"

"Bail!" Fortant yelled.

Colette found a tobacco tin, dumped out its contents, and bailed for all she was worth, but she made no headway. She felt for the breach under the water and was horrified at what she found. "The hole is huge!" she shouted at Fortant.

"There's an emergency kit under your bench!" he grunted.

A metal case was fastened right under the seat. Her hands were frozen, so it took several tries to unlatch it. Inside she felt the handle of a gun, which she yanked out of its clasps.

"Fire the flare! If there are ships out here"—Fortant sounded doubtful—"they will come."

She held the gun above her head, pointed at the heavens, and pulled the trigger. The light was so bright that she was blinded for a few moments. The flare floated lazily in the sky, reflecting on the water. The *Vendetta* had disappeared, but in the distance heads bobbed and occasional shouts for help could be heard.

"There are no other boats," Marlin said.

The water was now up to Colette's knees. The three of them bailed as hard as they could, but after a few minutes Fortant fell over. Colette and Marlin pulled him upright.

"We can't save the boat," Fortant sputtered. "Cling to the wreck."

"I'll fire another flare," Colette yelled, and pulled the trigger. What she saw by its light sent a wave of panic through her chest.

Shark fins. They were circling the boat, bright white in the moonlight.

"*Mon dieu!*" Fortant gasped. "My blood has attracted them! I am sorry—there is only one way to save you." Before Colette or Marlin could grab him, he heaved himself over the side.

"Chief Fortant! Chief Fortant!" Marlin cried, but the chief slowly swam away. He let out a scream and Colette and Marlin heard splashing and thrashing, then nothing more.

The lifeboat went on sinking. "We're too heavy!" Colette shouted. A wave hit, flipping the boat and tossing them into the ocean. The frigid water numbed Colette's thoughts. She flailed around, eyes burning in the salty water. Feeling something solid, she grabbed on to the overturned boat.

Marlin was already clinging to the other side. "Perhaps we've drifted far enough away from the sharks."

Her teeth were clattering too hard to reply.

"Don't kick!" he whispered. "They're attracted to motion."

He needn't have worried. Her legs were already frozen and still. The cold was forcing its way inside her body, cooling her blood, slowing her heart. The ocean was oddly quiet; the men had stopped shouting for help.

"Are they gone?" she said softly, but Marlin replied with a harsh grunt.

"Marlin!"

"I think one took my foot," he rasped. His eyes were wide with fear. "I'm too numb to be certain."

"Climb higher on the lifeboat!"

"I—" Then he was gone, sucked into the depths.

"Marlin? No! No! Where are you? Marlin?"

Something thumped into her leg and she stifled a scream. Don't move! Don't move!

Several shark fins passed near, then turned away. She felt an unexpected sensation, as if she were being lifted up, into the air. Something larger than a shark rose in the water below her.

2

The Familiar Intruder

Consul Gaspar Le Tourneau's wolfhounds were trained to protect him. He'd purchased them in Germany, and they had provided company during those lonely years at the French embassy in Berlin; they had traveled with him to New York and then to the embassy in London, which was now his home. Greta and Gunther sat with their ears raised. Their once sable backs were flecked with gray.

Gaspar knew he should be looking for younger replacements, but he had such affection for these two. And they had saved his life on more than one occasion.

They were restless today. Gunther padded over to the door, and it opened. Siméon, Gaspar's personal servant, stumbled in and the dogs began to bark. Gaspar rolled his eyes. The hounds *were* getting too old. He commanded, "*Halt den mund!*" and they stopped. They'd been trained by a German and responded only to that language. They watched Siméon with hackles raised.

"You should knock," Gaspar said in French. "You upset the hounds."

Siméon's thick face was dotted with beads of sweat. He held a tray of coffee and croissants, and looked fearfully at the dogs.

"Me thought you sleep," he replied in mangled French, his voice terribly hoarse.

"Are you sick? You can't even put a proper sentence together! Go back to your quarters at once! Don't bring your affliction into my study."

Siméon shook his head. "Not sick. Dog scared me."

"Are you drunk? I command you to put the tray on the desk and go."

Siméon crossed the room and the dogs growled even more. Gaspar shouted, "*Ruhe!*" and the wolfhounds fell silent. Siméon's waistcoat was untucked and his trousers were not properly pressed. "You are not presentable! Your appearance reflects badly on me and on all of France."

"Apologies me," the servant replied.

At the sound of his voice, the dogs bared their teeth, dripping slaver. Gaspar put a hand to his temple. All this commotion and he had not even had his croissant yet. "*Aufhören! Aufhören!*" he demanded, and the wolfhounds looked at him. "*Raus!*" He pointed to the door and they slunk out of the room, but not before Greta took a nip at Siméon. The servant jumped back, let out a little *eek*, and said, in English, "Bad dog."

"They only understand German, you fool."

Siméon closed the door, muffling the barks and yips. He set the tray down on the desk, wiped at his face, and drew a pistol from his inside jacket pocket, then said, in English, "I don't care what they understand. It's more important to me that you understand the situation."

"Siméon! Put down that weapon. What game is this?"

Siméon took a step closer, the pistol pointed steadily at Gaspar. "It's not a game and I'm not Siméon. You usually breakfast in the garden at this hour. Alas, today you changed your pattern."

As Siméon moved closer, Gaspar noticed that his servant's nose was a little wider than it used to be, his eyes not quite the same green.

"Who are you?"

"It doesn't matter. What I want from you is information."

The door rattled as the dogs scratched at it, but the man took no notice.

"What sort of information?"

"Two files. One on a woman named Colette Brunet. The second on Project *Ictíneo*."

Gaspar swallowed. No one on this godforsaken island of Englishmen was supposed to know about that project.

"And if I do not provide the information?"

"I'm a good shot. Not that it matters at such close range."

Gaspar nodded. "I would rather not die before drinking my first cup of coffee of the day." He casually reached under the desk and pressed the alarm button, assured that a bell would ring in the security room.

15

"The alarm is disabled," the man said.

"Ah, where is Siméon?"

"He's been . . . detained. Now, to the matter at hand. Get me those files."

Gaspar was well aware that he could be shot the moment he handed over the files and then the intruder would have the information and France would be short one ambassador. He searched his memory for what the files contained, what exactly he would be giving up.

"Now!" The man took a step closer.

The dogs continued to bark, pawing at the door. Why didn't I trust them? thought Gaspar. Perhaps their barking would draw that dunderhead Marcus, head of security for the embassy.

"I am—I am not certain I have the papers."

"Do not stall!" The man's gaze was steady and he thrust the pistol at Gaspar. The ambassador grimaced. There wasn't the slightest tremor in the man's hand.

Gaspar pushed away from the desk, the wheels on his wooden chair squeaking. He stood, hands held up, and walked slowly to the back of the room, so as not to alarm the man. He removed an etching of the Arc de Triomphe from the wall, revealing a safe. The combination was complex. Think! Think! His trembling fingers began to move. The lock clicked open. He would not give away everything. Just enough to make this man think he had it all.

But Gaspar was shoved aside. "I apologize, Mr. Le Tourneau, but you try my patience." With one hand the stranger reached into the safe; the other held the pistol pointed unswervingly at Gaspar. Francs, rubles, American dollars, maps, and more fell to the floor. Gaspar studied the stranger. He looked younger than he had first appeared, his sideburns now askew. They were fake.

"Aha!" The intruder clutched a brown envelope.

The office door burst open and the dogs were across the floor in two heartbeats, jaws open wide. As the man swung the gun toward them, Greta caught his wrist. He grunted in pain, dropping the pistol. Marcus stood in the door. "Sir, what—"

"You fool! Grab him!" But the intruder had slammed Greta against the wall and had lifted Gunther and thrown him toward the door, knocking Marcus to his knees.

Gendarmes ran in, some tripping over Marcus.

"Shoot him! Shoot him now!" Gaspar shouted.

"I apologize for the mess," the intruder said. Then he charged toward the gendarmes. They froze, but at the last moment he veered around them and leapt through the window, somehow bounding off the balcony and up toward the roof.

Gaspar howled, "Get him!"

"Yes!" Marcus yelled. "After him! After him! Gilles, to the street; Andres, with me to the roof."

As the guards ran off, Gaspar looked out the window at the tiny faux balcony. The intruder was extremely agile.

Gaspar searched the safe. All was accounted for, except one file and a map.

3

The Report

Modo clung to the edge of the sill and swung himself up, cursing his luck. He had come away with little more than a handful of papers, which would irk Mr. Socrates. It had taken a fortnight to plan and rehearse the assignment, and only a minute to botch it.

It was five stories to the street below. People were staring up, mouths agape, to see where the broken glass had fallen from. He swung over to another balcony, landed on both feet, and ran across the balustrade. The pedestrians were getting a show that rivaled anything playing at Astley's Theatre Royal. As he jumped and grabbed an awning and swung onto the roof, it occurred to him that the theft would be in the papers. Another mistake! The embassy would never report exactly what was missing, but Mr. Socrates was displeased whenever an agent caused enough stir to make the news. Blast it!

Modo bounded across to the next building and over a slanted roof, frightening pigeons. It brought him such joy to leap and dash over London's roofs. It had taken years of training under the watchful eye of Tharpa, his martial arts instructor, to make every step so sure, to perfect his balance. The six months he had spent practically living on London's rooftops had served to heighten his skill. He could get all the way to Buckingham Palace and back before a cab could complete half the trip. What other fourteen-year-old could do that?

Today he only needed to go a few blocks. He hopped onto the roof of Harrods grocer and lowered himself onto a balcony, unseen by the people on Brompton Road.

After removing his jacket, Modo examined the scratches and bite marks on his arm. Not too deep, and the bleeding had stopped. He'd had bad luck before with dogs; they didn't seem to be fooled by his disguises—no surprise since they relied on their sense of smell. He'd treat the wounds once he was back at Victor House. He turned his suit jacket inside out and pulled it back on.

"And now," he whispered to himself, "to become someone else."

He drew in a deep breath, gritted his teeth, leaned against the building, and concentrated, picturing his face shifting into one he called Mr. Dawkins, his "young lord with dimples" face. His bones ached, his muscles burned, and he sweated as his eyes grew larger, shifting from the squinty, tiny eyes of Siméon, who was at this point lying in an opium den. With the creaking, cracking of bones moving and enlarging, Modo's jaw grew longer, his nose wider. He ensured that his hated hump remained flattened on his back.

He'd been able to change his appearance since infancy. He'd trained for years to develop this "adaptive transformation" under the watchful eyes of Mr. Socrates, but it still took intense concentration. And it hurt. Oh, how the shifting hurt! He grimaced and grunted, hearing Mr. Socrates' voice: "You must perfect each face. No drooping eyelids or sagging cheeks, no sign of your true ugliness. Perfect it, Modo!" He didn't stop until every last bone was in place. He looked at least twenty-five years old now. He yanked off the sideburns, then took out a handkerchief and dabbed the sweat from his forehead. He didn't transform the rest of his body—if he did, his clothes would no longer fit. He had stashed a long, dark coat here. He pulled it from behind a chair and threw it around his shoulders.

The final touch was a collapsible top hat. With the press of a button it popped from flat as a fritter to full height. Modo placed the hat on his head, then climbed through the window and into an unoccupied room. In the next room he surprised a seamstress, who looked up from her work. "Oh dear!" she gasped.

"My apologies." Modo gave her a sweeping bow.

He made his way to the ground floor, stopping only to buy a jar of gooseberry preserves. He sampled them as he walked along the street. He could easily have traveled by rooftop, but he would be far too sweaty by the time he arrived at Victor House. Mr. Socrates wouldn't approve of that.

Modo had spent the past two days in the embassy, serving food and speaking little, as his French was only passable. Much of the time he pretended to be sick. He especially avoided the other servants, as they would likely have become suspicious. The ambassador and secretaries and commissaries hardly gave him a look because he was only a servant, which made his task easier. He had assumed the ambassador was out of his office, and intended to break into the safe; a nasty surprise to find Le Tourneau there. Mr. Socrates would not be happy with his poor planning.

Feeling bolder, Modo walked back down Brompton Road and Knightsbridge, past the embassy on the opposite side of the street. He glanced at the broken window on the top floor and snickered when he saw the gendarmes running back and forth along the street. London policemen were trying to gain entry to the embassy, but they were being barred by gendarmes. Carriages and an omnibus rattled past.

Then he heard barking and saw the two wolfhounds being led by Marcus, both straining at their leashes and glaring right at him. Modo nearly choked on a gooseberry. He cursed himself for being too arrogant and quickened his pace. He passed the gawkers and turned down the next street to hail a hansom cab. After twenty minutes of being jostled about, he was deposited in front of Victor House. Modo didn't know whether Mr. Socrates owned the grand mansion himself or if it was a possession of the Permanent Association, the secretive British group that managed agents all over the world. The Association had formed to protect Britannia from outside enemies. That was Modo's best guess, at least. Mr. Socrates was typically tight-lipped when it came to explaining the Association's goals. Modo mentally listed the estates of which he knew—Tower House,

Ravenscroft, Victor House—but he imagined there were many more. The Association was no doubt rich beyond his wildest calculations.

Right next to the iron front gate was a statue of Mars, the god of war, standing with a lance in one hand, a shield in the other. Modo rubbed the shield for luck. Mr. Socrates would frown upon such superstition.

At the front door, Modo knocked. It opened and Tharpa smiled, his teeth made brighter by his dark skin. Modo resisted the urge to hug his combat instructor. He hadn't done that since he was a child. "I recognize this face, young sahib," Tharpa said.

"One day I'll arrive with a face you've never seen."

"I will know you by your smell, Modo." Tharpa laughed. "Please come in."

Modo stepped into the front hall. "It's so good to see you, Tharpa! You'd be proud of how far I jumped, running along balustrades and swinging over flagpoles. Everything you taught me."

"Yes, as I have always said, young sahib is part monkey." Tharpa took Modo's coat sleeve and gently lifted his wrist. "Tch, tch. Wounded. Again." He rolled back the sleeve and looked over the scratches on Modo's arm. "Ah, always you are in trouble with dogs. Come to me when you are finished with your report. Mr. Socrates awaits you in the study."

Tharpa entered the study before Modo and announced, "Young Modo is here." Then he withdrew.

Modo strode into the circular study, trying to look confident. Mr. Socrates was seated at a table in his red satin smoking jacket, pipe burning, glasses on his nose. His white hair had been cut so short, it stuck straight out. For nearly fourteen years this man had been the closest thing Modo had had to a father. Every lesson, all the minutiae of Modo's education had been planned by Mr. Socrates.

Now his sharp eyes measured Modo, who felt as though his master's gaze was sizing up his deficiencies. Modo adjusted a button on his coat, wondering how old Mr. Socrates was: fifty-five? Seventy? A hundred? Mr. Socrates lowered his glasses.

"Welcome, Modo. Do have a seat," he said. Modo chose a chair next to the wall of books. It squeaked. The table in front of him was spread with documents and maps, lit by light from the nearby window.

"Please give me your report."

"Well, I began, as you suggested, by acting somewhat ill and surly so that others at the embassy would not suspect my disguise. I did my duties as a servant, but retreated to my room, feigning illness, when my features began to shift back to their usual state—"

"The results, Modo. What happened and what did you bring me?"

Modo recounted his last few minutes at the French embassy and produced the two papers he had stolen.

"This is all?" Mr. Socrates said.

"I didn't expect him to be in his study."

"Well, perhaps you should have carried on with your disguise."

"I don't believe I could have, sir. Some of the staff were

becoming suspicious. And once Consul Le Tourneau believed I was sick, I felt it would be some time before he would allow me back in his quarters."

Mr. Socrates nodded. "Yes, your line of reasoning is acceptable. Good."

Modo breathed deeply. That was as close as Mr. Socrates ever came to giving a compliment.

As Mr. Socrates examined the documents, Modo eyed the book spines beside him. *Intravascular Medicine. A History of Espionage. Britons and Britannia.* Outside the window, the midday sun shone down on the garden of Victor House. It being November, there were no flowers, but the vines and leaves were still quite green. "Well, this is something, at least," Mr. Socrates said, holding up a sheet of paper. "I wouldn't call your mission an unqualified success, but I can work with this."

"I'm pleased to hear that, sir." Modo leaned in to look at the documents, written in French, bearing the embassy stamp. Perhaps later Mr. Socrates would trust him enough to explain what they meant.

"I'm done with you now," Mr. Socrates said. "I imagine you're hungry. French pastries may taste like they are prepared by angels, but I find they never fill the stomach. Please go to the kitchen. If Cook is there, he will look after you. If not, help yourself. But the Roquefort is mine." He laughed.

Reluctantly, Modo stood. When he got to the door, Mr. Socrates cleared his throat. "One more thing, Modo."

Modo turned back. "Yes, sir."

"Your true features are beginning to show. Please let

them. You don't have to retain that form in front of me. I know what you really look like."

"Yes, sir." Modo plodded down the hall, undoing his cravat. How he hated his natural state. With each step, he let his body unfold. His hump grew, his back curved, his eyes widened and skewed, his nose flattened. By the time he opened the kitchen door, his hand was gnarled. He went over to the tin wastebasket and ran his hand through his dark hair, watching it fall out in clumps. Soon all that remained were the red tufts of his natural hair. His suit was too small now, so he undid a few buttons.

He rubbed his head and thought of Octavia. Just picturing her pale, perfect face made his heart race. A little more than two months ago, she had knocked at the door of his ancient room at the Red Boar, pretending to be someone else, and sent him on his first major assignment. Together they had explored sewers, faced the mechanical hounds created by the infamous Dr. Hyde, and stopped a giant machine that threatened the Houses of Parliament. She had pulled him, half drowned, from the Thames. He would always owe her his life. In the intense days of that assignment, he'd grown close to her. Because they were risking their lives together? Or was it something more?

He'd seen her only once more since then—on the balcony overlooking Kew Gardens, where he'd spent his mornings recuperating. She had asked to see his true face and he had refused; it wasn't a face for beautiful eyes to look upon. He wondered if she'd felt betrayed. She was the only fellow agent he knew, and he considered her a friend. But there would be no point in asking the ever-secretive Mr. Socrates about Octavia. He never shared information about other agents.

"This will heal your wounds," Tharpa said from behind him, making Modo jump. Zounds! Even after years of training at Tharpa's side, learning to slow his heart rate, to hear every twitch or creak of wood, his teacher could still sneak up on him.

Tharpa was holding a bottle and a jar of salve. Modo pulled back his sleeve and held out his arm for Tharpa to splash the wounds with alcohol. It burned, but then Tharpa applied the cool green salve.

"When will I learn to walk as silently as you?" Modo asked.

"When you learn to become the air itself."

Modo lifted an eyebrow and Tharpa laughed. "It sounded very wise, did it not?"

Modo heard footsteps, and a moment later Mr. Socrates entered the kitchen.

"Ah, good, Modo." He put his hand on Modo's shoulder, and Modo felt the warmth of his touch. It was so rare for Mr. Socrates to display affection. This is what a father would do, Modo thought, place his hand on his son's shoulder.

"I have transcribed what I can. After you eat, I want you to return to your room at the Langham. You're finished with this assignment."

4

Inside the Secret Room

On the last day of his life Matthew Wyle left his apartment on Lafayette Place, stepped onto the sidewalk, pulled his bowler hat down tighter on his head, and walked southeast. In his forty-eight years he'd seen wars in Afghanistan and skirmishes in India, had lost an eye to a Mexican saber and been shipwrecked on a Caribbean island. This afternoon he felt as though he'd risk all those misadventures to escape the brazen, ice-cold wind that tore through the bustling streets of New York. It made his bones rattle and dried out his glass eye.

A few short hours earlier he'd received a telegram from Mr. Socrates giving the location of a meeting room in the Astor Library, a favorite haunt of French *espions*. That made him chuckle; all this time spent secretly trying to unearth the various cells of international spies and agents that thrived in New York, and here was a cell, right in the very library he visited twice a week to relax and read Shakespeare. His orders were to discover what they did in that room and telegraph his findings to Mr. Socrates.

A faint cough a few feet behind him made Wyle bristle, but when he turned there was no one close to him. In his twenty years of being a spy, he often presumed, correctly, that he was being followed. Lately, however, it too often seemed to be his imagination, for he could never catch anyone at it, the way he used to. He knew of agents who'd been dragged off to the asylum, screaming about shadowy pursuers. Was this the first sign of his own madness? Even his sleep was no longer undisturbed. Last night he'd woken to the sound of a similar cough, right in his apartment. The sense that he was being observed had been overpowering, yet a search of the place revealed no intruder.

Wyle climbed the library steps. Inside, he caught a pleasant whiff of books that reminded him wistfully of his youth in Ottawa, Canada, before he joined the British Royal Navy. His mother had kept her own library and often read to him. For a moment he was a child again; then he guffawed. Here he was, a grown man, scarred by several battle wounds, with only one eye, thinking of his mother.

He passed a gathering of dapper men with neatly trimmed beards, and one steely-eyed young woman in a black dress. The woman looked familiar, but he couldn't place her.

As he climbed the stairs at the back of the library, it dawned on him: the young woman's upright, confident disposition reminded him of Colette Brunet, the French spy. She'd been just as confident, and extremely difficult to find.

He'd tracked her to New York, but a few weeks ago he'd lost her. A slippery fox, that one. How could he lose a half-Japanese, half-French girl?

The top floor of the library had the largest selection of books on philosophy in the city, but no one seemed to want to read them. He appeared to have the whole floor to himself. The morning light reflected off the windows of the building across the street, making him blink. His good eye had always been sensitive to bright light.

He found the door to the meeting room behind a long stack of books. It was ajar. And, oddly, a fedora lay on the floor just inside. His hand hovered over the miniature pistol in his breast pocket. Moving closer to the doorway, he noticed that the hat was smeared with a red stain. He grasped his pistol tightly and peered into the room. A curtain was open just a few inches, leaving much of the room in shadow.

He pushed the door, annoyed by the squeaking of its hinges. It hit something and stopped. He held his pistol at his chest and poked his head briefly around the door.

On the floor of the room was the body of a huge man, his muscular neck at a sharp angle. A knife lay beside him. Judging by the papers strewn about the room, and the overturned table and chair, the man had struggled before dying.

Wyle remained calm. He'd seen many such sights before. He breathed slowly, listening for signs of the killer. Nothing.

Wyle was able to open the door enough to squeeze past. A piece of paper floated through the air, which was odd; the windows were shut, so there was no breeze. Shelves on either side of the room held a few books. The table closest to the window was littered with papers, as was the floor. He listened carefully. Nothing. He reached down and felt the man's neck. Still warm. No pulse. A fleur-de-lis tattoo was on his right wrist: he'd been in the French Navy.

Wyle picked up papers from the floor as he walked over to the table. They were French documents, which he read easily as he thumbed through them. The killer was likely another agent. Russians? Germans? From the Clockwork Guild? This Guild was new to him, but the name had appeared in several of the messages from his masters. He knew very little about the Guild, only that he should keep watch for any insignia that looked like clockwork. Typically vague orders from above.

Among the documents was a map of the Atlantic Ocean, marked with red ink in the vicinity of Iceland. Scrawled across the top was the word *Ictíneo*.

He came across a page that read:
VSVYWBT KEUW 6035236
Code, obviously. He wouldn't have time to decipher it just now.

He heard a cough from the corner near the window and spun around, pistol cocked. It was the barking cough he'd been hearing over the past few days.

My imagination is becoming more vivid with age, he decided. He gathered the papers, stuffed them into his satchel, and left the room.

On the way back to his apartment, he checked several times to see if anyone was following him. He went in the building and climbed the stairs, his left knee aching. He unlocked his door, hung his coat on the rack, and sat at the table to work at the line of code. It was likely the Vigenère cipher, the preferred method of secret communication for the French. What they didn't know was that the British had cracked it years ago. After several minutes he noticed he'd left the door open.

"You're getting old," he told himself, and got up to close it.

He went back to the numbers and letters.

Grand poisson 6035236

Grand poisson was "big fish." But what were the numbers for? At once it came to him.

He felt a pair of hands close tightly around his throat. A man's voice said, "Ah, that is the information I've been trying to decode." There was a hint of an English accent. Wyle flung himself backward but was thrown to the ground, his face shoved into the floor so hard he felt his nose snap. He didn't get so much as a glimpse of his assailant. He felt a knee jammed into his spine as fingers closed off his windpipe.

"What do the numbers mean?" the voice hissed. "Tell me!"

Wyle answered with a cough and a valiant attempt to suck in air. I don't want to die without seeing my attacker's face, he thought. He twisted around but saw nothing. The last thing Wyle heard as the final bit of air puffed out of his lungs was eerie, childlike laughter.

5

The Assignment

Alone in the dining room at the Langham Hotel, Modo finished his breakfast of cheese scones and apples, wiped his lips with the napkin, and let out a satisfied huff. He was wearing his Mr. Dawkins face again—a face that was handsome enough, but not overly so. No sense attracting unwanted attention.

This was the life! It already felt as though years had passed since he'd last seen Ravenscroft, the house in the country where he'd been raised from a toddler until he was a young man. Mr. Socrates had told him he was likely fourteen now, because he had rescued him during what appeared to be Modo's first year of life. But no one could be certain. He had never celebrated a birthday. Maybe he was fifteen! Time was always playing games with him. The years in Ravenscroft sometimes seemed so short because every memory he had of his early life had taken place in the same three rooms.

He'd spent all that time indoors, reading history, learning how to change his shape, training with Tharpa, and working on his acting skills with his governess, Mrs. Finchley. Only eight months ago, Mr. Socrates had taken him from Ravenscroft and left him in London to fend for himself.

He did like the Langham. It was so much better than his first, rat-infested room at Seven Dials. And, after all, Octavia had stayed here. It was the place they'd first met face to face. That made him laugh—well, it wasn't this face she'd seen, but another he called the Knight. Had Mr. Socrates sent her somewhere else? She could be in Wales for all he knew. Or France. That would be disconcerting. Surely Mr. Socrates wouldn't send a girl out of the country.

He feared he might never see her again. He pushed away from the table and went up to room 327, where he found a note left under the door: *Report to Victor House at once. You no longer need the room or your accoutrements. They will be handled by my staff.*

Another assignment already? It had only been two days since his last visit to Victor House. Modo burned the note in the sink and undressed. His dining suit had been specially tailored by Norton & Sons on Savile Row, and he hoped he would be able to wear it again soon. Mr. Socrates would store it at one of his many properties. Modo pulled on cheaper clothes and a dark jacket and let his features slip away, his face changing to its real shape, his hump rising on his back.

There was no point in retaining this shape any longer; Mr. Socrates would only ask him to revert to his normal appearance once he arrived. Modo chose a flesh-colored mask. No one but Tharpa and Mr. Socrates were supposed to see his actual face.

Grabbing a haversack, Modo took one last look at his room with its green satin curtains, red bedspread, and brass gas lamps. He'd been here for several weeks before the French embassy assignment, resting and preparing, with all the comforts. Hot and cold running water! Silk bathrobe! Now he would leave all that behind.

He walked down the stairs, receiving odd looks from the very staff who had nodded politely to him earlier. He found the mask to be a useful weapon. He could glare through the eyeholes and silence anyone who had too many questions.

Soon a cab left him in front of Victor House. Just as Modo was lifting his hand to knock, Tharpa opened the door, then led him to the main room.

Mr. Socrates was sitting at the library table with Octavia Milkweed. Modo drew in a long breath, and his hand automatically flew up to his mask to be sure it was in place. It had been nearly two months since he'd last set eyes upon her, and now he couldn't stop looking. She had on a green satin dress, her hair tied up under a green bonnet, and she wore white gloves. He straightened his back as much as possible, his twisted spine complaining.

"Ah, Modo, please join us for tea," Mr. Socrates said. "You remember Octavia, I presume."

"Of course, good morning to you, Miss Milkweed." He bowed slightly, intending to look princely.

She gave him a mischievous smile. "Good morning, Modo, you haven't changed a bit in the last while. In fact you don't look a day over . . . twelve."

"What?" Modo sat awkwardly on a chair. Something about her put him off balance. "I'm older than that!"

"Ah, yes, so you say. I see you are masked, yet again. Playing a villain in a play?"

"Yes," he said, searching for a clever counterquip. Nothing. He couldn't think of the name of a single drama. "Yes, I am playing a villain."

As though it were the end of a boxing match, Mr. Socrates rang a small dinner bell. "Tea will be right up," he said, a hint of a smile on his face.

Octavia looked quite full of herself. The last time Modo had seen her he'd been nearly certain she was going to confess that she cared deeply for him. Or, at least, for his visage of the day. If he were to show her his real face, she would be disgusted.

Cook entered, holding a tray of sweet biscuits and tea. He was a small, barrel-chested man, his face a mass of scars. He poured tea and retreated to the kitchen.

"It's a fine blend of black tea flavored with bergamot oil," Mr. Socrates said. "My own recipe; a secret that will go to the grave with me."

It was tricky for Modo to drink with his mask on, but he'd done it often enough that now he expertly dipped his head, lifted the mask with his left hand, and sipped. "It does taste delicious, sir. We'll raise a cup in your honor when you die."

Mr. Socrates smiled. Modo was pleased by his master's

reaction, and even more pleased to see that his teasing had brought a smile to Octavia's lips. He took a satisfied sip of tea and swished it about playfully.

Mr. Socrates held his teacup perfectly still. "I suppose you are wondering why I have asked you here." He took a slow sip. "My intention is for you two to marry."

Modo spurted his tea back into his cup.

Octavia said, "Each other?"

"For espionage purposes only, of course."

"I have no desire to be married—again," Octavia said indignantly, giving Mr. Socrates a cool stare. "I'm sure you'll remember that my last husband died."

"Pardon me?" exclaimed Modo.

"Yes," Mr. Socrates said. "I haven't forgotten that, and I understand your hesitance. Perhaps you'll have better luck this time. I'm certain that Modo hopes so, for his own sake. You two will travel to New York, and you must keep up appearances. After all, unmarried men and women do not travel together without a chaperone." He sipped his tea. "I already have tickets on the steamship *Abyssinia*, departing this afternoon. It's a twelve-day trip, and you'll have a stateroom and study. You'll take on the roles of Mr. and Mrs. Warkin. I have passports, papers, and money for you. Modo, because your disguises last only for a few hours at a time, Octavia will fetch your food."

"I look forward to it, sir," Modo blurted out happily, while Octavia snapped, "I don't fetch!"

"My error," Mr. Socrates said. "I used the wrong word. Octavia will be kind enough to bring food to the room, because you shall be playing the part of a somewhat ill man. That will allow you to remain in your cabin most hours."

Modo still couldn't get his mind around it. He would be on the ocean. Going to America. With Octavia!

"I've never been on the ocean before," he said.

"Not entirely true, Modo," Mr. Socrates said. "You did cross the Channel as a child."

"I did?" Modo gripped his teaspoon a little tighter. His only childhood memories were of Ravenscroft. "When?"

"That's not important now."

"Who are we supposed to be meeting?" Octavia asked.

"Ah, you always have your mind on the task, Octavia. Good. Good. Mr. Wyle, who has been an employee of mine for many years. I was expecting communication from him, but it hasn't arrived. You shall go and find out what the delay is. I've prepared a dossier, which you will memorize, of course."

He handed a paper to Octavia, who looked it over quickly and tossed it to Modo.

"You have it memorized already?" he asked.

"Of course."

Modo stared at it a bit longer, then set the paper down.

"And your wedding rings." Mr. Socrates opened a small envelope and handed one ring to each of them. Modo's gold band was a little loose.

"Does it do anything?" Modo asked.

"The ring? Yes, if you fall in the water it will expand into a cork float."

"Truly?" Modo said. Octavia rolled her eyes. Modo blushed. "Ah. You were joking."

Mr. Socrates actually grinned. Modo ran his fingers over the gold ring. Married. He nearly laughed out loud. Then it dawned on him: he would be sharing a room with Octavia! He began to sweat profusely.

Mr. Socrates placed a photograph on the table. Modo leaned forward to more closely inspect the grainy image of a man in a French military uniform, a woman and a young girl beside them. The woman was Japanese and wore a kimono. The girl's face was circled, and Modo could clearly see that she must be their daughter, as she had both the determined look of the man and the beauty and coloring of the woman. At the bottom was written *1869, age fourteen; Hakodate, Japan.*

"This is the Brunet family. Captain Alphonse Brunet died of wounds sustained during the Boshin War. His only daughter was Colette Brunet. She is eighteen now and works as a spy for the French government. She is highly regarded despite her youth, and she has risen to the top of the ranks."

"What does she have to do with our assignment?" Modo asked.

"Patience, Modo. I'm coming to that. Miss Brunet is searching for something called the *Ictíneo*. Since the French have given her the job of finding it, that would strongly indicate it's their top priority."

"I assume it's important to us, too," Octavia said.

"Yes, the French are allies, but we cannot allow them to gain any advantage over us, especially on the seas."

Octavia adjusted a lock of her hair. "In other words, you

want to gather up all the toys before the French have a chance to play with them."

"Ah, such cheekiness." Mr. Socrates no longer seemed amused. "These *toys* are what decide the fate of the empire." He looked at Modo. "Can you guess what the name *Ictíneo* means?"

"Uh, it's Greek, correct?"

"Yes, but what does it *mean?*"

"Well, an *ichthus* is a fish. *Neo* is 'new.' So it's a new fish."

"Yes, perhaps that's what it means. The root of the second word could be *naus*, or ship. So it may mean 'fish ship' or a fish as big as a ship, a blunt translation. There are rumors of a sea monster."

"A sea monster!" Modo said. "A whale, like Moby-Dick? Or is it more like the kraken?"

"Mrs. Finchley allowed you to read too many flights of fancy," Mr. Socrates said sadly. The sense of shame made Modo shrink inside. But they were good stories, he wanted to say. He couldn't imagine his childhood—or his life now—without books. Every line of Coleridge was stamped in his memory.

"In any case," Mr. Socrates went on, "I doubt that Miss Brunet is pursuing an actual sea monster, though I admit one can never be certain what the depths of the ocean will produce. I have myself seen squids the length of a ship, whales as large as an island. One theory from other members of the Association is that they have replaced the ivory tusks of narwhals with metal ones and trained them to sink ships."

"Is that possible?" Octavia asked, her eyes large and distractingly beautiful. Modo bit his lip, trying to keep his mind on their task.

Mr. Socrates nodded. "A few months ago I would have said no, but our encounter with the Clockwork Guild has opened my eyes. After all, they melded flesh and metal in ways beyond human comprehension."

Modo swallowed. He didn't like to think about the Clockwork Guild. They had nearly destroyed the Houses of Parliament and, worse, had attempted to kill him several times in the space of a few short hours. Just the thought of Miss Hakkandottir and her metal hand was enough to make him shudder. She lived on in his nightmares; more than once he had woken up in a cold sweat from a dream in which she had plucked out one of his eyes with her sharpened metal nails.

"Attaching metal spears to whales sounds like something they would do." Octavia was tapping her fingers on the table. "After all, those hounds of theirs were half iron, half flesh. That idea would certainly be in keeping with what we know of them."

"I'd be quite happy never to have to set eyes on one of those hounds again," Modo said.

"Don't be frightened, Modo," Octavia said. "I'll protect you."

"I'm not frightened! I was only stating a fact."

"There's no indication that the Clockwork Guild is involved," Mr. Socrates said. "The Guild is, as we say in the business, sleeping. They've disappeared down the rabbit hole. But one can never be too cautious. In the meantime, we will act on what we know. The papers Modo retrieved from the embassy include the last transmission from Brunet, which I have deciphered to mean that a ship was sent for her to command. We need to know where she went."

"And will Agent Wyle have the answer to this question?" Octavia asked.

"He should have reported in by now. You, Modo, must discover his whereabouts. Octavia shall assist you."

"I'll lead the investigation, you mean," Octavia said.

Mr. Socrates shook his head. "Modo will take point. You will work together. If you are not able to make contact with Wyle, then it will be your mission to pursue Colette Brunet and discover the story behind the *Ictíneo*. We must either have that technology or destroy it."

"Destroy it?" Modo asked.

"Yes. I cannot overstate this. Our nation is built on sea power. We must control the seas. Modo and Octavia, this is not a small assignment. You will be the eyes and the ears of the empire."

"Me peepers are me own," Octavia said with the accent from her pickpocket days.

"This is no joke!" Mr. Socrates raised his voice ever so slightly, but the change made Modo sit up straight. Octavia, too. "I don't send you on this assignment lightly. I have arranged for clothing for you. All is packed in the next room. And there is one final thing." He opened a box on the table. "This." He took out a leather item from which hung a safety chain.

"A wallet?" asked Modo.

"Open it," Mr. Socrates said.

When Modo did so, he found that the top half of the wallet encased a square mechanical device. The change pouch of the wallet held an electric cell.

"What is it?"

"A wireless telegraph," Octavia said. She smiled at Modo's surprise that she should recognize it. "I've seen one before, but this one is amazingly small."

"You are very observant, Octavia," said Mr. Socrates. "That's exactly what it is."

"But how does it work?" Modo asked. "How far will the messages travel?"

"Alas, the distance isn't great. You must be close to a telegraph line. It will work, occasionally, on the ocean; you'll be able to communicate through the transatlantic cables. You keep it, Modo, since the husband always carries the wallet. Secure it in a safe place on your person."

"I shall."

"And I also have this." From the same box Mr. Socrates took out what looked like black netting, but when he shook the fabric, two eyeholes appeared in it. "A mask. Much easier to transport than your papier-mâché ones. You can keep it in your pocket and it will stretch over your face, concealing any shape."

"That is excellent, sir!" Modo folded the mask carefully, surprised by the suppleness of the material.

"Now you must go and make yourselves ready. A cab is waiting to take you to the train to Liverpool. At two o'clock this afternoon your ship departs."

6

The Crossing

Modo did not have to pretend to be ill on the voyage—he spent the first three days seasick. He slumped on the bed in their stateroom, the fancy satin blankets and swansdown pillows providing little comfort. His net mask was a damp sponge of stale sweat that clung to his face like a starfish. He could eat the occasional orange slice or cracker, or bits of a sugar biscuit, but that was all. Octavia had brought him lemonade, but just the smell of it made him retch.

"The deviled kidney is excellent," Octavia said, sitting at the glass dining table in their room, cutting the kidney with a silver knife. Modo gritted his teeth, biting back a snide reply. "The fried onions are straight from heaven," she added.

"You are intentionally being cruel, Miss Milkweed."

"Oh, suddenly so formal, Modo. Is our marriage already on the rocks?"

He ignored her. "I should sleep on the floor," he said. "You have the bed. I'm well enough now."

Octavia laughed. "Don't be foolish. I've slept in worse holes." She had used the sofa as her bed for the voyage. They'd been given a Chinese privacy screen, which Octavia pulled across the room at night.

Modo had insisted the lights stay low. In his state, it had become impossible to shift into a more attractive appearance; he had tried twice and nearly passed out both times.

He remembered Mrs. Finchley, the closest person he had to a mother, wiping his forehead whenever he was sick as a child. How he missed the sound of her voice, the touch of her hands, and the way she used to hold him. It seemed a hundred years ago. But even then, even with a fever, Mr. Socrates would make Modo test the limits of his abilities to transform.

"You're deep in thought," Octavia said. "Reliving the plot of some penny dreadful?"

"At this point I'm a living penny dreadful."

Octavia laughed, and Modo was pleased with himself.

"You said you were married before." He gripped the sheet. He'd punch her first husband, if the fellow wasn't already dead.

She shrugged. "It didn't last; my beloved was old."

"Beloved? You—you really were married?"

"Ah, it was just another game for Mr. Socrates. My husband was an old Chinese agent called Mah. We were investigating a triad—a Chinese underground society."

"I know what a triad is," Modo huffed, wishing his voice didn't sound so whiny. "How did he die?"

"Not arsenic, in case you were worried. As I mentioned, he was old. One day, over breakfast, his heart gave out and our investigation was over."

"Sounds horrible!"

"Well, I didn't actually see him die—I was still sleeping behind a screen, not unlike this one. He was overbearing, opinionated, and loud, and he drooled. Otherwise, I was sad to see ol' Mah go. Mr. Socrates was very angry with him for having the audacity to die while on assignment, so neither of us should ever do that!"

"Don't even joke about dying. When were you married?"

"A few months before you and I met. Now, enough questions. It's time for my little penny dreadful to sleep," Octavia said.

"Must I?"

"You can hardly keep your eyes open. I'll entertain myself by strutting up and down the deck and dining in the Paris café, where the young lords and gentlemen will no doubt watch me like hawks."

The thought made Modo clench his fists under the sheet. "A married woman shouldn't be out on her own!"

"Tut, tut!" Her hand was on the doorknob. "I'll tell them I'm getting my sick husband some tea. Sleep well, my lord," she said, then was out the door.

Modo did fall asleep, but it took longer than usual.

That night he woke up and listened to Octavia's slight snore. It was such an odd feeling to have her right in the same room. He had thought about her so often since their first meeting and, in the months that they were apart, between assignments. He had wandered the streets of London, swung from rooftop to rooftop for hours looking for her, hoping for a glimpse. And now here she was only feet away. What was she dreaming about? Him? The thought made him choke back a laugh. No, she had much better things to dream about. Men with faces that were permanently handsome, for one.

By the fifth day he was able to keep meals down and he felt almost healthy. He found too that he could finally change his face into the one Octavia knew, a man he called the Knight. So, while she was out, he'd managed the transformation, then daubed on sweet-smelling lotions and dressed himself in his finest morning jacket and black trousers.

When she returned, he was sitting at the glass table, playing solitaire.

"Ah, you are alive, and sans mask. This is a momentous day!"

She sat across from Modo and stared at him for so long that he felt nervous sweat beading on his forehead. "Why are you looking at me?"

"You seem different somehow."

"In what way?"

"I can't quite put my finger on it. Perhaps you just look older. You might pass for sixteen."

"Sixteen?" he said with a huff. "I'm twenty!"

"That's a lie, Modo. One day I'll figure out your age. For now, though, shall we go out for a stroll and get our morning vittles?" She said this last bit in a falsetto. Modo wasn't quite sure whom she was imitating, but he smiled.

He stood and nearly fell over. "Ah, you're still a touch weak on your pins," she said. "I'll give you a hand."

He leaned on Octavia's shoulder as she helped him out of the cabin. He caught a whiff of his own sweaty stink. Was she wrinkling her nose? If he hadn't felt so tired, he would have rejoiced at being this close to her. She led him onto the gangway. The wind was brisk and cold. He gazed at the horizon, the greatest uninterrupted distance he'd ever seen. He had peeked out the porthole in their room, but this was his first panoramic view of the Atlantic.

"No wonder ancient sailors believed there were waterfalls at the end of the earth," he said.

"Yes, it's something, isn't it?" Octavia agreed. "Though after five days, I've had my fill of endless nothingness. I want to see America, to walk the streets of New York and be a part of the great hubbub! Imagine, New York! Maybe we'll like it so much we'll just stay there."

"Don't say that! We have an assignment!"

"Ah, you are such a fussy duffer some days! You need a good meal. We're off to the Paris café."

She led him along the gangway and to the center of the upper deck. A smokestack loomed above them, sputtering out smoke from the depths of the ship. In the café, several gentlemen and their wives sat at tables, eating breakfast. Modo and Octavia found an empty table near a man reading the *Times*.

"That's not today's paper, is it?" Modo quipped.

The man looked up, squinting through his monocle at Modo. "It most certainly is not," he said, then put his nose back in the paper.

"It must be hard being such a dummacker," Octavia whispered. "Never a smile or a chuckle. Did you know there's a thousand third-class passengers on the decks below us and only a hundred of us up here enjoying the sun?"

"That doesn't seem fair."

"Oh, it's not fair." Octavia shrugged. "But it's not a problem we can solve now. We've got bigger fish to catch." She laughed at her own joke.

When the waiter arrived, Modo ordered porridge, while Octavia asked for eggs and a croissant.

"So we search for an agent who, in turn, is searching for a creature from the great depths," he said; then, remembering all the literature he'd memorized, he recited, " 'Full fathom five thy father lies.' "

"Shakespeare again, Modo? How trite."

"It's not trite!" he hissed, surprising himself at how loud he could be. "It's art!"

"Pfft!" Octavia waved her hand. "You know my thoughts on Shakespeare. It's like reading mud."

He was silent until their breakfast arrived, then asked, "Do you have any guesses about what happened to Mr. Wyle? Do you think he's been captured?"

"Oh, he's likely blewed, slewed, and tipsy."

"What?"

"Drunk. That's my guess."

"I can't believe one of Mr. Socrates' agents would get drunk. That would be unprofessional."

"I see it all the time. These older agents get burned out and turn to the bottle."

"Hmm. Well, we'll just have to wait and see if your theory is correct. Speaking of theories, what do you think of this *Ictíneo*? Is it a giant fish?"

"I have no idea. Obviously Mr. Socrates doesn't either."

"Why do you think Mr. Socrates sent us together?" he asked.

"Because he knows you need someone to look after you."

"That's not true!"

"Who pulled you from the Thames? Tharpa? Mr. Socrates? The Queen?"

"It was you, Tavia," he said. "Must I thank you every day?"

"Yes. Morn, noon, and night. You can take Sundays and Christmas off." She laughed. "If you really want my best guess, it's that we're his youngest agents. He needed two people who could convincingly behave as though they were married. We were his most logical choice. Some of his other agents are so ugly, no one would believe they'd find spouses."

She grinned, but Modo found it hard to respond in kind. "Yes, I suppose some of them are ugly."

"I must admit, Modo"—she motioned around the ship—"I like this upper-class life. Perhaps if I found the right rich gentleman, I'd retire."

"You'll never retire," he said, trying not to picture her married off to some rich, rotund nob.

"Perhaps, perhaps not." She eyed him closely again. "What I still don't understand is how you change your appearance."

"Magicians don't give up their secrets."

"No, I suppose they don't, not even to their friends."

More than anything, Modo wished he could explain why he couldn't show his face. He would certainly be the ugliest of all the ugly agents.

When they were finished eating, Modo said, "I'm already

49

worn out. We should retire to our cabin." Octavia nodded; when they stood up, she bumped into the man with the paper.

"Sorry, so sorry," she said, giggling. "I find ships so topsy-turvy."

The man glared at Modo. "You ought to keep a better watch on your wife," he snapped. "Women are delicate, clumsy creatures."

"Good day to you," Modo said.

As they walked back to the cabin, Octavia began to giggle again, and by the time they stepped inside she was full-out laughing.

"What's so funny?" Modo asked, smiling. "That man was rude."

"He said to keep a better watch on me," she said between giggles. With that, she produced a golden pocket watch hanging from a fob. "He should have been watching his own watch!"

"You stole it?" Modo cried. "We could get into trouble!"

"That dunderhead will never figure it out. I wish I could be there to see the look on his face when he checks the time."

And, imagining that, Modo joined her in laughter.

7

The Arrival

odo gazed from the forecastle of the *Abyssinia* out at
the port of New York City, the late-November wind
sending a chill down his spine. He was wearing his gentleman's winter clothes and his Knight face. Mr. Warkin, he reminded himself. Octavia—Mrs. Warkin—was at his side, a
thick muffler around her neck. Modo's legs felt as though
they were made of India rubber, but he stood as tall as he
could, wanting to capture every detail. Steamships from various countries plied the waterway, as did sailing ships and
tugboats; they seemed to miss each other by inches. The
Abyssinia passed a sandstone fort: Castle Garden. It was the
immigrant landing depot, where all passengers from foreign
ships had to go through an inspection. Line after line of
piers filled the southern side of the island, and beyond them
were the buildings of the city, some so tall they boggled
Modo's mind. How would he be able to climb them? The

city looked orderly, though, compared with London, each street in a perfect line.

"It really is a wonder," Octavia said. "It looks so . . . so new."

"It is new," he agreed. "This was farms and a village not long ago." He searched his mind for any tidbits he remembered from his studies. "There are over a million people here. Maybe more."

"And one of them is our Mr. Wyle. I do hope he knows how to make tea."

A short time later they disembarked. Modo saw the third-class passengers waiting in long lines in the cold and dragging all their own luggage. He felt a stab of pity as he and Octavia were directed to the first-class arrival line. Porters carried their portmanteaus, and they were speedily ushered through Castle Garden. He was careful not to cough around the border agents, as he knew they were always on the lookout for passengers with infectious diseases.

Soon they were in a hansom cab, the horse's hooves clomping on cobblestone streets. The cab itself was much like any he'd seen in London, but the driver wore a bowler. Modo stared out at the people on the street—so many! The men's hats were shorter than was the fashion in London, and the cut of their jackets was different. Several men wore striped gray trousers with black frock coats. They dressed as if they were going to a picnic, though they were entering the doors to the city hall.

The cab rattled down another street and finally turned onto Lafayette Place, where Modo and Octavia got out and paid the driver with the American money Mr. Socrates had supplied. Modo grabbed both portmanteaus and stood on the sidewalk, glancing up and down the street. It looked like a safe enough lane, but he plotted an escape route anyway. Over the years Tharpa had drilled that necessity into him.

"Let's not dillydally," Octavia said. They went to the address Mr. Socrates had given them, entered the building, and climbed several sets of stairs to the third floor. Modo set down their luggage as Octavia knocked on the door of Mr. Wyle's apartment. She banged again. No answer.

"He must be out," Modo said.

"Who are you?" A middle-aged man was coming up the stairs, wheezing with each step. A red handkerchief, neatly folded, peeked out of his front pocket. Modo took a measure of the man. Short, maybe a hundred and seventy pounds, and no weapons in his hands or visible in his jacket.

"He's the caretaker," he whispered to Octavia.

"Oh, aren't you the master detective," she whispered back. "Look out, Scotland Yard."

The man stopped on the landing, removed the handkerchief, and dabbed at his balding forehead. "Are you here to see Mr. Wyle?"

"Indeed, we're here for our honeymoon," Modo said. "We had intended to surprise him."

"He's my brother," Octavia continued. "We're visiting from London."

"You are much younger than Mr. Wyle."

"I'm the youngest of a large family."

"Ah, well, I should introduce myself. I'm Jonathon Trottier, the caretaker here."

"It is a pleasure to meet you," Modo said, extending his

hand. Trottier's palm was sweaty, his grip weak. "We are Mr. and Mrs. Warkin."

"Well, I have some bad news. I'm sorry to inform you"—he took in a wheezy lungful of air—"that Mr. Wyle has passed away."

Octavia started back. "No!"

"How?" Modo asked.

"He was found in his room nearly two weeks ago. I'm afraid . . . that . . . he was murdered."

"Oh, dear Lord! How horrible!" Octavia was looking suitably pale. "Murdered? Why would anyone want to hurt him?"

"My dear, my dear." Modo embraced her. He looked at Mr. Trottier. "Did they catch the murderer?"

"No. Not that I know of. And I follow the papers and have had contact with the inspectors."

Modo patted Octavia's back as she wept quietly. "Was it a robbery?"

"No. There seems to be no reason, but another man was murdered at the Astor Library on the same day. The authorities say there may be a connection." He patted his forehead again. "I was told the police couldn't find any next of kin for Mr. Wyle."

"We had fallen out of touch," Octavia said, lifting her head from Modo's shoulder. "He was . . . a quiet sort."

"He was, at that. I'll let you into his apartment. It, uh"—he paused to wheeze—"it has been properly cleaned, but perhaps, Mrs. Warkin, you would prefer not to be in the place where the foul deed took place."

Octavia sniffed and patted at her eyes with a handkerchief. "No. I must see his room, if only to believe that he is gone."

Mr. Trottier produced a set of keys and opened the door. It was a smallish apartment, with a window that let in the morning light. The furnishings were spare; the walls bore no artwork or hangings. Octavia motioned to several books on the shelves and whispered, "He always liked reading."

The man stood at the door, and it became clear that he had no intention of leaving. It would be impossible to find clues under his watchful eyes.

Octavia began to weep impressively, leaning on the table. Modo put a hand on her shoulder and she turned and rested her head against him. Her hair smelled of perfume. "Darling," he said, the word slipping out so easily, "this is too much. Too much for your delicate spirit." He turned toward the caretaker. "Would you be able to bring us some tea, Mr. Trottier? My wife needs something warm to soothe her."

"I can make coffee. Would that do?"

"We would appreciate that so very much."

The moment he was out the door, Octavia lifted her head, wiped at her tears, and began searching through cupboards. "Be quick, Modo. That old duffer could return any moment."

"Yes, dah-ling," he said, but swallowed nervously. He didn't exactly enjoy picking through a dead man's possessions. "So who killed Wyle?" he asked, his voice breaking.

"The enemy, of course," Octavia answered in a whisper. "Sadly, that doesn't narrow down our suspects. Perhaps the French knew he'd been following them."

"But a man was killed at the library."

"Wyle could have killed him. Then someone followed Wyle to his apartment."

"Who? More French agents? Or are other agents involved? The Germans? The Clockwork Guild?"

"Let's hope it's the Germans. I don't fancy tangling with the Guild again. Now shut it and keep your mind on the task, Modo."

"Well, you don't need to get peevish!"

"Just concentrate! That's what Mr. Socrates would tell you. We don't have much time."

"Well then, what are we looking for?" He opened the closet. Three suits, a pair of boots, a raincoat.

"I don't know. A hint of what he may have discovered. If anything."

Modo checked the suit pockets. A bill from R. H. Macy & Co. Was that important? He picked up a pair of boots, knocking on the soles to see if there was a concealed compartment. Mr. Socrates had a knife hidden in his shoe. Could these be the boots Wyle was wearing when he died? Modo set them down.

Octavia tapped the top of a dresser. "Aha!" She had pulled a drawer out and was feeling behind it. "There's a hollow space here." She removed a square box and opened it to find several papers and a few notes, which Modo tucked inside the pocket of his jacket.

They heard a sharp cough. Modo slipped to the door and peeked out, but there was no one in the stairwell. Someone must be downstairs, in the entrance. When he turned back, he saw papers on the table that he hadn't noticed before.

"Were these always here?" he asked.

"We must be going blind!"

One was a drawing of a fish; another showed fancy handwriting that Modo thought might be a woman's. It said *VSVYWBT KEUW 6035236*. The third piece of paper had *Grand poisson 6035236* scribbled in a large, quick hand. Several other words had been crossed out as though someone had been trying to solve a puzzle.

"It looks like a cipher," Octavia said.

"I bet this page is Wyle's handwriting. And the code has already been partially solved. Big fish—that's nothing that we didn't already know. What do the numbers represent?"

"It must be another code."

Modo heard footsteps on the hardwood in the hall. "Quick!" Octavia said, and Modo was able to tuck the papers into his jacket before the caretaker returned.

"Your coffee," he said. "You must forgive me, I didn't express my condolences."

"We are in debt to you," Octavia said sweetly. "You are being so very kind." She and Modo sipped their coffee. Modo had never understood the attraction of this bitter drink over tea, but he thanked Mr. Trottier anyway.

"Is there lodging nearby?" Octavia asked. "We must rest and . . . and tell my family the news."

"Yes. The Mercer Hotel is a few blocks from here."

After receiving directions, they bid the man goodbye. Modo grabbed their luggage and they went down the creaking stairs. They needed to send a telegram to Mr. Socrates with all the information they had found so far.

Modo grimaced, testing the suppleness of his face. His

muscles weren't tired—he was in control of his transformation. It had been three hours since he'd shifted into the Knight form. He'd have just another few hours before he'd have to slip his mask back on.

"Open the door for me, husband," Octavia said when they reached the outside door.

"But my hands are full," he answered.

"I am a lady and you will open the door."

Modo rolled his eyes and balanced the portmanteaus so that he could twist the knob, letting a bit of a cold breeze through. "Let us go, then, my delicate wife," he said. "We have much work to do."

8

Other Eyes

In an apartment across the street from Lafayette Place a young man sat looking out the window, playing with a roll of gauze, occasionally wheezing out a cough. He'd been keeping an eye on the building for weeks. On this particular afternoon he was contemplating calling his masters to suggest they move him on to more interesting work, when a young couple carrying luggage stopped outside Lafayette. They were clearly visitors. As soon as they entered the building, the man dropped the gauze. There was no time to prepare a disguise or dress properly. He would go as he was, despite the cold.

He ran over and crept up the stairs. They were inside Wyle's apartment! He heard a male voice say, "I can make coffee. Would that do?" and watched as the caretaker emerged and climbed the stairs to his third-story apartment. The young man stealthily took the remaining stairs and positioned himself next to the door. He stilled his breathing, and listened. He overheard the conversation between the two strangers and discovered that their names were Modo and Octavia. It was soon obvious they were agents, but their English accents meant nothing. They could be working for anyone. They mentioned a Mr. Socrates. Another code name? He would take things into his own hands and trick these two into decoding the numbers for him.

The young man cursed Agent Wyle for dying so easily. He had intended to squeeze critical information out of him first. And now he had no idea what the numbers on the paper meant. He'd telegraphed his masters for guidance but had not yet received a reply. What was the point of having a telegraph if not to obtain instant answers? No one was giving him any direction!

And so, brazenly, he had stepped right into the apartment while their backs were turned and placed the papers on the table. He walked as though he had no weight. He retreated just as quietly, but couldn't stop one cough from squeaking out. Damn his lungs. He hid in a doorway and listened as they found the papers and argued over their meaning. Fools! he thought. I'm playing you!

He waited around the back of the stairs as they clomped down them, and smirked as Modo opened the door for Octavia. They had no idea he was stalking them. It was almost too easy.

He approached the door to observe their direction; then, cursing the cold, he followed.

9

The Indecipherable Cipher

Octavia believed she was about to go stark raving mad. Or perhaps she would just get mad, at the very least. She picked at the crusts from her beef sandwich. For the past hour they had been sitting in O'Bryan's Eatery, examining Agent Wyle's papers. There was one note about losing the trail of Colette Brunet, and another about the Red Horse, a saloon that French sailors frequented; and finally there was the code: *Grand poisson 6035236*. The numbers were completely vexing!

Modo had the page in his thick hand and was staring at it as though his eyelids were glued open. She took a moment to examine him. There had been a subtle shift to his face; it seemed fleshier, somehow, and a rashlike redness had appeared on his forehead. She knew he had some unnatural way of manipulating his appearance. Was that what he was doing now?

He was the oddest, most exasperating man she had ever met. No, she corrected herself, he wasn't a man. He was a boy who looked like a man. She was certain that he was younger than her own fifteen years.

"You're breaking out in a rash, husband," she said.

The panic on his face surprised her. He patted at his forehead, peeked at her through his fingers. "I'll soon have to wear my mask again," he said.

"What's happening to you, then? Why can't I see what you really look like?"

At this, his eyes narrowed.

"Let's not discuss that," he said, somewhat coldly. "You know I can't show you. Now, come on, we must solve this code. Mr. Socrates will want to know the answer."

"We're going in circles," she complained. "It'll take greater minds than ours. We should contact our lord and master at once and wait for our orders. Use the wireless telegraph he gave you."

"Not here in the open. Besides, I want to solve the puzzle first."

"Don't be stubborn, Modo," she said.

"Fine. We'll say that it's your decision."

"Of course it's my decision. I *am* the senior agent."

Modo let out a raspberry, loud enough that other patrons looked their way, and quite suddenly both of them began giggling. They continued to chuckle as they walked down the street to the Mercer Hotel.

"We have to be on our guard," Modo said, still smiling. Octavia was impressed by how easily he carried both portmanteaus. "If someone was trailing Agent Wyle, they may be watching us."

"Oh, Modo," she said lightheartedly, "Mr. Socrates has you boxing with shadows. We're completely safe." She wished she could believe her own words. After all, she didn't know New York; she felt safer in London. At least there she knew good places to hide. Any one of the hundreds of people on the street here could be the enemy.

They checked into their room at the hotel, and once they'd unpacked, Modo withdrew the wireless telegraph from his pocket and opened it. At the top of the device was a small switch and three keys. "Now to get this to work," he said.

"Do you want me to do it?"

"No. Mr. Socrates gave it to me for safekeeping." His fingers hovered over the keys. "It uses electromagnetic induction to jump the signal to the nearest telegraph line."

"Really? Ain't you a longheaded professor! How do you get it going?"

"Oh, that's easy!" Modo pressed a key and nothing happened. Then he tapped the side of the machine. "I believe a wire is loose."

Octavia reached over and flicked a small switch. A light bumblebee-buzzing noise was followed by a hum.

"I was just about to do that!" Modo said. He slowly typed out a message. "There! It's done."

"How will he reply?"

"That's the problem. This can't receive messages. He'll send a telegram to the hotel."

"So we have to wait. We should go browsing books, then, my dear," Octavia suggested.

They went back to Lafayette Place, dodging carriages as they crossed the street, and strode toward the Astor Library. Octavia wondered what it was that made New York so different; it wasn't just the people. The air was clear and crisp. She was so used to fog and coal smoke; she found she actually missed them.

The library wasn't the largest she had visited, but it seemed popular. Some gentlemen and ladies sat at tables, while others perused the shelves. Octavia led Modo to the top floor, to discover that no patrons were there.

"That's the meeting room," she said, motioning to a door.

"It's the only room up here," Modo said. "Scotland Yard, watch out!"

"Oh, still stinging from that one, are you? Well, if you're not too upset, please pick the lock. I'll keep an eye out." Modo pulled a set of pins from his belt, and he and Octavia were soon in the room. It was sparse: a table, curtains on a window, and only a few books on the shelves.

"Well, this was a waste of time," Octavia said. She paused to wonder if she was crossing the place where the Frenchman had fallen.

Then she heard a slight cough and a scuffling sound. She turned. "Are you sick?" she asked.

"It was you who coughed," Modo said without looking up from a book.

"I don't cough," she said. "I expel air daintily."

"Lucky you, then." He threw up his hands. "I don't

believe we'll find anything here. It was all cleaned up weeks ago."

His forehead glistened in the light coming through the window, and his skin was pink.

"You're looking a little flushed, Modo. Is it the seasickness?"

Modo put his hand to his cheek and with a small gasp turned his back to her. He dug in his jacket pocket, then brought his hands to his face again. When he turned around he was wearing the net mask. He seemed slightly smaller and hunched over.

"What's happening to you, Modo?"

"You know I can't answer that."

"Yes, but I like to ask, husband dear. I'm an odd fish that way."

· He was especially hard to read when he was wearing a mask. She'd stared at the net thing for over a week and was sick of it.

They returned to their hotel room, ordered a roast chicken to be sent up, and ate quickly. Octavia remained at the table, tapping her fingers on a map of the world that had been intricately carved into the mahogany. She traced a line from London to New York. "The waiting will drive me off at the head," she said. "Would you like to play a hand of snap?"

"I don't play cards. Mr. Socrates didn't feel that those games were necessary to my upbringing."

"Oh, that old parsimonious codger! No one's to have any fun in his Permanent Association. I sometimes believe that their real objective is to bore the world to tears."

She was pleased to see Modo laugh. "Well, husband,

what am I to do with you? I'll have to revert to children's games. Let us give 'I'm Thinking of Something' a go."

"How does that work?"

"We used to play it while we pounded laundry at the orphanage. We ask one another questions and try to guess what the other's thinking. I'll start. Ready?"

"Ah, sure."

She decided that he was so staid, it was time to stagger him. "So, Modo, do you understand love?"

She nearly laughed at how he goggled. Even the net mask couldn't hide his shock.

"Do I what?"

"Do you understand why we mortal vessels feel love? Or, more important, how does one such as yourself dupe others into believing you are the romantic prince of their dreams?"

He scratched at his shoulder. "What brought this on?"

"Mr. Socrates had me read Shakespeare and Dickens, especially *Great Expectations*. He wanted me to understand how humans want love." She began to imitate Mr. Socrates, feeling pleased with her tone and accent. "The key to being a good agent is manipulating your targets into giving you information. Use flirting. Use words that imply love. All their emotions are tools that can be used against them."

"That's a horrible thing to do. Did Mr. Socrates really say that?"

"Oh, he said some such similar thing. Perhaps we female agents get different lessons. We are so much weaker than you men, so we have to rely on trickery. I'm curious, though— has anyone ever . . . loved you?"

"Of course."

She tapped her finger on the table. "Who?"

"Uh. M-Mrs. Finchley."

"The governess? She was paid by Mr. Socrates to raise you. So how can you be sure that she loved you?"

"You're wrong about her!" he snapped.

I'm being cruel, she thought. Why? And yet, she couldn't stop. He could be so innocent at times. He had to wake up to the reality of the world around him. "I'm only suggesting that one must examine one's beliefs. Does Mr. Socrates love you?"

"No. Of course not. I'm an agent."

His eyes were glimmering, as if filled with tears. Shame made her swallow her next words. Why was she lashing out this way? Because he wouldn't show her his real face? Because he didn't trust her completely?

"I'm certain someone *has* loved you, Modo," she said finally. "I mean, *does* love you. Mr. Socrates hides much more of his feelings than he shows. And that—that governess, too."

"Her name is Mrs. Finchley," Modo said after a long pause. "If we follow your logic, one should never trust one's own assumptions about other people's feelings. Thank you. Lesson learned. Good night, Octavia." He unfolded the privacy screen between the sofa and the bed, hiding from her eyes.

After several minutes she whispered, "Modo? Modo?"

Silence.

"Modo."

"Yes." He sounded groggy.

"I'm sorry. I was just having a lark. I did not mean to upset you."

"You're forgiven," he said.

"Thank you," she answered, with all sincerity. "Modo, you called me Octavia just a moment ago."

"Yes."

"Remember, you can call me Tavia. It's what my friends call me."

He sighed. "Good night, Tavia." That was the last she heard from him that evening.

10

Commandeering a Ride

Modo awakened several times in the night, sweating and trembling from nightmares. At one point he unintentionally slipped off his mask and tossed it to the floor. He heard Octavia moving about on the other side of the privacy screen. In a panic he felt around until he found the mask and pulled it over his face, then slept fitfully until morning.

In the bathroom he changed his twisted face and body back to the shape of Mr. Warkin, gritting his teeth and smothering his groans of pain. He dressed and, looking in the mirror, decided it was time to surprise Octavia. He oiled his hair, parting it in the center instead of at the side. He grinned. It suited the aquiline features of this face.

"Tavia, are you awake?" he asked.

"Yes, Modo, you can fold up the screen."

She was already in a dark gray dress, and was tying back her hair with a ribbon. These were the sorts of things a husband was privy to, his wife fixing her hair.

"Good morning to you," she said. Her eyes looked heavy, suggesting she'd also had a restless sleep. "Your hair is extremely fashionable. I shall be proud to take your arm as we promenade about New York."

Modo smiled. "I spent an extra ten seconds on it." Something moving under the door caught his eye. An envelope. "It looks like work has found us."

He opened it and removed a telegram that read: erwaiv sfzmsyw STOP Pex&prsk STOP Qsria xs QRF STOP Lmvi wlmt rs p&p ex srgi STOP Xeoi tlsvs iuymt STOP Fi tvsjiwwmsrep STOP

"What is it?" Octavia asked.

Modo took a moment to decipher the message, using a simple code system Mr. Socrates had taught him years ago. "The note says, 'Answer obvious STOP Lat&long STOP Money wired to MNB STOP Hire ship to l&l at once STOP Take photo equip STOP Be professional STOP.' "

"Even in telegrams Mr. Socrates has to lecture us," she said. "I can almost see him wagging his finger."

"I should have guessed the numbers were latitude and longitude!" he said.

"Oh, Modo, don't beat yourself up. Sometimes the simplest answers are the hardest to find. Now, where exactly are we supposed to go?" She sat at the mahogany table, and looked down at the carved map.

"Assuming this is accurately carved, it's right here!" He tapped on a point about an inch below Iceland.

"Sounds dreary and cold; good thing we get paid such riches to do this job."

"You get paid?"

"Mr. Socrates said he is setting aside a fund for my retirement. I assume he has done the same for you."

"I didn't know we could retire."

"That's the whole lark of it all, Modo. Most of us won't get to live long enough to retire. Ah, well, it's better than pickpocketing, I guarantee that!"

After breakfast they went to Merchant's National Bank, where Modo withdrew seven thousand American dollars, filling his wallet and stuffing the rest in his portmanteau. They gathered up their luggage, took a cab to shop on Broadway, bought photographic equipment, then returned to the port. They were deposited near Castle Garden.

The landing was noisy, with draymen and deckhands shouting and fruit vendors, their baskets on carts, bellowing out their prices. Travelers streamed into the city. Occasionally a steam whistle cut through the din, loud enough to shake the very docks.

"Passenger liners won't alter their course for us," Octavia said, "so we must hire a smaller ship."

Modo nodded. "It would be best to have a steamship. Anything sailing under canvas would be far too slow."

"Then let's find our ship, Modo. Look for the ones with smoking funnels. That means their boilers are being stoked and they'll soon leave port."

"I know that," Modo snapped, which was true, for he'd read enough sailing novels. He was growing tired of how she always tried to teach him things.

Partway down the docks they found a ship called the *Hugo*. Smoke puffed out of its smokestack. It had a rusted iron hull and was so shabby it looked as if removing one rivet would make the entire ship collapse and sink straight to the bottom.

"Almost seaworthy," Octavia said.

"Maybe there's something better." Modo lifted their luggage and continued down the pier, but they returned a half hour later to the *Hugo*. "There's really no other choice," he said, "and Mr. Socrates did say we should go at once."

They approached several seamen and dockworkers. "I would like to meet the captain of the *Hugo*," Modo said, and the men stared at him without moving. Octavia coughed and pointed at her palm. Modo reached into his wallet and brought out a dollar bill. "For your troubles."

A few minutes later they were being rowed in a boat by a husky sailor who reeked of whisky. His red-rimmed eyes were glued to Octavia. Modo wanted to poke the man's peepers out, even though Octavia ignored the sailor, gazing out across the water, umbrella in hand. They pulled up to the huge side of the *Hugo*, and the seaman seemed to shake the boat as much as possible as Modo and Octavia stood up to grab the gangway ladder.

When they'd climbed to the top, Modo looked down to see the drunkard teetering and waving his arms as though bothered by insects, before falling into the water to the laughter of the seamen remaining on the dock. That'll teach you! Modo thought.

The wooden deck of the *Hugo* was scarred by weather

and littered by a mess of rope, boxes, and nets. A crate of black, rotted bananas had broken open amidships. "We'd like to speak to the captain," Octavia said to the first deckhand they met.

"Yes, we would," Modo added quickly, to show he was in charge.

They were taken up a set of stairs to the upper deck. The sailor knocked on the door and shouted, "Captain, guests here to see you!" Then he left them standing alone.

Nothing happened for several moments. "Do you think he's there?" Octavia asked.

Modo shrugged and knocked again. "Captain! We're here about passage on your ship!"

The door swung open to reveal a short man in trousers and a shirt with the sleeves torn off. His arms were tattooed with coiled snakes. He was thin as a ferret, his eyes two black coals, and his matted, oily hair was parted in the middle. Modo guessed he was another deckhand.

"Is the captain here?" Modo asked.

"I *am* the captain, you fool! What are you doing on my ship?"

"We—we— What is your destination?"

"Hamburg."

"Ah, that's perfect," Octavia said.

"Perfect?"

"Ah, yes, we have—" Octavia began, but Modo cut in.

"A wedding to attend," he finished. He shot Octavia a look. As the husband, he was supposed to make such arrangements man to man.

"I don't take passengers. They talk. They eat. They get in the way. Not even if you offered me two hundred dollars."

"What about two thousand dollars?" Octavia said. Again, Modo scowled at her.

The captain's eyes widened. He pursed his thin lips and ran a hand over his greasy scalp, then stepped back and bowed. "You are so very welcome on my ship. Captain Goss at your service! You'll find the *Hugo* may not look like much on the outside, but she'll do twelve knots with the boilers fully stoked and the sails set."

"Twelve knots? That is fast!" Modo exclaimed, knowing they'd be lucky to hit ten knots. "We are Mr. and Mrs. Warkin. I'm a photographer and my wife is my assistant. I wonder . . . on our way to Hamburg there is a particular ocean vista we would very much like to photograph. A place where the slant of light reflects in an amazingly perfect way on the capturing lens of the camera. It's simply stunning, I am told."

"Where is this 'vista'?"

Modo told him the latitude and longitude.

"That will be another thousand dollars," Captain Goss said without hesitation. "It's a day out of our way. I have to pay my crew a bonus, and there are coal supplies to consider. I myself make nothing."

"Agreed," Octavia said.

"Agreed!" Modo repeated, giving her the eye. She would never be able to play the wife correctly!

"My men will bring your bags aboard and my first mate will show you to your cabin." Goss whistled, so loudly that Modo's ears rang.

Forty minutes later the ship was moving out to sea. They had been given the first mate's cabin, after paying him a hundred dollars so that he would sleep on a bunk in the seamen's quarters. The cabin was tiny, with a small cot that Octavia claimed, saying, "It's your turn to sleep on the floor, husband dearest."

"I'd have it no other way," Modo replied with false sweetness. A smoke- and coal-smudged porthole looked out on the ocean. Modo's stomach churned, but not nearly the way it had on their first crossing of the Atlantic. Soon his face began to burn and ache and he was forced to put on his mask. He drew a thick cloak out of the portmanteau and threw it over himself to hide all his bumps and humps from Octavia's eyes. How he hated the way his back twisted! The cabin was so small, he was certain Octavia would eventually see every iota of his ugliness. Whenever her eyes flitted over him, he wanted to retreat like a rat into a hole. He set up a sheet in one corner for both of them to change behind when they needed to.

The *Hugo* splashed and fought its way northward. The farther they traveled, the shorter the daylight hours became. Modo spent most of his time in their wretched room. He would change his shape to go for an infrequent walk, then return to the cabin, feigning illness. Meals were brought right to their door, but were never hot and never good and mostly seemed to be made of an unidentifiable overcooked meat. "It must be buffalo," Octavia declared after several meals. "I've heard it's quite stringy."

Occasionally the captain invited them to "sup" at his private dining table, which was little more than a slab of wood in his cabin. The metal plates were nailed down, and it looked as though a decade had passed since they were last wiped. "I did have a lovely basket of apples," he told them when the salted pork was done, "but they disappeared down someone's gullet. The lash will get to the bottom of it. So drink lots of lemonade instead; that'll keep the scurvy away." He smiled wryly.

The next day, while Modo walked around the deck, he tried to picture a life at sea and decided it wasn't for him. No place to climb if there was danger. Well, that wasn't true—there was the crow's nest, at least. Without a second thought he scrambled to the top, joining the bald seaman who sat on his perch staring out into the vast distance. "You climb well, for a fancy gentleman," the man said.

"Thank you," Modo answered. "I just wanted to get a good look at this watery world."

"Go ahead. Feast your peepers! There's nothin' and everythin' to see."

Modo could feel the sway of the ship much more up here, but it didn't bother his stomach. He enjoyed the familiar wonderful feeling of being above the world. And his "peepers" could see much farther than they could from the rooftops of London. The water seemed endless. The sun was setting, even though it was only six o'clock in the evening.

Down on the deck he saw two men toiling away at the daily swabbing. Then he counted the lifeboats. Six. All together they might hold thirty men. There were at least a hundred people on the *Hugo*.

"There are only six lifeboats," Modo said. "What happens if we sink?"

"Well, gent"—the man smiled broadly, exposing a missing tooth—"on a civilized boat it'd be women and children first. I can't vouch for this bein' a civilized boat, if it were to come to that. Best to just make your peace with Jesus, Joe, and the Good Lord." He chuckled. Modo's stomach suddenly didn't feel very good. The ship had made many journeys without sinking, he told himself. It would be fine. Just fine.

On the morning of the seventh day of the voyage, the *Hugo* gave a great shudder, the engines slowed, and the anchor was let down with a thunderous rattle of chains. Someone pounded on Modo and Olivia's door. "We've arrived, Mr. and Mrs. Warkin!" They recognized Goss's voice.

"We'll be right out," Modo shouted. He was still in his nightclothes, the net mask, and a nightcap.

"You're quite the picture," Octavia kidded. "Now avert your eyes."

He did so as Octavia took two steps from the cot to get dressed behind the hanging sheet. Modo hid under his own blanket to change his features. He was still sleepy and had to struggle to remember the right face.

"I wish you would tell me what you're doing," Octavia said.

She was already dressed! "Just the usual ritual," he said between clenched teeth. When he was done, he wiped his forehead, and lowered the blanket.

She smiled. "Well, whatever you did worked. You look very dashing."

Cheeks burning, Modo changed behind the hanging sheet and led the way out, carrying the photographic equipment.

It was after nine and the sun was only beginning to rise over a rather unremarkable, gray stretch of ocean, nothing but rolling waves in the distance. The captain and three of his men were standing near the mainmast. "Not sure why you wanted to see this amazing 'vista,' " Goss said, "but here it is."

"Are you certain they're the correct coordinates?" Octavia asked.

Goss furrowed his brow. "Of course!" He pointed north. "That way is Iceland. I know the sea like the back of my hand. Remind me what you want to do here?"

"It's all about the light," Modo said, unfolding the wooden legs of his tripod. Octavia held out a light meter. "This latitude and longitude and the refraction from the curvature of the earth create perfect light." Modo was pleased with his use of baffling jargon.

"Perfect light for what?"

"For portraits, Captain Goss. Portraits! Your crew would make good subjects for our study."

"A photograph? Of those dogs?" Goss's eyes lit up momentarily, and Modo seized on what he saw as the captain's vanity.

"Not them so much, sir, as you. *They* will be good background material. You should be front and center."

"Your face is very Roman and powerful, Captain," Octavia added. "Such cheekbones and a strong jaw." She turned to Modo. "He's truly perfect, my husband."

Goss blushed slightly. Modo raised an eyebrow at this.

"Are you dressed appropriately? Your image will be recorded forever, you know," Modo said.

Goss patted at his hair. "Give me a moment. I forgot my sash. Should I wear a saber?"

"Do you even have to ask, Captain?" Octavia said. "Of course you should! We need to capture the drama of your occupation."

Once the captain had scurried off, Modo and Octavia went to the rail of the *Hugo* and looked out over the water.

"Well," she said, "we're here. Now what?"

One of the men sneezed. It seemed rather close, but when Modo turned, the nearest sailor was several yards away.

"Frankly, Octavia," Modo said, "my guess is we're just supposed to get the lay of the land, so to speak. I think it's a long shot if Mr. Socrates believes some fish will just suddenly rise out of the ocean to greet us. The *grand poisson* could be anywhere. We'll take a few photographs of the area. Perhaps Mr. Socrates will have some use for them."

The *Hugo* lurched to one side and Modo grabbed the rail. Octavia latched on to the same spot and their hands touched. "What was that?" she asked.

"I don't know."

The first mate shouted, "We've lost our anchor, sir!"

Captain Goss burst out of his cabin and marched down the stairs, holding his belt, a scabbard clicking against his heel.

"Lost our anchor? But that's impossible."

"The chain has been cut, sir."

"Cut? By what?" He turned to the nearest deckhand. "Tell the engineer to put on steam! Move, you lackey!"

Modo was about to shout out that they'd paid to come here, they needed to stay, when the ship was hit on the port side so hard that it tilted toward starboard. The railing Modo was holding, worn by time and rusted by salt, broke, and he slipped over the edge.

Octavia grabbed his shoulder and he whipped out his arm just in time to catch hold of a piece of the broken railing, leaving him hanging in midair. He pawed the rusted side of the ship until Octavia was able to grab his free hand. Something splashed into the water below.

"Don't let go, Modo!" she cried as the last bit of railing creaked under the strain of his weight. It wouldn't hold long; both of them would fall. Where were those bloody seamen? Couldn't they see their passengers' predicament?

Modo looked into Octavia's eyes and saw her determination—she wouldn't let go. He couldn't have her fall into the water too.

He pictured his wrist expanding, growing larger, and a moment later it began to do so.

"What are you doing?" Octavia screamed as she lost her grip on him.

He tried to find some final, memorable words to leave her with, but all that came out of his mouth was "*Uhh-ooh!*" as he fell into the Atlantic.

11

The Cold Truth

Octavia watched Modo fall and disappear into the waves. She nearly tumbled after him; only by gripping the remains of the railing and pushing back did she manage to stay on the *Hugo*. She leaned over the edge as far as she dared, watching for him.

She began counting silently. Come on, where are you? Not until she hit twenty did Modo's head bob up a hundred yards away. He flailed his arms. What to do? She glanced around, grabbed a nearby wooden barrel, and hefted it over the side, shouting, "Modo, hold on to this!" But he wasn't even looking in her direction.

"Ah, good lord!" Captain Goss rushed to her side. He was sweating, his scabbard bouncing off his heels. "That's bad luck!"

"Bad luck!" she cried out. "Your ship is a wreck!"

"Don't blame the *Hugo*. We've been attacked! All because you and your husband wanted to come here." He waved at Modo and howled, "Keep moving or you'll freeze. We'll send help."

"Kick, Modo!" Octavia yelled. "Keep kicking! We'll be right there."

"Madame," Goss said, his voice surprisingly soft, "Madame, the cold truth is he's beyond our help now."

"No!" She grabbed his arm. "Turn this ship around. We can pick him up."

"Mrs. Warkin, calm down," he said, pulling her hand off his person.

At first she didn't even know whom he was addressing, having forgotten her married name. She clenched her fists. "I won't calm down."

"You must understand, our anchor has been cut, so we can't stop properly. Our ship has been rammed—the hull is punctured. We have little time before the chambers fill to a dangerous level—we must immediately get to port. A rescue attempt would use up time we don't have."

"If you won't go, I will! Lower a rowboat. Now! I insist!"

"Madame, that would be a death sentence. I can't allow it. Our only hope is to travel with all speed toward Iceland. Perhaps we'll encounter another vessel on the way. If not, we can alert the Icelandic authorities and give them the coordinates. They can conduct a more systematic search."

It was all Octavia could do to stop herself from diving in after Modo. He was out there, alone. He wasn't even visible anymore. Her eyes blurred with tears.

"Madame, Madame, please don't weep," the captain said soothingly.

Octavia couldn't hold back a sob. Modo!

"There, there. Moments ago I ordered the engineer to go full speed. We have good winds, too. We're about sixty leagues from Iceland. Rescuers could be back by this evening."

Octavia sighed and wiped her eyes. She had been taught to cry at will if the situation demanded it. But these were real tears. Tears wouldn't accomplish anything, though. "It is all we can do, isn't it?"

"Yes, Mrs. Warkin. I'm sorry. It was wise of you to throw that barrel to him. Let's hope your husband is floating on it right now. If he can keep most of his body out of the water, he'll last much longer. He looked like a fit man. He'll have a better chance than most of surviving." The captain paused. "Is there anything else you need? I could have one of my men bring you tea."

"Tea? No. I'm fine."

"Then please excuse me. I must look after my ship. I would suggest returning to your cabin. It would do no good for you to catch a chill."

"Thank you, Captain." She looked toward the ocean one more time. There was no sign of Modo. It was as if nothing had happened at all. She sent her warmest thoughts, her brightest wishes out over the water. Be strong, Modo. We'll do everything to rescue you.

Then she remembered the wireless telegraph Mr. Socrates had given them. She might be able to send a message to him—maybe he could alert the Icelandic authorities imme-diately. She ran back to their cabin, searching madly through their luggage and drawers, but she was unable to find the device. It would be in Modo's pocket. She collapsed on the cot and pounded her fists into her pillow until feathers flew everywhere.

12

When Hands Become Claws

On his way down Modo had the presence of mind to take a deep breath. He hit the water with a huge splash and plummeted like a cannonball deeper and deeper into the shocking cold, then kicked and kicked his way upward. When he finally broke the surface, he sucked in a breath, then treaded water. His eyes stung from the salt water. He blinked until his vision cleared. Then, as he was lifted by a cresting wave, he saw that the *Hugo* had already drifted hundreds of yards away. He could make out Octavia and the shorter figure of the captain beside her, both shouting and gesturing. Then Modo fell with the wave and it seemed forever before he rose high enough to spot the *Hugo* again. Octavia was so far away, he couldn't imagine her being able to see him.

Minutes later he could still hear shouting and the rumble of the engine, but could no longer see the ship. The next thing he saw was a funnel of smoke on the horizon.

"Don't leave me! Don't!" he shrieked, swallowing a mouthful of seawater. He hacked for a minute, trying to keep his chin above the surface, until his throat was cleared. Then his world fell silent. Good lord, he was alone now. Even the smoke had vanished.

Over his right shoulder there was a splash. Sharks? Would they go for his legs? Oh no! Oh no! He kicked hard and swam until his limbs ached and his lungs wheezed.

Keep your thoughts clear! Tharpa had told him that a thousand times over the years. Modo paused to gather his wits. He treaded water in a circle, scanning every inch of its surface. No fins. Therefore, he deduced, it was unlikely there were any sharks. Octavia's voice echoed in his head, "Look out, Scotland Yard." Unbelievably, for an instant, he smiled.

Suddenly he was aware of the drag of his clothing, so he struggled out of his jacket and kicked off his shoes. Think, Modo. What next? The ship wouldn't come back, and in any case he would be very hard to spot.

There would be no rescue, unless they were able to send another ship in the next hour, and then, by some miracle, the crew would have to pick him out in the vast rolling waves. Would it be soon enough? He was shivering so hard that his teeth clacked together. Just keep moving! Keep yourself warm. Since Modo's last assignment, Tharpa had taught him how to swim properly at Forest Hill Baths. But the ocean was much colder than the plunge pools at the spa.

He had read so many stories about men being stranded at sea, then captured by pirates. But pirates liked islands. Under Mrs. Finchley's tutelage he had memorized the map of the world, and he knew there were no islands in the area. Ergo, no pirates.

Maybe Mr. Socrates would save him! Yes! Yes! With a balloon! He'd float down out of the sky. With Tharpa. Who would lower a rope and lift him out of the water. . . . Madness! He shook his head to dispel the daydream. Stay calm, stay calm. Think! Think!

It was after nine in the morning, which meant the sun was in the east. If he swam north he'd be heading in the direction of Iceland, but it was miles and miles from here, and no one could swim that far in this frigid November water.

Unless I change my shape into that of a dolphin! More madness! He nearly slapped himself. He could think more clearly if it weren't so cold! He didn't understand why he hadn't already frozen to death.

Perhaps it is my odd ugly body! This thought made him chuckle. It might be that some quality of his adaptive transformation made his body less likely to freeze.

He was growing colder and colder. His hands were as gnarled as claws; he couldn't straighten them. Though he was exhausted, his features remained in the form of the Knight, as though the cold had frozen him that way. Wouldn't that be something—to die with this face, forever handsome.

He thought he heard another voice. Or was it the onset of real madness? In the next few minutes his legs cramped, each sharp pain the only feeling in his universe. At least that meant he was alive. Within a half hour his feet had arched and twisted into throbbing hooks. Even his toes were crossing, frozen in place. Each breath became harder.

Say goodbye, Modo, he thought. Goodbye to Mr.

Socrates, the enigma of a man who had rescued him from a traveling sideshow and raised him as a son. Well, not a son, but as close as one could be. Mr. Socrates, you struggled so hard to teach me, and I am failing you now, sir.

Then Tharpa. Young sahib, he always called Modo. Young master. Had there ever been a man as strong, quick, and light on his feet as dear Tharpa?

Mrs. Finchley. She had raised him like a mother. *Just one more cookie! One more.* He could see a cookie jar floating on a wave just out of reach. He splashed toward it, but the jar vanished.

And Tavia, who had such perfect eyes. It was as though she were there. He wished he had remarked on her hair, told her that it looked fine that day, that she was dazzling.

A hissing cut through the air, a fountain of water spouted some hundred feet away, and soon he felt himself lifted slowly from the water, higher, higher, as though to heaven.

His knees cramped again and bent. There was something solid underneath him. A large, dark blue whale was surfacing. It took all his strength to cling to it. Another column of water shot skyward. His mind wandered to Jonah, then to Moby-Dick and Captain Ahab's need for revenge.

Finally he remembered: this was the metal-sparred whale Mr. Socrates had spoken of! From his prone position Modo couldn't see much of it, just the many bumps along its back. Barnacles.

His fingers were fused together by the freezing water. A cramp ran alongside his spine and he cried out in pain. The whale was like a block of dark blue ice that vibrated. A shiver? The swishing of its tail? He'd heard of shipwrecked men who'd swum to an island, only to discover when they lit a fire that the island was actually a whale that had been sleeping there for years. Could that be true?

His eyes were half frozen shut; the glinting of the dull sun made him blink. Only one eye was working now. He blinked again. His vision cleared momentarily and he saw that they weren't barnacles on the side of the whale after all, but glittering gold flecks across the dark blue skin.

He touched one with numb fingers. A nut. It was a brass nut, fastening a steel plate.

The sight shocked him, gave him a spurt of energy. He spotted a small rail a few feet in front of him; a rounded section protruded from the metal. He crawled to the rail and hung on. Then he saw the circular door at the top of the protrusion.

He worked his claw-fingers into the latch. It wouldn't turn. Locked! He summoned up his last spark of strength and pulled. He half expected his fingers to break and fly off. His every muscle was knotting up, but he heard the metal begin to grind. Then came a *snap* and he pried the lid open. Inside was a ladder. A light. Safety.

Something struck the side of his skull, hard. As he tried to raise a hand to protect himself, he was hit again. He grabbed at the ladder, but his stiff hands couldn't catch the rung, and he fell headfirst down the hole.

13

The True Meaning of *Ictíneo*

When he opened his eyes, Modo wondered at first if he'd gone blind. He blinked, quivering. Darkness. Perhaps his eyes were frozen. He could feel warm air surrounding him, but every inch of his body trembled. He touched his face and traced the familiar lumps, his concave nose, his elongated ears. He had shifted back to his normal self.

He patted his chest and discovered he wasn't wearing a shirt. He ran his hand over his back. The hump was still there; even his numbed claw-fingers recognized the shape. His underclothes had been removed and he was naked under a prickly wool blanket. He tried to wiggle his toes but felt nothing. Had his toes fallen off? He reached down and counted all ten.

Someone had undressed him. Who? Had they seen his ugliness? The thought of someone else's eyes on him made him sick.

The room was so humid he wheezed each breath. He was on a mattress of sorts. He felt a wooden frame, decided he was on a small cot. He waved his hands in the air and they brushed something cold and wet as an eel. It seemed to hang in the air above him. He stuck one hand out to the side and found a wall.

At that moment a light burst to life above him and he raised a hand to shield his eyes. He saw the outline of a small dresser at the end of his cot. Someone knocked heavily on the door. He yanked the gray blanket up over himself and pushed his back against the wall, peeking out of the shadows. The narrow door swung into the room, banging against the cot.

A man squeezed inside, his frame thick, a black beard striped with gray beneath his round glasses. He was wearing a blue military uniform without any stripes or markings. He looked like a clerk who'd been raised by woodsmen. He set a steaming bowl and a cup on the dresser, then spoke, but his words were guttural and unrecognizable, another language.

Modo said nothing in response. . . .

"English, then," the man said, his steady gray eyes measuring Modo. "You speak English?"

"Yerr," Modo answered. His tongue was withered with dryness. "Yeerrrsss."

"I should have guessed. I've brought you a bowl of soup. Eat it slowly with the bread. Wash it down with the tea. Why do you hide yourself?"

"I—I'm naked."

"I know that. I removed your clothing and hung it to dry." The man pointed above Modo's head. Modo saw that it was his own wet trousers that he'd mistaken for an eel. "I apologize for doing so without permission, but you would never warm properly in your wet clothes. Why do you hide your face?"

"I—I suffer from an ailment."

"What kind?"

"A facial deformity."

"I saw no such thing. You did suffer a blow to the head. Is it affecting you?"

"No." Though now that he thought of it, his temples throbbed. "My deformity comes and goes. It's like a rash."

"Well, do not feel that you must hide your condition. That is the old way of thinking. You are among equals— there are no deformities here." The man said this in such a matter-of-fact manner that Modo felt as though he'd been chastised. "I've brought some clothing that I hope will be suitable. It is not as stylish as your own garments, but we are not concerned about fashion. You should consume your food—it will bring you back to health." He pointed a thick index finger at the bowl.

"Where am I?"

"The captain will inform you of any details you need to know."

"When will I meet him?"

The man shrugged two lumpy shoulders. "When the captain decides."

"May I ask your name?"

The man's smile was friendly. "Anselm Cerdà," he said, then backed out of the room and closed the door.

Modo pulled on gray trousers, a thick wool sweater, and

a seaman's wool cap that covered his ears. He massaged his toes; they were gray and cold, but he could move them now. He put on the socks and thick-soled shoes the man had provided.

Modo tried to lift the bowl of soup, but his shaking hands spilled so much that he had to leave it on the dresser and lean over it. Then he couldn't control the spoon. The few drops he got into his mouth were salty and heavenly. Finally, he lapped it up like a dog, which left some unfamiliar vegetables and a white fishy meat at the bottom. He scooped these out with trembling fingers. When he was done he felt a little more energetic. The tea was salty and sweet, with a faint orange flavor.

He lay down again. The ceiling light was bright and contained in a circular, glass-enclosed compartment. There was no flame, so it was neither gas nor oil. The whole room thrummed, and a sense of gentle vibration came from everything he touched.

It was a ship, of sorts, and if this wasn't all a dream, it was a ship that could travel under the water. He'd read about attempts at underwater exploration, but those vessels had been tiny and powered by pedals. This was surely powered by steam. But if it was, how were they venting the coal smoke? He couldn't imagine any other way to move such bulk through the depths of the ocean.

It was the kind of technology that Mr. Socrates had hoped they might find when he'd sent them on this assignment: a steamship that traveled underwater, ramming ships from below. Whoever had an army of these vessels would rule the seas.

Modo leapt from the cot and dug into his wet vest pocket. He pulled out the wallet—soaked, of course—containing the wireless telegraph. Surprisingly, the telegraph still looked usable, but he assumed the electric cell had been destroyed by seawater. He set the telegraph under the cot to dry.

Someone banged on the door. "Come out," Cerdà commanded, "the captain wishes to meet you."

"Yes! Yes, one moment." Modo felt in his wet pants pocket and found the net mask. He squeezed out the seawater and pulled it over his face, then put the seaman's cap back on.

His legs were wobbly and threatened to cramp up, but he forced himself to the door. He stepped into a narrow corridor lit by three more of the mysterious round lights. Cerdà looked down at him. "You cover your face."

"I must," Modo said. "I'm ashamed of my rash."

Cerdà nodded and led Modo down the corridor. The walls were gray metal, with railings every few feet; the floor was hardwood that shone in the light. Bolts protruded from the wood, providing traction. They passed several more cabins and came to a winding iron staircase that took them into a large, darkened oval chamber. Modo limped, and occasionally a sharp pain shot up his legs, making him grit his teeth.

It was twelve steps to the bottom. He'd also counted each of his steps from the cabin so he could guess the length of the ship, presuming his room had been near one end. Now he tried to figure out what this room was—the only light in the chamber was entering through a cluster of glass portholes. He squinted, had the impression that there were levers and perhaps a wheel to one side. Then he saw what was on the other side of the glass: fish!

He shuffled as quickly as his body would let him across the room to look out. Gray fish with bulbous eyes goggled back at him as if they were just as surprised to see him. How deep in the ocean could the ship be?

"It is a marvelous sight," a woman said.

Modo spun around to see that he had walked right past two women standing in the shadows. I let my surprise overcome my training, he thought. How stupid! Tharpa had drilled into him that he should always take full stock of any room he entered.

He was taking stock of the first woman now. Tall, dressed in black, with a red sash across her waist, a small cutlass in her belt. Her hair and eyes were dark, her skin ivory. "Yes, it is quite the sight," Modo agreed. She glared at him, her gaze not wavering. She was at least thirty years old, but the bags under her eyes made her seem older.

Beside her was a young woman in a long skirt who wore her dark hair pulled back in large barrettes. She seemed angry too. Her familiar features were vaguely Oriental. Then it came to him—the photograph! The woman standing before him was the French spy, Colette Brunet!

14

Nifleheim's Circle

The five-and-a-half-hour journey to Iceland seemed a lifetime to Octavia. When she wasn't staring out the porthole, she paced the deck, but they didn't see another ship until they were at Reykjavik's port. She stared at the capital of Iceland, no bigger than an English town, the tallest building being a church on a hill. The houses were small and brightly colored. She surveyed the port for a steamship, but there were only sailing ships with great masts. It was as though she'd gone back in time.

Once the *Hugo* had been tugged into the harbor and secured to a wharf, she ran down the gangway. She stopped a fisherman carrying barrels from his ship. "Where's the port authority? I must know now!" He shrugged and shook his head, and muttered something in Icelandic. Ah, he didn't speak English. And she didn't know a single Icelandic word, so she shrieked across the dock: "Please, please, someone tell me: where is the port authority?" A skinny man in a thick gray sweater pointed toward the town and said, "Red house. Over there."

Octavia dashed past him, avoiding fishermen unloading their stock, and burst into the red two-story house without knocking. A huge man with tiny glasses sat behind a desk, wearing a dark blue sweater. He looked up and said something in Icelandic.

"Do you speak English?" she asked.

"Yes."

"Good!" She told her story quickly, finishing with the coordinates of Modo's location.

The man shook his head. "I am sorry. You won't find anyone willing to rescue your husband," he said. "We call that area Nifleheim's circle. No Icelandic vessel has ventured there in over a year."

"Don't you have military ships? Or a steamer?"

He shook his head. "We cannot go there."

"I'll find someone else, then. There must be at least one brave fisherman in this godforsaken place!"

She stormed onto the street without bothering to close the door. She still had fifteen hundred dollars, so she went to a post office and sent Mr. Socrates a telegram, then marched down to the docks and ran from ship to ship, begging fishermen to take her to Modo. The few who did speak English just shook their heads sadly or shrugged. Within the hour the sun began to set, and by a little after four that afternoon, the long Icelandic night had begun.

Octavia slumped to her haunches at the end of a dock, knowing in her heart that no one would be willing to venture out into the treacherous night and that Modo would soon freeze to death, if he hadn't already. She began to sob.

15

The Captain

Modo gawked at Colette Brunet, his mind racing. What was she doing here? She was a French agent. Was this a French submarine ship? The young woman stared boldly back at him. He hadn't expected her to be so tall; she was at least as tall as Octavia.

The older woman rested her hand on the hilt of her cutlass. If she drew her weapon, Modo's best course would be to run, but where?

"I am Captain Delfina Monturiol," the woman said with a slight, unfamiliar accent. "What is your name?"

"Robert Warkin. I'm a photographer."

"Well, Mr. Warkin, you damaged my ship!"

He was momentarily dumbfounded. "Oh, the entrance hatch? I apologize. I—I was desperate and freezing to death."

"With a good deal of trouble, we were able to repair the latch." Her hand remained poised on the cutlass. "I assume you were a passenger of the *Hugo*. Your vessel was trespassing."

"Trespassing? But these are international waters. We struck something and I was thrown from the vessel."

"What struck you was the spear of Icaria," she said. "If that ship had lurked any longer in my waters, it would be at the bottom of the sea right now."

"Yes," Colette said in perfect English, "our dear captain does not hesitate to kill." Modo glanced at the French spy, puzzled by her tone, and by the fact that she spoke with no discernible accent.

Captain Monturiol let out a sigh. "I am sorry, I should have introduced you. This is Colette Brunet, and she is, in her usual dramatic way, telling the truth. I take the defense of my country very seriously."

"Your country?" Modo asked. "Are you from Iceland?"

"No. Not every country exists above the land. The world will know that this area is to be avoided. My homeland of Icaria shall be defended at any cost."

"The seamen on my ship were harmless," Colette snapped.

"They were soldiers, Miss Brunet. As I have explained before, we watched you for days and saw through your countrymen's disguises. Then we struck as we would at any invader." She turned to Modo. "As for this *Hugo*, it was not a military vessel, so we cut her free. Her men will now tell others not to trespass here."

"That's why you rammed her?"

"Yes, but we did not penetrate her hull below the waterline. It was only a warning."

For an instant Modo thought of Octavia. Had they made it to port? He couldn't bear to think of her going down with the ship.

At one end of the chamber, a light flickered on. Cerdà stood at a desk, filling out a chart, seemingly oblivious to the conversation. Next to the desk, the wheel of the ship was lashed in place.

Modo gestured around him. "I've never seen such a vessel. What is it?"

"It's a submarine ship," the captain said matter-of-factly. "Welcome to the *Ictíneo*. You were not invited, but please consider yourself our guest anyway."

"By guest she means prisoner," Colette added.

"Prisoner?"

"I do tire of your sharp tongue, Miss Brunet," said the captain. "My apologies, Mr. Warkin. I am afraid in her short time here she has grown impatient. Should she offend you at some time during your visit, I apologize in advance on her behalf. The French are not good at apologizing."

Colette opened her mouth to say something, then pursed her lips. What had she meant by that "prisoner" comment? Modo's legs were trembling. He tried to ignore his exhaustion.

"I—I wonder if I could be taken to Iceland," Modo said, his voice shaky. "I would like to join my wife there."

"That will not be possible at the moment," Captain Monturiol answered. "We shall discuss the length of your stay at another time." She paused, her eyes appraising him. "Comrade Cerdà informed me that you have some sort of deformity that causes you discomfort. I assume that is why you wear the mask. I shall respect your wishes, but all people are welcome here, able-bodied and disfigured. In Icaria citizenship means equality for all. The old, the weak, the crippled. There are no poor and no rich in our country."

"Thank you," Modo said, though he wasn't quite certain what land she could possibly be speaking about. The disfigured equal to everyone else?

He looked about—it was important to learn as much as possible about the vehicle. The more he knew, the better he would understand his situation. "About this ship, I must say I'm stunned! I've photographed many ships—even warships. This is unlike any of them."

"Yes," the captain said proudly. "It sprang like Athena fully formed from my father's mind. Come!" She finally took her hand from the cutlass and led Modo to the largest porthole. It was disconcerting to know that water was only inches away.

"Why doesn't the ocean pour in?" he asked. "The pressure must be overwhelming."

"The glass is ten centimeters thick and tapered so that the pressure of the water wedges it into place."

"Ten centimeters?" He had never learned metric measurement. Mr. Socrates considered it "foolish French nonsense."

"It's about four inches," Colette said. "Metric is a much more efficient system, but I know you English are slow to adapt to new ideas." Modo thought he detected a note of teasing humor in her voice.

"Yes indeed! Finally, Colette and I agree on something," Monturiol said. "This is why we use the metric system in

Icaria. The old ways are dead." She tapped on the large portal. "A solid system, a solid ship. The eyes of the *Ictíneo* will not crack or break, even at a thousand meters below sea level. Here, have a better look." She turned a golden key and illumination blossomed outside the window. Fish scattered, shocked by the sudden appearance of an underwater sun.

"What kind of light is that? It can't be gas," Modo said.

"Ah, you are an inquisitive one. Good! Good! Perhaps that comes with being a photographer. Your questions will be answered in time."

Modo stared out the porthole, trying not to gape, but it was amazing. A large squid floated by, its tentacles waving. Modo couldn't see the surface of the ocean, and had no idea how deep the submarine was.

Modo stepped back and noticed, above the porthole, a bronze plaque etched with a star rising out of the water. *Plus Intra Plus Extra* was inscribed below it.

"The deeper the better," Modo translated.

"Oh, an Englishman who can read Latin," Colette said. "That's rather rare." Her intense eyes measured his reaction. Did she really hate the British so much, or was she just playing the part?

"Yes," he answered, "and Greek. The *Ictíneo*. Well chosen. This really is a fish ship."

Captain Monturiol laughed. "My father had a way with words."

"He's a brilliant man to have designed all of this."

Her face darkened. "He *was* a brilliant man."

"Oh, I'm sorry."

"It is the past. And we must build upon the past, that is

something he often said. Enough of such talk. I want you to know that as a guest you are welcome to spend time on the bridge. And in your cabin, of course. The engine room at the aft of the ship is out of bounds, along with the crow's nest at the bow. We have a library you are welcome to visit. Please remember to sign out the books."

"A library?" Modo couldn't hide his surprise.

"Icaria is a land of thought, philosophy, and spirit. True human spirit. You will be very comfortable and completely accepted here. Forgive me, there are matters I must attend to. I will leave you in the care of Miss Brunet. I am sure she will be only too happy to have new company." Monturiol disappeared up the spiral staircase. Cerdà continued his work at the helm.

"So you're English," Colette said. "I forgive you for that."

"What's wrong with being English?"

She laughed as though the answer were obvious. "Were you working on that ship?"

"I was a passenger. With my wife."

"Ah, that explains the ring. And why did the crew drop anchor at this location?"

Her questions were so probing and her stare so fierce that he stepped back. "I—I was inspired by the way the light reflected off the water. It was the perfect slant for portraits. I couldn't capture the effect if the ship was moving."

"You must have a golden tongue to have convinced your captain to stop."

"If you must know, I greased his palm."

She chuckled. "Ah, money! The ultimate motivator. You will find yourself wishing you could bribe your way off this ship. The *Ictíneo* is hospitable, if you enjoy living like a sardine."

"How big is this ship?"

"It's about fifteen meters wide and tall. As for the length, there's no way to tell. Neither forward nor aft is accessible to us good guests of Icaria. Shall I show you the library, or take you back to your prison cell?"

"Are we really prisoners here?"

"As the hours turn into days, then weeks, you can make up your own mind about it."

Modo didn't like her answer. Even here, in this large chamber, the walls were beginning to close in around him. Sweat trickled down his neck. The humidity made the mask cling to his face. "Well," he said with forced jauntiness, "if it's going to be a long stay, I'd better have something to read. I'd love to see the library."

He followed Colette down a second spiral staircase, into a room where three chandeliers illuminated thousands of volumes. He perused the shelves and found books in Latin, Greek, Spanish, and French; all manner of histories, novels, collections of songs, and scientific manuals. "This is remarkable!" He ran his hand along the spine of a book titled *Geosophy*. "And what is this Icaria she spoke about?"

"A dream inside her head. She is quite mad, but of course you have likely come to that conclusion yourself."

"I don't know enough about her yet," he said. "How long have you been here?"

"Twenty-eight days and four hours, not that I'm counting. I hope you like reading books and looking at fish."

"I do like reading, though not every hour of every day.

Captain Monturiol said that there were soldiers on your ship. Was it a military vessel?"

She narrowed her eyes and Modo suddenly felt like an insect under a magnifying glass. "You may be a photographic artist, but you have a detective's mind." She let her gaze linger on him for a moment before continuing. "Like you, I was just a passenger. My father is back in the United States. He's an attaché to the French ambassador. I was returning home to visit my mother."

"I assume you sailed out of New York. Wasn't there a more direct route?"

"We were traveling to Iceland for diplomatic reasons. And smoked cod, of course."

"And what happened?"

"The *Ictíneo* rammed our ship below the waterline. The *Vendetta*, which was two thousand eight hundred tonnes, went down in under five minutes. To my knowledge, I am the only surviving passenger."

Modo noted that she knew the exact tonnage. "It must have been a frightening experience."

"Frightening?" She huffed. "No. I reacted to the situation as it unfolded. I was with two seamen in a lifeboat. It had been damaged, though, and it sank. The men were taken by sharks, and the *Ictíneo* rescued me because I was a woman. At least, that's what our dear Captain Monturiol said. She thought she'd found another downtrodden comrade, but quickly discovered I had teeth. I've been trapped in this metal coffin ever since."

Colette had delivered her story without a trace of emotion. Modo, trained to detect emotion in the slightest twitch, saw nothing. "A horrible, horrible experience," he ventured.

She shrugged, and Modo couldn't help feeling respect for this woman. In the briefing, Mr. Socrates had said she was eighteen years old. The tension in her face made her look older.

"Do you know how they attack the ships?" Modo asked.

"Well, I believe they have some sort of pincers to cut anchor chains. And there must be a battering ram at the bow of the ship that is used to puncture hulls. Who knows how many vessels lie at the bottom of the ocean because of this madwoman. *Sacre bleu!*"

"It does sound very unsportsmanlike, not to mention illegal, to sink ships without warning."

"Indeed. Bloody rude, as you English might say."

Modo grinned. "I must admit that I'm stunned by all of this." He touched a gold statue of Poseidon used as a bookend. "The likely cost of this vessel astounds me. I have so many questions. Where was it constructed?"

"You may have better luck with the captain than me. I've learned little. The men and women who run this ship—the comrades—are tight-lipped. Tell me a bit more about you and your employment, Mr. Walkin?"

"It's Warkin," Modo corrected, wondering if she wasn't trying to catch him out. "I have worked as a photographic artist for three years now, with my wife as my assistant. I've captured scenery from the Arctic to Egypt to England. We want to preserve glorious man-made monuments and nature in stereoscopic images."

"It sounds *très excitant.*"

He smiled, then remembered his mask. She couldn't see his reaction. "It's rarely as exciting as today was. Imagine the pictures I could take through the portholes." He paused. "I do hope my dear wife is well."

Modo heard footsteps on the stairs and turned to see Cerdà stopping at the bottom step. "You are both invited to dine with Captain Monturiol at nineteen hundred hours, Icaria time."

"That is very kind," Modo said. "What time is it now?"

"Sixteen hundred hours," Cerdà said, pointing at a wall in which a clock had been embedded. Its hands were two lightning bolts and there were twenty-four hours on its face. Modo had heard of this style—it was called an Italian clock. "There are clocks in every room; they were my idea," Cerdà said. "I will have a comrade bring you. Until then, please relax."

After Cerdà had gone back up the stairs, Modo asked cheekily, "Is Icaria time a real measure of time, or is it imaginary?"

"Ha! Icaria may be imaginary, but the time here is real. It's Greenwich mean time minus one hour." Colette grinned and Modo noticed that her dark hair was carefully combed and knotted up on her head. Even though she had been here for weeks, she kept up her appearance. If Monturiol suspected Colette of being a spy, Modo wondered what her fate would be.

"I must say I find it very curious to be talking to a masked man," she said.

"I—I have a rash."

"I hope it's not too forward, Mr. Warkin, to mention that

you have soulful eyes. I suppose a photographer needs them."

"Uh . . . I suppose so."

She laughed, her eyes trained on his. "Well, I shall retire and prepare for *le bon repas*. One does not get to dine with the captain every day. Remember, a good Icarian is never late."

Modo watched her wind her way up the stairs until the last of her long skirts disappeared.

16

Under Observation

After spending some time in the library, Modo climbed the stairs to the bridge. Several men and women in blue uniforms stood at various stations. One man was looking through a brass-plated viewing device that had been lowered from the ceiling. A periscope, of course. One woman was at the helm, and another read numbers aloud from a dial. He was fairly certain she was speaking Spanish—it was a language of which he had learned only a few words.

Modo searched his brain for the little he knew about submarine ships. There would have to be some sort of ballast tanks to control buoyancy. He assumed some of those levers emptied or filled the tanks. Mr. Socrates would want to know. And, at some point, such knowledge might be necessary to his own survival.

Modo climbed to the top of the stairs and went down

the passage. The door to his room was open a crack. He was certain he had left it closed. He slowly pushed it open. His tiny cabin was empty, the cot still unmade, the drawer on the dresser pulled out an inch. Someone had been through his room, clearly not caring if he knew it. He closed the door, patted under the mattress, and found the wireless telegraph. At least that was safe.

In a code Mr. Socrates would recognize he typed: *Agent Modo stop aboard submarine ship stop.* There was no way for him to receive a message. And this would only work if the *Ictíneo* happened to be passing by one of the transatlantic cables. What chance was there of that? He typed the message again, and a third time, then slid the wallet under the mattress.

Mr. Socrates would be pleased to learn of the *Ictíneo*'s existence. An underwater ship such as this would make Britain the master of the world's oceans. The Germans, the French, and the Russians wouldn't dare cross swords with an empire that could sink ships with such stealth.

The *Ictíneo* thrummed and sat perfectly balanced in the water. Modo's only complaint was the humid heat, probably caused by the buildup of human expelled air.

Feeling stifled and tired, Modo decided that a short nap would restore his energy—maybe then he'd be able to shift his face. Since there was no lock on the door, he turned his back to it and removed his mask.

He heard a gasp. With his heart racing, he slipped the mask on again. The door was closed, the room empty. Perhaps there was a pinhole and someone was watching him through it. He searched the walls from floor to ceiling, then climbed onto his cot, looking in every corner, shielding his eyes from the light. Nothing.

When he turned back to the door, it was ajar. A spy! Modo shoved the door closed. It was clear someone had seen his face and been shocked, but who? He removed the small oval mirror from the wall. Nothing unusual there. No pinholes. Had the spy been peeking in the door?

He felt betrayed. In his few minutes with Captain Monturiol he had realized that she was ruthless with her enemies but had an honorable side. Spying didn't seem to be her mode of operation.

At the moment, nothing could be done. He would have to dine with her soon, and that meant uncovering his mouth to eat. His muscles were tired, and though he no longer felt the chill, he was still weak from his ordeal in the frigid water. Maybe if he concentrated on just his face and hump, he could at least make himself more presentable. And so he worked on his muscles and bones, making his nose rise, smoothing his jaw into the noble line of the Knight, forcing his hump to recede. When he was done, he pulled on a jacket. It was too large, which was good since it hid his imperfections. His reflection in the mirror was respectable enough.

The lightning-bolt hands of his clock pointed to five minutes before 1900 hours. He went out into the hall. One of Monturiol's men was already waiting.

"Hello, sir," Modo said. On second glance he saw that the man was in fact a square-jawed, broad-shouldered woman with a grim countenance. She shook her head; either she didn't want to talk or she couldn't speak English. *"¡Hola!"* he said, hoping for a response. She motioned for him to follow her down the corridor toward the bow. They took the catwalk across the *Ictíneo*'s bridge, where the comrades were still at their stations. He was led down a corridor with a dozen or so cabins on either side. If each held one sailor, Modo calculated, there would be at least twenty on the ship. Unless, of course, there were more cabins on the lower deck. Or more men per cabin.

They stopped in front of a large door. The woman knocked, then slid the door aside to reveal a small dining room. Colette was already seated at a shining maple table, set with the finest cutlery, golden goblets at each of the six settings. Having guided Modo to his seat across from Colette, the comrade left.

"Ah, you do clean up well, Monsieur Warkin," Colette said. "And you aren't hiding behind your mask."

"My affliction was temporary."

"Well, I'm glad to hear that. I feel much better talking with you now that I can see your face."

The door slid open and Captain Monturiol walked in. She sat at the far end of the table. "Greetings. First, I feel I must clarify something. I do not want you to think this is the head of the table. I would have placed a round table in here, but that was not feasible with the dimensions of a submarine ship."

Once more the door slid open. Cerdà and a young comrade with short bristly hair entered the room.

"Ah, here you are," the captain said. "Comrade Cerdà and Comrade Garay will be joining us tonight. I dine with different members of the crew each evening. No one person is more important than the next."

The men took their places. Comrade Garay nodded to Modo and his eyes lingered on Colette. She gave Garay a wide smile, which, to Modo's surprise, left him a little envious. Remember, he told himself, you're a married man! Besides, why would he feel jealous? Octavia most certainly had his heart.

A side door leading to the galley opened and a female comrade brought in two silver-plate dishes and set them down on the table. "*Gràcies*," the captain said. It sounded Spanish, but Modo knew *gracias* was the proper word. What language was she speaking? Monturiol lifted the lids. "Please, Mr. Warkin, as our newest guest, you may serve yourself first."

Modo squinted at the steaming meat: some sort of dark organ, cut into six pieces, all exactly the same size. He served himself a section, along with what looked like squid and an unfamiliar red and black leafy vegetable.

"May I ask what this meat is?" he said.

Captain Monturiol laughed. "An Icarian specialty. Please try it. I am curious to hear your thoughts."

Modo found that it melted in his mouth, leaving a pleasant briny aftertaste. "It's wonderful!"

"It is seal liver. The other is squid and the salad is dulse seaweed harvested off the coast of Ireland."

"Seaweed?" Modo poked it with a fork.

"Yes, everything is from our mother the ocean. She is rich beyond all imagination. While the capitalists fight over the carcass of the earth, we live on the ocean's bounties."

"Well, it's certainly a fine meal," Modo said, sipping his wine.

"That is aged fish wine," Cerdà explained. Modo didn't mind the taste, but had no desire to learn how fish wine was made.

"I'm not accusing anyone," Captain Monturiol said, looking at Modo and Colette, "but some of our stores have gone missing. Fruit, in this case. Rescued from a sunken ship. Aboard the *Ictíneo*, we are to share all food, all riches, equally."

"I didn't take it," Modo said.

"Nor I," added Colette.

"I am only making you aware of the theft. It could very well have been a citizen of Icaria."

Comrade Garay coughed uncomfortably.

"I am not accusing anyone at the table," Captain Monturiol repeated. Then she smiled, as if to dismiss any unpleasantness, and raised her goblet. "Welcome aboard, Mr. Warkin."

They clinked goblets and Modo sipped more wine. He rarely drank alcohol, so he wanted to be certain to not have too much. "I have a question," he said.

Monturiol lifted her goblet again. "Please, ask. We will answer anything within reason."

"Well, you are the captain of the vessel, correct? But every other—uh—seaman, seawoman I've met is called a comrade. I thought ships had coxswains, masters, ensigns, and so on."

"Ah, there are no ranks here, though every comrade has his or her job. I was elected captain five years ago for a ten-year term. So, in consultation with my fellow comrades, I make the decisions for the *Ictíneo* and all of Icaria."

"So it's like being a queen," Colette said.

Monturiol set down her goblet so hard some of the wine spilled. "It is nothing like that! We Icarians are from all stations in life—barrel makers, factory workers, soldiers, poets, engineers—and from many different countries. But we all had one dream: to throw off the class-system shackles of the modern world. Our research and actions are all directed toward the creation of Icaria."

Modo tasted some of the seaweed, which was salty and had a spicy dressing. He decided it would be best to change the topic. "You said you would explain what powers the lights of your craft. I have never been inside such a well-lit ship."

"May I answer?" Cerdà asked.

"It is only right," Monturiol said. "You installed the system."

"Based on your father's designs."

"Yes, but you gave it life. Such modesty does a disservice to your contributions."

Cerdà shrugged. "You want to know about our secret agent?" he said. Modo's stomach did a somersault—had they seen through him already? Even Colette was gripping her fork tightly, her face momentarily frozen. But Cerdà's smile was friendly and he spoke enthusiastically. "The agent we use to power nearly every apparatus aboard this ship is electricity."

"Electricity?" Modo squeaked in relief, then cleared his

throat. "But how is that possible? It can only be used to power small devices."

Cerdà pointed to the light above them. "It was only a matter of being inventive. We have harnessed this power and bent it to our use. No massive stores of coal to carry. No belching steam engines to fill our ship with smoke. Electricity is the very soul of the *Ictíneo*."

"But . . . but . . . ," Modo said, "how can you produce enough?"

Monturiol laughed. Both she and Cerdà were looking at him as though he were a child. "The answer is all around you," Cerdà explained. "The ocean itself. We have developed a process that uses the chloride of sodium in the water. It is an endless supply. I can explain no more than that, for the rest is a rather complicated state secret."

The thought absolutely staggered Modo: ships that could travel the length and breadth of the ocean without stopping for coal! This would change the world. He had to contact Mr. Socrates.

"You are shocked, my friend," Monturiol said, then stifled a small laugh. She raised her goblet toward Modo again. "It is an honor to have an artist among us. We happen to have photographic equipment that will be of use to you. Mr. Warkin, we would like you to capture photographs of Icaria."

"Oh, wonderful," Modo said, trying to sound pleased, when the truth was he knew little about photography.

"Yes, what sort of photographic device would you use for underwater landscapes?" Colette asked. "What plates would work on the ocean floor?"

"I don't actually know of any equipment that would work, Mademoiselle Brunet," Modo said. "Water would, of course, ruin the . . . the insides."

"The camera would also require a lens that could capture imaginary countries," Colette said.

Monturiol smiled coldly. "You mock me still. Tomorrow, you'll laugh from the other side of your mouth. I'll show you the real Icaria. Both of you, if you are willing, shall take a walk with me."

"On an island?" Modo asked.

"No, Mr. Warkin. We are going to walk upon the Icarian ocean floor."

17

A Message Received

Mr. Socrates was seated at the dining room table of Victor House. He had just finished a late dinner of roast duck, garlic potatoes, and turnips. He sipped his tea. His mind was working on several problems at once. The French had made private inquiries into whether the British government knew anything of the robbery at their embassy. It was obvious they were groping for answers, so Modo had done his work well. Then there was the death of Agent Wyle in New York, which was troubling in a number of ways. First, someone knew that the British were pursuing the *Ictíneo*. Most likely the French, but it could be the Germans or this new deadly enemy, the Clockwork Guild. Second, Wyle was an experienced agent. This meant that whoever had killed him was likely even more experienced, and therefore dangerous. And finally, Mr. Socrates had liked Wyle. The man had been tough and competent and someone he trusted implicitly. Wyle's only weakness had been that he was growing too old for the game.

At that, Mr. Socrates smiled grimly. Old? He had at least twenty years on Wyle. Maybe *he* was getting too old. No, this was a permanent post in the Permanent Association. All the members had sworn an oath to stand guard and defend their country until the last beat of their hearts. The prime minister, the politicians, the military, even Queen Victoria, were all unable to adequately protect it. They could not act with impunity, as there were so many eyes watching them. But the Permanent Association was invisible and could act wherever and whenever it wanted. The order that Britannia had brought to the world was good and necessary.

Cook entered with a dish of roly-poly, a rolled-up suet pudding with custard on the side. It had been a childhood favorite of Mr. Socrates, and always reminded him of his years in the navy, too. His fellow officers had called it deadman's arm.

As Cook set the pudding on the table, someone rang the door chimes. A moment later Tharpa entered with a telegram. Mr. Socrates set down his spoon and opened the envelope. He quickly decoded the message: *Octavia reporting stop ship rammed by unknown unseen enemy stop Modo lost in ocean stop hiring searchers stop need funds stop orders stop.*

Mr. Socrates read it again. "He's dead," he whispered.

Tharpa stepped toward him. "The young sahib?"

"Yes. He fell into the ocean more than eleven hours ago. He would be frozen to death by now. All that work, lost. And that foolish girl believes he might still be alive. I did try to teach her to be logical, but clearly she doesn't listen."

"Are you certain that she is the one you are angry with, sahib?"

Mr. Socrates scowled and looked up at Tharpa, who stood there, arms crossed. His gaze was steady, calm, but the glimmer of a tear rested on his cheek.

"Exactly what are you daring to suggest? With whom do you suppose I should be angry? Myself? Or is this more Dalit mysticism?"

"I am speaking as your friend."

"Friend?" The word took Mr. Socrates aback. *Friendship* was not a term they had ever used to describe their relationship over the years. He had lifted Tharpa from the muck of Bombay, from a miserable life as part of the untouchable class, and this was how the man repaid him? By accusing him of . . . of . . . Mr. Socrates wasn't exactly certain what.

"Yes, friend. You are my sahib, but you are my friend, too. It is not impossible to be both. I concluded that long ago. Just as Modo is both my friend and my pupil. If he is dead I will mourn him deeply."

"*If* he is dead? This is too much, Tharpa." Mr. Socrates stood up with a grunt of exasperation. "Cable Octavia in Reykjavik. She is to cease all activities and return to London immediately for reassignment."

"If that is what sahib wants."

"Yes, that is what I want! Please send her the message now!"

Tharpa nodded solemnly and left the room.

Had everyone gone mad? Mr. Socrates looked down at the roly-poly. Dead-man's arm. His stomach turned and he pushed his chair back from the table.

He climbed the stairs to his room, his limbs heavy. He had to be resolute. This day was far from done, but here neither Tharpa nor Cook would bother him.

Looking at himself in the mirror, he saw that he *was* older. All that work training agents, setting them on their assignments. His great struggle against the enemies of Britain. Many had died serving the cause; Modo was just another death. Another sacrifice.

His eyes strayed to the portrait on the dresser of his wife, Margaret, dead now for twenty years, and below that the golden bracelet he'd bought for the baby, the boy his wife had died giving birth to. The child had taken his last breath only moments later. Mr. Socrates could still feel the child's lifeless body in his arms. His child. His son. Dead.

Modo dead? It couldn't be. Surely he had been prepared for the risks better than that.

Are you certain that she is the one you are angry with, sahib? Tharpa was always speaking in riddles. It was infuriating. Just what was he insinuating?

Octavia was acting out of passion, not reason. She deserved his anger. And Modo was not his son. He was a highly trained agent of the British Empire. Mr. Socrates crossed his arms. He was, above all else, the stalwart commander of the most powerful agency in the world. He had to move the pieces on the chessboard without succumbing to maudlin sentiment.

Despite these conclusions, he found himself moving

across his room, opening the door, and walking down the hall, to the top of the stairwell. He spoke without knowing if anyone would hear him. "Tharpa"—his voice was a hoarse whisper—"wire Octavia five hundred pounds. Tell her to continue the search."

He heard Tharpa answer from the shadows below. "I shall, sahib."

18

Thievery and Secret Pacts

When Modo returned to his cabin, the door was closed and everything seemed to be in place. But when he looked under his mattress, the wireless telegraph had vanished. Stolen! How could he confront the captain without admitting what he was missing? She wouldn't believe it was a piece of photographic equipment. Anyone with basic technological knowledge would spot it as a wireless telegraph. Cerdà would recognize it in a heartbeat.

But had the theft been at the captain's orders? Was the dinner a ruse to give them time to explore his room?

There were other potential suspects. Colette couldn't have taken it, since she had been seated at the table with him and had left when he did. Then Modo remembered her beguiling smile and the way Comrade Garay had responded to her with a blush. She had been on board for a fortnight. Time enough to bend a crewman to her will.

Without the telegraph he was, for all intents and purposes, a prisoner on the *Ictíneo*. It wasn't as though he could just open a hatch and be on his merry way.

He felt a little slaver collect on his lip, a sign that his face was beginning to droop. He looked in the mirror. Already his features were melting like wax.

A knock at the door. He shuddered.

"Yes?"

"It's Colette. I need to speak with you, Mr. Warkin."

Angrily, Modo tried to stop the changes. No, having a temper tantrum wasn't helpful. It clouded the mind. Mr. Socrates had told him that a thousand times. He focused, forming the Knight face again.

"Mr. Warkin?"

"Just a moment." Modo quickly straightened his eyes, a bead of sweat running down his cheek. He ran his fingers through his hair, relieved that it wasn't falling out yet. He was certain he could hold this form for twenty minutes at most.

He opened the door an inch, but Colette pushed her way in and closed it behind her. The room felt very small. "No one saw me come here," she said, "but there isn't much privacy on this death ship."

Modo backed away from her, leaning up against the far wall. Her dark, almond-shaped eyes burned into his. "I apologize for the intrusion."

"Yes, well, how may I serve you—I mean, be of service?" he asked.

"By telling me the truth," she said.

"The truth? It's inappropriate for us to be alone together. I'm a married man."

"Liar!" She said this with such force, Modo felt as though he'd been slapped.

"I am!" he squeaked.

"What color are your wife's eyes?"

"They—they're . . ." He paused, picturing Octavia. "Green. Green!"

"Hmmph. I'm particularly gifted at observation, Mr. Warkin. The ring on your finger is too big for you, and very shiny."

"We were just married. I've been meaning to get it sized properly."

She grabbed his arm. "Stop it! You're being pointlessly evasive." When she let go, his arm stung. Her strength surprised him. "Your ship dropped anchor at the exact coordinates we were investigating. The Atlantic is too vast for such a coincidence."

"We were photographing the sea. The light is perfect and—"

She put up her hand. "Nonsense! Stop this charade, Mr. Warkin, if that in fact is your name. Captain Monturiol can't see what's right in front of her nose, but I can. You watch the others. You analyze. You are inquisitive. My guess is that you've been trained in these arts; the question is, by whom?"

"I don't know what you're talking about."

Colette grabbed his hand this time, but held it gently, as though they were old friends. "Please, don't lie to me," she said softly. "We're the only two sane people on board, and we could be trapped here with this madwoman for the rest of our lives. Tell me the truth."

Modo took a deep breath. She had a point. "Well," he said, removing his sweaty palm from hers, "I suppose France and England are not officially at war. And we have cooperated in the past. The Crimea being but one example."

Her smile was dazzling. "I knew it! I knew it! Trained by the Brits, of course. You're all so wooden."

"Wooden?"

"You're not natural *acteurs*. Honestly, it's as though you've all got rigor mortis. There's something about the fog and cold that makes you stiffen up."

"I must say, I'm insulted." As he said it, though, he couldn't help laughing. Her brown eyes flashed.

"We must make a pact, Mr. Warkin."

"What sort of pact?"

"We'll get out of this coffin together, that is our pact! Come hell or high water." Modo raised his eyebrows. Colette was trained to be devious. "All right, but just so no one gets the advantage, we'll inform our countries simultaneously about the existence of the *Ictíneo*."

"I'll shake on that," she said, and so they did. Her hand was warm, her grip vise-tight.

"The question is," she went on, "how do we contact our countries? I've never seen the crow's nest of this ship—it's somewhere in the bow. There may be a means of communication there. Or we may have to send a message some other way when we surface. It may be a note in a bottle." Modo enjoyed her sardonic tone.

"How often does this submarine ship surface?"

"Every three days, to refresh its oxygen. There's a slim chance we'll surface near land or a friendly ship."

"There is something else," Modo said.

"Which is?"

"I have a device that will allow us to communicate with outsiders."

"Really? What is it?"

"I can't tell you that."

"Oh, Mr. Warkin. I see. Your wireless telegraph is a state secret."

Modo's eyes twitched. He paused to consider his options and chose to give in. "How did you know?"

"I have my ways. Where is it?"

"Well, that's the thing. It was stolen."

"Stolen?" She furrowed her brow.

"Yes, it was hidden under my mattress."

"Then Monturiol knows. And she would certainly recognize the device. She's playing a game with us."

"Is it possible one of the crew searched my quarters and has kept it, not knowing its purpose?"

"Perhaps. Though you will find that these Icarians, as they call themselves, are slavish to their duty. It seems unlikely one would keep this secret."

"But suppose the thief just wanted something that none of his comrades had."

Colette pursed her lips. "Still, we must assume she knows—but she's very blunt, so it's not like her to hide her motives. We'll have to wait until she plays her hand."

"How many men and women are under her command?"

"I've met twenty-two different comrades. But this labyrinthine vessel could hold a hundred at least. There are cabins on both levels, some with four bunks each."

"Are there other ways off the ship?"

"I'm not aware of any, but they keep the aft and the bow under lock and key."

"Then we shall have to assume the only way out is through the top hatch."

"Yes." She touched his hand. "My word is my honor, Mr. Warkin. Do you trust me?"

Modo tried to read her intentions in her face. "Trust? Between agents?" His chuckle was cut short by the severe look in her eyes. "I give you my word too."

"Then what is your real name?"

"It's Modo." The moment he said it, he cursed himself. Mr. Socrates would never want any foreign agent to know his real name!

"It's a pleasure to meet you, Modo." She shook his hand again, this time lightheartedly, her eyes scanning his face. Was it still holding its shape? "Mademoiselle Colette Brunet is my real name, but you may call me Colette in private. When I was dragged, half frozen, into this ship, I let them know my real name without thinking. But these Icarians know nothing of my true background."

"I—I must admit I know who you are," he muttered. "I studied you. I . . . ." He didn't know what to say and was surprised when he blurted out, "I'm sorry that your father died."

Colette's face went pale and she quietly said, "Thank you." Then she turned, pausing at the door. "One final thought, Modo. If Monturiol knows that you're a spy and is suspicious of me, then this proposed walk under the ocean may be a trip to our own execution. Think on that."

She left and closed the door.

He did think on it, throughout most of his fitful night's rest.

19

Hard Truth

Octavia dragged herself to a boardinghouse that overlooked the bay, paid the elderly woman for a room, and turned to go upstairs, only to find the *Hugo*'s captain sitting in the drawing room by the fire, a mug of coffee in his hand.

"Mrs. Warkin," Goss said, "please sit down."

She did, and it was the first time since leaving the *Hugo* that she had allowed herself a moment's rest. Goss poured a mug of coffee and handed it to her.

"Your luggage is here," he said. "You left it on the ship, you were in such a hurry. I presume you were unable to find a rescue party."

"No one dares go back to that area!"

He nodded. "I have spoken with several other captains and with the port authority. Many ships have been struck there. Some have gone down. We're lucky we weren't one of them. Still, my condolences once again on your loss."

Octavia froze. "Condolences?"

"Well, yes, I'm so sorry that your husband has perished."

"No!" She couldn't control the emotion in her voice. "No. He's still on that barrel."

"Since age eleven I have lived on the sea. No one could survive in that water for more than a few hours."

"Then a ship has picked him up. I know it in my bones."

"No captain worth his salt would dare go there." Again his voice was soft. "The truth is hard, I know, but it would be better for you to face it."

She set down the coffee cup and stood up. "Thank you for the coffee, Captain Goss," she said before climbing the stairs to her room, where she collapsed on the bed, not even taking the time to remove her shoes.

Later that night Octavia heard something being slipped under the door. When she read the telegram from Mr. Socrates, she didn't know how to interpret it. Did he believe Modo was alive, or did he just want his body? Either way, she would have to hire a boat. She dared to feel a tinge of hope. Then something Goss had said came back to her. *No captain worth his salt would dare go there.*

It was time to find a captain who wasn't worth his salt.

20

A Stroll at Full Fathom Five

Colette had breakfast in her cabin, delivered by a female comrade. The Icarians were often hard to tell apart, given their uniforms, but this one she'd nicknamed Big Chin. She was as mute as all the rest of them, and so dull and stolid that Colette was certain she was part ox. Colette ate two slices of seaweed bread, all the while thinking, My heart, my soul for a croissant. She longed for eggs from a chicken, not a turtle. And lamb, too! After twenty-one days of fish-based meals, she would have killed for lamb chops.

She had spent much of the night trying to figure out who Modo was. She believed him when he said he was an English agent. She had placed his accent as London upper class, but couldn't get any more specific than that. She'd had her suspicions upon first meeting him, and they had been confirmed by his behavior at the dinner table. And it was especially obvious that he had only a rudimentary knowledge of photography.

She wondered if he was younger than he appeared to be. The rash confused her, though. Was he faking that? For what purpose? As an agent it wasn't a good tactic to draw attention to yourself. And that mask certainly drew attention.

As she swallowed the last mouthful of bread, someone knocked on her door. She opened it to find Cerdà. "Captain Monturiol thought you should come early to the lock chamber. It will take some time to dress, and it is best to be suited up while no men are present."

"Ah, how modest of Monturiol," Colette said wryly.

Cerdà led her down the corridor; he was so large that both his shoulders nearly brushed the walls. Anselm Cerdà was a hard one to peg. Despite the fact that none of the Icarians wore any insignia, he seemed to be Monturiol's second-in-command. Colette had gathered bits and pieces of information: he was an engineer and had brought this ship to life, using Monturiol's father's schematics. He spoke Catalan, French, Spanish, and English fluently. And he had no sense of humor. At least, Cerdà never responded to any of Colette's quips. He answered all questions in a matter-of-fact way and was, it seemed, emotionless. The perfect Icarian.

They descended the spiral staircase through the bridge. Colette stole a glance at the pressure gauge. It was at ten atmospheres, so they were one hundred meters below sea level. Her father had taught her marine science, so she knew each atmosphere of pressure was equivalent to 10.6 meters of water pressing down on the gauge.

They went through the library, and for the first time, Colette was allowed into the lower hall leading to the aft of the ship. She kept her eyes wide open, counted her footsteps. From this she calculated the overall length of the *Ictíneo* to be at least fifty meters. There were more cabins on either side of her, and new clusters of gauges.

The journey didn't feel particularly ominous, but her heart skipped a beat when she allowed the idea of an execution to invade her thoughts.

"Is it . . . sunny out today?" she asked to distract herself. Cerdà glanced down at her. "We do not experience the ravages of the sun in Icaria."

"It was a joke."

Cerdà's footsteps echoed on the hardwood. "Oh. I see. Yes, that is humorous."

He led her through another portal. Each section was designed so that it could be tightly closed if the ship took on water. They entered a larger room, oval in shape. Various kinds of machinery and what looked like harvesting instruments lined one wall. And there was the captain, along with a female Icarian who was helping the captain get into a strange metal suit.

"Ah, Mademoiselle Brunet," Captain Monturiol said. "Good morning." She sounded pleasant enough, but Colette would not give her the benefit of a smile. "Comrade Girona and I will help you into your aquasuit." The two women removed a suit from hooks and shelves along the wall. Then the captain stopped to study Colette's face. "You have a mind like an oyster, did you know that?"

"What do you mean?" Colette replied.

"It is closed. But I know there are pearls inside. I eagerly await the opening of your mind today."

"I'm sure you do," Colette said.

Cerdà had left the room. Girona handed Colette a rubber suit, which she could only get into by stripping down to her chemise and pantaloons. It fit like a second skin, and she wished she had a mirror. "Well, this is *très* fashionable," she declared, barely containing her contempt.

"We are only concerned with practical fashion in Icaria," Monturiol said, "but I am pleased with the design. And now, your armor." Girona and the captain picked up a large copper collar and breastplate, which they lowered over Colette and fastened around her. It was followed by a series of narrow metallic sections that they strapped to her legs. She lifted one leg and it fell with a thud. "It's so heavy. How will I be able to walk?"

The captain smiled as they continued to strap on more metal. "You are a strong woman, and the water will lighten your suit." Soon Colette's arms, too, were covered in copper plating.

The door opened; Cerdà and young Comrade Garay entered. Following a step behind them was Modo, in trousers and a white shirt that showed off his powerful shoulders. No mask, Colette noted. He was indeed handsome. He glanced around the room like a curious child. Then his eyes found hers.

"Mr. Warkin," she said, giving her dark hair a flick so that it spread across the shoulders of her armor. Modo's cheeks turned a deeper shade of red. Aha, she thought, he finds me attractive. "The captain was kind enough to invite me here early, since it would be improper to dress in front of you masculine creatures."

"Oh, I see." He seemed to be at a loss for words. "Uh, the um, the undersea suits are simply brilliant."

"It's water armor," Monturiol said. "Cerdà and I designed it. The plateau we will be walking across is fifty meters below the surface. The pressure is enough to squeeze the air out of your lungs." She knocked on the copper plating of her own suit. "This aquasuit will prevent that."

"Ah, good," Modo said. "How long will we be gone?"

"No more than three hours," Monturiol said. "But you will be different people when you return."

"I wait with bated breath," Colette said, winking at Modo.

Cerdà helped Modo into the India rubber suit and attached the copper plates, which made him look to Colette like an ancient warrior hero. Perhaps it is you who finds him attractive, she chided herself. But was he older than her, or younger? They both stepped into metal shoes that Girona strapped onto their feet. Finally, Cerdà helped Comrade Garay into his aquasuit. "It is Comrade Garay's first underwater perambulation," he explained.

A blush crossed Garay's freckled face. Colette grinned at him. "I'm certain that Monsieur Garay is as happy as I am to have such elderly—er, I mean, veteran—sea walkers to guide us."

Garay smiled back until Cerdà tightened a strap, making him grimace.

Monturiol tapped the tank on the back of Colette's aquasuit. "You'll be even happier to have the Emilia device. It will give you several hours of oxygen."

"The name, is it Latin?" Modo asked.

"I named it after my mother, who gave me life. My father discovered that manganese dioxide catalyzes the decomposition of potassium chlorate into potassium chloride gas and oxygen gas."

"There's chloride in this tank?" Colette asked.

"Yes." Monturiol pointed to a tube. "But it is expelled. You will be breathing only the oxygen. We have tested it a thousand times without a problem. Speaking of oxygen, you must be a bit of an oddity, Mr. Warkin."

Modo immediately touched his face in several places. Colette found that strange and took note in case she should, one day, have to use it against him.

"What do you mean by oddity?" he asked.

"Well, I keep exact records of the oxygen levels on the *Ictíneo*. Since your arrival, more oxygen has been consumed than usual. Has your lung capacity ever been measured?"

"Uh . . . no."

"Well, you do have a large chest. The amount of oxygen needed for your bloodstream may indicate that you are an aberration. The Emilia device will solve this puzzle. If you consume more oxygen than us, we'll know."

"I won't run out, will I?" His voice quavered slightly.

"That would be inhospitable of me," Monturiol said with a half smile.

"What is our lovely destination?" Colette asked.

"Soon, my friend, you'll enjoy the pleasure of strolling through Icaria."

The last item for them to put on was a spherical helmet with small, round glass windows at the front and sides. Cerdà, who had dressed himself in his own aquasuit, was holding two of the helmets.

"Before we clamp your aquahelms into place," Monturiol said, "I should point out that there is a light on each of our helmets. The electric cells will last eight hours. These suits are heavy, but we will be much lighter in the water. Perhaps we shall even dance." And at that she threw her head back and laughed. This was as giddy as Colette had ever seen her; she was clearly looking forward to the journey.

"Well, Mr. Warkin," Colette said, "I hope you're a good dancer."

"I am looking forward to being the first Englishman to waltz upon the ocean floor!"

Before Colette could comment, Cerdà lowered the aquahelm over her head. She looked out the little window. Her breath was already fogging the glass. Her heartbeat doubled and she sucked in air, but that only misted the glass more. She could hear the blood rushing through her ears.

The captain motioned for them to move, and Colette struggled step by step into a smaller chamber, where the five of them stood close together. Girona closed the heavy door, which had a porthole, and turned a spoked wheel.

Colette glanced at Modo. His eyes seemed to show the same fear and exhilaration she was feeling. There was a hissing; then a cold sensation began moving from the soles of her feet to her knees and her hips. When she looked down, she saw water filling the chamber. Soon it was up to her arms and her neck. A tingle of panic rose in her stomach, and she thought of her father teaching her to swim. *Always be the master of your breathing.* She made herself breathe extra slowly, counting each breath. By the time the water rose above her head, she was calm again. The window in her helmet cleared.

With a muffled clunking sound, Cerdà opened the door in front of them and Monturiol gestured for Colette and Modo to follow her. The lights of the *Ictíneo* lit up the ocean floor.

Colette's first step sank into the soft bottom, but a few inches down she hit something solid and she soon got her footing. A bright orange starfish sat near her feet. Bulbous purple and red plants surrounded her, and others with spiky or cottony coverings. Orange mushroomlike plants waved back and forth. Gray fish darted out of the way. She didn't know her sea species very well.

She followed Monturiol and Cerdà, surprised at how light her suit felt, though it still took some effort to move. Modo was just behind her, and she gave him and Garay a friendly leaden-handed wave. The ocean bed wasn't as flat as she had expected, and they seemed to be climbing. Something large floated in the distance, but her light didn't penetrate that far. What if it was a shark? An image of the sinking *Vendetta* flashed through her mind, and the fins cutting through the water. Her stomach lurched, but she continued to put one foot in front of the other.

After fifteen minutes of walking, they entered a grove of

tall seaweed. Captain Monturiol stopped, knelt down, and appeared to pray. Cerdà knelt beside her and was clumsily joined by Comrade Garay. Colette glanced behind her at Modo, who gave an almost imperceptible shrug. It wasn't until Colette had taken another step that she saw the gravestone. *Narcís Monturiol I Estarriol* was carved across it. The grave of the captain's father. The inventor of the submarine ship. There were five other graves as well, perhaps belonging to fallen comrades.

Colette's father had been buried in Japan, in a grave she had visited only once. She felt tears well up, and then it seemed the most natural thing in the world to kneel and lower her head.

When she opened her eyes, she was surprised to see Monturiol standing over her, holding out her hand. Colette took it and was lifted to her feet; then Monturiol turned and motioned for them all to trudge on.

Colette was cold, but moving through the water warmed her. She felt light-headed, happier than she had in a long time, and she wondered if the mix of gases in the Emilia device was somehow responsible. Then it occurred to her that she was actually exhilarated—she was walking on the amazing ocean floor! There was so much to see and to feel. Somewhere far above them the sun was shining, but only a glimmer of light reached these depths.

Another large shape appeared above them. Colette watched in terror as it shot straight at Modo. He put up his hands, and at the last moment the shape veered around him. By its profile she realized it was a dolphin. It glanced back, smiling playfully. Monturiol had stopped, and through the window of her aquahelm Colette could see she was laughing.

Several bright white lights appeared ahead, surprising Colette. With each step the lights grew larger and so bright, it became clear that no creature of the ocean could be the source.

When they had trekked close enough for her to see what the light revealed, she gasped, astonished at the genius and the pure audacity of what stretched out before her.

21

Inside New Barcelona

Captain Monturiol raised her hands as if to say, "Look, look what I've created. Isn't it wondrous?" And Modo could only agree. Even Colette had turned to look back at him. Down in a valley, twelve white mineral towers rose from the ocean floor, each bubbling at the top and looking like an oversized chimney. Wrapped around the towers, like pearls tossed by Poseidon, were twenty or so dome-shaped bronze buildings of various sizes.

It was the beginning of an underwater city. Two people in aquasuits stood outside one dome, welding a section into place. How they were able to weld underwater, Modo had no idea. A third aquasuited person was screwing large bolts into a steel plate. The entire set of buildings glittered and glowed with light and life.

All this at the bottom of the ocean!

They arrived at a stairwell cut out of the sea floor and descended slowly. Modo was so busy soaking up the sights of the city that he stumbled twice. Light glowed in round glass windows. Windmills—or rather water mills—turned on several of the roofs. The group passed a yellow and red flag on a pole, swishing back and forth in the current, fish darting around it. They stopped at a round door with a large spoked wheel. Cerdà spun the wheel until the door opened, and they stepped into a large lock chamber.

Once Cerdà had closed the door behind them, Captain Monturiol lowered a lever on the other side of the chamber. Hissing and bubbling, the water was soon below Modo's viewing window, then his chest and his legs, and seconds later it had all drained away. The suit felt much heavier; his legs were rubbery and tired. Cerdà removed his own aqua-helm and helped the captain take off hers; then they both helped Modo and Colette. Finally, Cerdà lifted off Comrade Garay's helmet. "That was wonderful!" Garay said. "A marvel and a joy!"

"I agree," Captain Monturiol said. "There is nothing like a good walk to clear your mind." She turned to Colette with a mischievous look. "And how is my oyster-minded friend?" Cerdà was grinning too.

"Oh, *je suis assommée,*" Colette answered. She was astounded. Modo was pleased to put all his years of French classes to work.

"It's beyond belief," he said, and Colette added, "Truly and utterly, I am speechless and stunned."

The captain shrugged as if to say "Of course," then spun a knob and the door into the interior opened. Waiting for them in a brightly lit room were three women in white robes. Modo blinked, then held a hand to shade his eyes. Monturiol clanked in, and they all followed, making a glorious racket.

"Welcome home, Captain Monturiol," a rosy-cheeked, middle-aged woman said. Her two companions looked about the same age, their skin soft and pale. One reminded Modo of Mrs. Finchley, but this woman appeared happier and plumper. The women assisted them in taking off the aquasuits and hanging the various pieces on wall hooks. Soon Modo was stripped down to the India rubber. Without the weight of the suit he felt as though he would float up to the ceiling. He snorted up as much of the cool, refreshing air as he could, realizing now just how hard it had been to breathe in the suit.

"I have work I must attend to," Cerdà said. "Our recent need to patrol our waters has meant we have neglected some of the repairs our city demands."

"Yes, Cerdà, I hear what you are saying," Captain Monturiol said. "And I agree. We shall patrol less and get to work on the plaza soon."

He nodded. "I look forward to that. Come along, Comrade Garay. We are on welding duty today." Cerdà bowed to the women and left the room, with Garay a step behind.

Modo glanced around, soaking up every detail: the same glowing circular lights as on the *Ictíneo*, except much larger; an arched roof; red curtains along a wall; paintings of the underwater world hanging on every open wall space.

He eagerly took a glass of water offered by one of the women.

"It is purified seawater," Monturiol said, raising her glass. "A toast to my friends! Welcome to New Barcelona, the first and greatest city of Icaria."

Modo took a sip. "It tastes marvelous!"

The sound of running water drew Modo's attention and he turned to see a waterfall set in a corner. "That is purified seawater too," Monturiol said. A skylight, or rather, an oceanlight, was set into the ceiling, and on the opposite wall was a large window. Both presented brilliant views of the ocean. A squid squirted by, and several schools of fish swam past.

"How is all this possible?" Modo asked.

Monturiol laughed. "Anything we imagine is possible. That is what my father taught me."

"But how were you able to build it?" Colette asked.

"Ah, she speaks!" Monturiol chided, a twinkle in her eye. "You have never remained so silent for so long."

Colette drained her glass. "Icaria has certainly surprised me! Now, I must admit, the *Ictíneo* is a wondrous machine, though it's not the first submarine ship. No one has ever lived beneath the ocean. It's a huge leap in technology! To even conceive of it, never mind making it a reality."

"Yes," the captain agreed, "our collective imaginations and our collective will made it possible. There are systems from the *Ictíneo*—for example, our air supply and energy— writ large here. These are what allow us to breathe at fifty meters below sea level." She paused. "Speaking of air . . ." She went to the wall of dripping aquasuits to examine the gauge on Modo's. "That's odd . . . you don't seem to consume any more oxygen than the rest of us. Perhaps it happens when you sleep."

"You could sleep in an aquasuit to find out," Colette suggested in her usual wry tone. "Wouldn't that be comfortable."

"I'd rather not, thank you," said Modo, and turned back to Monturiol. "How long have you been developing New Barcelona?"

"Seven years. Cerdà and I found this life-giving sector with the *Filomena*, a prototype to the *Ictíneo*. I had been looking specifically for hydrothermal energy. Everything is constructed on a plateau—the valleys on either side would be too deep for us to conquer at this point in time." She gestured at the white rocks towering above them, clearly visible through the oceanlight cupola. "These natural chimneys are hydrothermal vents, some as tall as the tallest buildings in New York. They vent water at two hundred degrees Celsius, which we use to heat our living capsules. For a hot bath all you have to do is turn a tap!"

"That is the height of civilization," Colette said enviously. "The showers on the *Ictíneo* are ice cold."

"It keeps the comrades awake! Here, though, our food floats by and we catch it with nets, not ever having to leave the comfort of our homes." Monturiol paused. "Anything is possible, my friends, with human comradeship. This is just the first of many cities to come."

"But how do you create oxygen?" Modo asked.

"We use the same process as with the tanks that got you here, though on a much larger scale."

"How many live here?" Colette asked.

"We could easily support five hundred, starting today. And we would have no problem finding citizens, given that our arms are open to the rejected and the oppressed."

She led them into a room that smelled of bread. A man and a woman who wore white robes with yellow and red stripes were hard at work, kneading dough. The woman offered a baked sample to Modo and Colette. Modo took a piece, spread it with a dark lumpy paste, and devoured it. "This bread is exactly what I needed!" he exclaimed, having enjoyed every mouthful.

"Oh, that is not exactly bread, Mr. Warkin. It is made from ground coral and mermaid's purse—that's the pouch that holds shark eggs. Oh, and ground whalebone. The butter is black Lumpfish caviar."

"Caviar?" Colette asked. "Isn't that rather expensive?"

"Here it's free. I get particular pleasure from eating something for which the rich pay exorbitantly."

Modo couldn't believe that something that sounded so strange could taste so good. He greedily accepted a second piece.

When Modo had eaten, Monturiol took them down an arched hall and up a wide staircase that had been cut into the bedrock. Beautiful fossil shapes had been carved into each step. Monturiol then led them into a large room. Modo looked around to see that they were, in fact, inside a great dome. "Welcome to Icaria's National Museum," chimed Monturiol, obviously pleased with herself.

Ship models hung from the ceiling. A model of a submarine, made of wood, sat on a platform. "That is what the

Adelaida looked like," Monturiol said. "It was my father's first submarine ship, and it held only four people. You had to pedal hard just to get out of the docks." She laughed. "Oh, the hours I spent pedaling! We would picnic at the bottom of the reef, away from the city and all its politics. My father hated the 'clay curmudgeons of bureaucracy'!" Sadness crossed her face. "It was named after my older sister, who died of consumption. That was a long time ago."

Modo searched for words to comfort her, but Monturiol had already moved on, her face no longer showing any sign of emotion.

He glanced away and looked through the portholes on each side of the museum. They gave an impressive view of the rest of New Barcelona. Noticing his gaze, Monturiol said, "This is the highest point of the city."

Modo peered up at the giant oceanlight in the ceiling. He couldn't tell if the sun was shining. Somewhere out there was the real world.

" 'In Xanadu did Kubla Khan a stately pleasure-dome decree,' " he quoted. " 'Where Alph, the sacred river, ran / Through caverns measureless to man / Down to a sunless sea.' "

Monturiol and Colette clapped. "Ah, Coleridge," Monturiol said. "All of his works are in our library."

Modo tapped his temple. "I keep it up here. It's as if Icaria has brought his poem to life." He could see the pride in her eyes. Deservedly so.

"I'll admit an English monkey can occasionally write a good poem," Colette said, her eyes piercing his, "but in the end it is still written in *English*. I shall have to read you a

French poem. It's such a language of romance." She reached up to touch a large bell-shaped object made of wood and strengthened by metal braces. Weights hung on hooks around the circumference, to make the bell sink deep into water. Its interior was made waterproof by India rubber. "That's a diving bell," Colette said. "I've seen the marines use these."

"You have?" the captain asked. "Where?"

"With my father. We were traveling with Ambassador Vernier and we were escorted to Morocco by marines. They used the bell to reclaim the guns from a ship that had sunk. The bell is weighted so it sinks bottom-first and traps air inside. Then divers swim down to the bell and use it as an oxygen station so they can dive even deeper."

"Yes, a primitive but effective way of traveling underwater. This diving bell was used off the coast of the Cap de Creus, near my childhood home. Come along."

As they walked out of the museum, Modo asked, "Why are you showing us all this?"

"Because I want you to understand the destiny of Icaria. This is the future of mankind. Rather than fighting over the refuse above us, we'll work as one, in the womb of Mother Earth. Each of us equal. All of us one. The complete emancipation of men, of women, of the strong and the crippled." Modo couldn't help feeling the same desire for such a utopia.

Monturiol pointed out a porthole. "I don't know if you saw the people welding and working outside the city. Some are elderly, but in the water they shed their years. Some have lost limbs, but with the support of the ocean they can work." She paused. "We'll also have historical and archaeological museums about the Old World above us, collections of the greatest works of art that mankind has created, the drawings of da Vinci, the formulas of Galileo. It will all be safe here forever." She pointed to the statue of a naked goddess with her arms lifted to the sun. "Diana. Discovered in the wreck of a trireme."

How could they possibly afford to build such a city? The sheer volume of metalwork alone was staggering to Modo. Smaller nations couldn't finance it: how could so few people find the resources? It became clear in an instant. "You paid for the construction with undersea treasure, taken from wrecks."

"Yes, Mr. Warkin," Captain Monturiol said, nodding. "You have come to the right conclusion. Think of all the warships mankind has put to sea over the centuries: triremes and quinqueremes carrying gold for Caesar, the great Spanish armada, British frigates off Cape Trafalgar. I have walked among the wrecks and carried back the Old World's treasures to build this new world."

"So thieves do prosper," Colette said.

Modo expected Monturiol to snap at her, but the captain only smiled. "You cannot steal from the dead. Your world covets gold, not mine. I have been to your Paris, the air blackened by belching coal, the starving children begging for food. New York. London. Ugly, ground-dweller cities with their Babel towers."

"My mother lives in that ugly city of Paris." Colette's voice was breaking.

"I have people I care about too," Modo said, but it felt

as though a year had passed since he had last thought of Octavia. "My wife, Octavia. And . . . and my father. And I have my photograph collection in London. I'm not a famous artist, but it's my life."

"Well, it is gone. Vanished." Monturiol waved her hand as though the flick of fingers could erase their memories. "You must leave the past behind. Icaria is your new world. This is why I'm showing off our beautiful city. You will come to love it here."

"I can't forget my wife!" Modo said, surprised by the depth of his own anger. It wasn't just Octavia he was being asked to abandon. Mr. Socrates! Tharpa! Mrs. Finchley! "Captain Monturiol, my whole world is out there."

"A dead world," she responded nonchalantly. "I understand the loss of loved ones. Do you think I walked away from Catalonia without second thoughts? But it must be done. A clean cut."

Catalonia—so that was where she was from. A province of Spain. Once its own country.

"Sometimes it's the cleanest cut that kills," Colette said, "because you don't notice you've been wounded."

Monturiol raised her index finger. "Or it severs the limb from the trap. We have room for you both here. We have photographic equipment, Mr. Warkin. Imagine the blue whale, its image taken from the ocean floor. It would be a first!"

"But my wife, she—"

"Would not deny you this opportunity, if she knew. And Mademoiselle Brunet, you must also live as though you had

152

no previous life. That is what all of us surrender. You will not be allowed to return to the Old World to tell them about our creation."

"So you are imprisoning us for life?" said Colette.

"You can't do that!" Modo said, shaking his finger at her.

Monturiol laughed. "This is not a prison. This is Utopia." She glanced at a clock on the wall. "As always, the visits are too short. We should return to the *Ictíneo*. New Barcelona needs to be resupplied, and we must defend our borders."

As Monturiol led them down a long hall, Colette pulled on Modo's sleeve. He slowed his pace so that they were several feet behind the captain. Colette leaned in to Modo and whispered, "I'll pull out the tubes on her air tank halfway back. No one will keep me a prisoner forever."

"You can't do that," he replied. "The Icarians would kill us both."

"You're right. But there will be a time to escape." Then she paused. "Together," she added.

When they returned to the lock chamber, Monturiol helped them into their aquasuits. "Where's Cerdà?" Modo asked.

"He has duties here. I shall send for him when I need him."

"You can communicate with New Barcelona from the *Ictíneo*? How?"

"I send a message in a frequency the dolphins understand and they deliver it by Morse code, tapping on the glass."

"Really?" Modo asked.

Monturiol laughed. "No, my friend. I was being amusing. My father had quite a sense of humor. I inherited some of it."

"Some, is right." Colette wore a grim little smile.

"To answer your question," Monturiol said as they clomped into the lock chamber, "we communicate between the city and the *Ictíneo* with sonic messages. It's similar to an underwater speaking trumpet."

"But how would Cerdà join you?" said Modo.

"Ah, you ask too many questions, Modo. I suggest you put on your helmet." Monturiol stood at a bank of levers and began flipping them up, then slipped on her helmet. Modo did too, hoping he had fastened the clasps correctly.

Soon he was following Captain Monturiol across the plateau toward the *Ictíneo*. Dolphins played around them, and he wondered at it all. A world where he might actually be accepted for who and what he was, if the captain was to be believed. Where he wouldn't have to change from face to face, shape to shape. No more fighting. No more assignments. A world of peace.

If only Octavia could be here. The thought of her gave him a pang of guilt, for he'd been thinking more often of Colette. Could Octavia be so easily forgotten? Could the rest of the world be left behind? If he was to be trapped under the ocean, Colette was beautiful and interesting, perhaps even enough to spend a lifetime with.

But what about Mr. Socrates? And Tharpa? What would life be like without them? And what would Mr. Socrates think of New Barcelona? Modo desperately wanted to tell him about it. He pictured Mr. Socrates saying, "You've done well, Modo."

He wheezed, his throat a little tight. He coughed and felt a prickling at the back of his neck. Oh no! He was changing. He tried to slow the process. His bones were shifting and his flesh was pressing against the armor. He was breathing so rapidly, he feared he would pass out.

Finally, he spotted the *Ictíneo* and lumbered as quickly as possible toward it, pushing seaweed out of his way. The others, recognizing that something was wrong, caught up to him and climbed into the lock chamber after him. Soon the water drained out of the lock chamber and the door opened. Modo threw himself onto the floor, choking for air.

22

Not Worth His Salt

Octavia awoke, her mind made up. She had shed enough tears. Whether Modo was alive or dead, she had a task to perform. She dressed quickly, but took the time to comb her hair properly and tie it up in a bonnet. She pulled on her warmest jacket and gloves and dug into her portmanteau for money. With what she had, plus the funds Mr. Socrates had just wired her, she intended to make her way back onto the ocean, even if she had to buy a boat and sail it herself!

She had woken several times in the night, trying to puzzle out where she'd find a captain. Finally, the solution had presented itself and she'd been able to sleep soundly.

Instead of walking to the docks, she turned and strode into town, past the green-roofed cathedral. She soon found the building she was looking for. The wooden sign was written in Icelandic, so she couldn't read it, but a ram's head and a goblet had been carved into the wood. In all languages, that meant one thing: a pub.

Taking a deep breath, she pushed the door open. Peat moss burned in the fireplace, dung-scented smoke clouding the air. Two patrons were slumped across a table. She went up to the innkeeper, who was holding a mug of coffee. "I'm searching for a captain brave enough to sail to Nifleheim."

The man laughed. He stopped when she handed him a five-dollar American bill; then he pointed to a darkened corner of the room, where a man sat. Well, he's upright, at least, Octavia told herself. When she got to the table, she discovered that the man was using his detached wooden leg to prop himself up. If not for that, he'd have been slumped across the table like the other two. His eyes, a mass of red veins, rolled slowly toward her. He grunted something that sounded like "Valkyrie."

"No, I am not a Valkyrie," she said, "or an angel. I need a captain brave enough to sail into Nifleheim's circle."

He blinked slowly. His teeth were crooked, but she could see that he had once been handsome. Time and drink had scarred his face. "Only the dead go to Nifleheim."

"I mean the place on the ocean. Not the realm of the dead." Her answer surprised her. Proof she'd actually been paying attention to Mr. Socrates' lectures on Scandinavian culture. Maybe learning to read would finally pay off.

"Hel awaits in her hall," the man muttered. "She serves a dish called hunger."

He was mad! He believed in the Norse fairy tales. "If you were a brave man, you would take me there."

He let out a raspy chuckle. "Even Hermod could not save Baldur from Hel."

Octavia recognized it as an argument, one that she must somehow win. She put money on the table and he stared at it balefully, then swept it onto the floor. There was a tattoo above his wrist, the shape of a hammer.

"Well, that's nasty," she said. Then she remembered a name from her studies. "Thor would not fear. Thor would go. He would take his hammer and strike a blow."

That sparked a light in the man's eyes. He stood abruptly and wobbled on one leg until he had strapped on his wooden leg. He thumped and clumped toward the door.

"Bring my money," he said over his shoulder.

23

The Voice Inside His Head

"Mr. Warkin, what's afflicting you?" Colette asked. Modo ignored her. He had to act fast—he felt his chest expanding to fill the armor cavities. He unsnapped the helmet and dropped it to the floor, then tore at the buckles that held the aquasuit in place.

"Mr. Warkin! Be careful with the equipment!" Monturiol shouted, holding her helmet in both hands. "Speak! Tell us what is wrong."

"Too small, too tight!" he hissed. Pain burned in his bones as he tried to make them maintain their shape. He kicked off the leg armor, his mind clouded by the agony of the transformation.

"Mr. Warkin!" Colette cried, and he turned away from her. She mustn't see him like this!

He tossed the breastplate to the floor and slurred through his thickening lips, "I go to cabin! I must! My affliction!"

He burst past two of the beefy Icarians and down the narrow hallway, scampering through the library and bridge, up to his room, where he slammed the door closed. He threw his back against it and breathed heavily.

There was no stopping the transformation now. It had come upon him so quickly, and earlier than usual. His arms were growing thicker, his hump pressing against the door, his spine curving as each nerve tingled with pain. He tore off the India rubber suit, fearing that it would constrict his arms and cut off his blood. The little mirror reflected his sagging features. One eye was slightly larger than the other. His lovely dark hair was falling out, and tufts of red hair poked through his scalp.

"Mr. Warkin," Colette whispered from outside the door. "Mr. Warkin, are you well?"

"Go away," he slurred.

"Modo," she whispered, "what's happening?"

"I'm ill," he said, wanting to slam his fists against his hump. He pressed hard against the door. "I need time alone." If only he could turn off the light, but the ship was in its daytime cycle.

"Please, let me in."

"No! No one comes in!" He let out a gasp. It was torture every time he twisted back into his original from.

"Modo!"

He struggled to make his mangled lips and throat form words. "I. Will. Not. Dine. Tonight. Please, Colette, go."

There was silence on the other side of the door. Modo's breathing was more controlled now.

"I will go, then," she said, "but I expect a full explanation."

"You. Shall. Have. It," he promised, not exactly sure what he would tell her. He assumed she was gone. He rubbed his shoulder—he'd half dislocated it getting out of the aquasuit.

Another knock. "Please, go!"

"Mr. Warkin!" Captain Monturiol's voice was stern. "Explain why you damaged that highly valuable equipment! What is the matter with you?"

"I—I felt smothered. The suit too small. Ocean too deep."

"That is all in your head. You must get past it. Icarians have no fear of the sea. She is our mother."

Modo took a deep breath. The pain subsided slightly. "I—I apologize, C-Captain. I really am sorry. Understand, these experiences are new to me." He sucked in another wheezing lungful of air. "I've walked on the ocean floor. I never dreamed of such a thing. It was such a wondrous city."

"Yes, yes, it is understandable. I should have prepared your minds for the overwhelming journey. Perhaps I am partly to blame. I will have food delivered to you. Soup?"

"I would appreciate that."

"You rest, Mr. Warkin. Settle your thoughts."

When he was certain she was gone, he sat on the bed, still catching his breath. His spine had twisted, and he shifted to find a comfortable position.

What to do now? There seemed to be no way out of the submarine ship. New Barcelona had been amazing. Mr.

Socrates would want to understand the science that had been used to create the city. Modo pictured such cities all across the Atlantic. Mining kelp, gathering coral, harvesting pearls, deep-sea fishing. A whole new world, much richer than even the Americas had been.

His foot bumped something under his cot. He bent over, picked it up. The wireless telegraph—in two pieces! Was this some mind game the captain was playing with him?

He examined the pieces. Nothing was seriously wrong; he could put it back together. But what was the message in this? Was the captain signaling that she knew about the device, and therefore knew that he was an agent? Or was it someone else who—

"You're quite the ugly sot, aren't you?"

A male voice! He snapped his head left and right, but no one else was in the room. He got up and pressed his ear against the door. Only the metallic creaking of the submarine ship. The person must be spying through a pinhole in the wall.

Light laughter from the far corner. Modo spun around to look in that direction, but no one was there.

"Looking for me, are you?" The voice was singsongy, playful, with a slight English accent. "That's the thing, I can't be seen. Can't be found."

"Who are you?" Modo scrambled to find his mask. "Where are you?"

More laughter, this time from right beside him. Then the voice fluttered out from across the room. "I move like the wind. I've been watching you for weeks. Weeks! You're enamored of that coquettish Colette, aren't you? What would Octavia think?"

"Octavia? How do you know her name?" Modo wondered if he was going mad. "Tell me where you are!"

The telegraph pieces rose up from the bed and floated together, then drifted apart. Modo gaped.

"I tried to make the wireless work, but there's a trick, isn't there? A trick. And then it broke. Very flimsy. Very flimsy." The pieces floated back down to the cot.

"Who—who are you?"

"Who am I?" And again that high-pitched laughter. "Why, I'm a little experiment that bends light."

"But—but it doesn't make sense."

"Of course it does. It's just that your brain is too tiny to comprehend the wondrous being in front of you. I'm Griff, the first invisible man, and I'm pleased to make your acquaintance."

24

A Tale Transparent

Griff couldn't suppress a giggle. The monstrous freak before him was so slack-jawed he looked like a puppet. His crooked eyes were wide with fear. Fear of me! Me! Griff had never seen such ugliness; the chimpanzees altered by Dr. Hyde were handsome by comparison. This agent's features made Griff want to retch.

"Ah, I messed up my introduction," Griff said. "Silly me! It's been so long since I've spoken to anyone. I am Griff, Invisible Man the First. Get that? I am the first! And we are agents under the same flag."

He watched Modo snap his head from side to side again, searching the room. "Where are you? Please stop this game."

Griff shrieked with laughter. "Oh, don't gape like a country bumpkin! I'm right before your very eyes. Ta-hee!" This is how lesser beings behave in the presence of greatness, Griff realized. This underling's dim intellect cannot even begin to comprehend my existence. I shall have to provide proof! Griff yanked a sheet from the bed and wrapped it around his shoulders, over his wiry muscles, displaying his shape. Modo watched him in awe. Yes! Yes! He was beginning to get it.

"This is impossible," said Modo.

"Nothing is impossible; it's all probabilities. That's what the brilliant doctor taught me."

"Doctor?"

"Yes, for the Association."

"The Association?" Modo looked positively bewildered.

Griff smiled, invisible lips pulled back from invisible teeth. Was it really going to be this easy? "The Permanent Association, Modo. Your masters. *Our* masters. I'm on your side." He had heard Octavia use the name in New York while he'd been crouching in the corner of their hotel room.

Modo leaned against the dresser. "You're an agent of the Association?"

"Quick little boy, aren't you? Yes, I am. I'm their majestic experiment. You and I have much in common, don't we? I'm guessing that your particular talent, which I've now observed closely, has been with you since birth. They trained you in some secret location, didn't they? Mr. Socrates is the one who yanks your leash."

"You know Mr. Socrates? Did he—did he raise you?"

"No. No. I know *of* him. I've not had the pleasure of a face-to-face with the ol' boy."

Modo took a deep breath. And another.

Good, good, Griff thought. You're calming down.

Modo brought his hands up to hide his lower jaw.

"Are you concerned about your looks? I've seen worse," Griff lied.

"How long have you been following me?"

"Since New York. I was haunting the library, told to find Colette Brunet and this mysterious *grand* fish. I followed you onto the *Hugo*. I snatched food here and there. I was right beside you when the ship was rammed, and I fell over the edge before you. Nearly froze to death in the water. And when you ripped open the *Ictíneo*'s hatch, I went in along with you."

"You mean before me. And you struck me on the head!"

"What can I say?" Griff raised his arms, lifting the sheet. "I apologize for the blow, but you have a thick head and I was desperate. There was no time to explain who or what I was. I recovered in the library and have kept myself well hidden since then. The food is awful here. I hate fish. At least this ship is warm." He coughed. Ah, he could never escape his own lungs, the hated cough they produced. It was truly the bane of his existence. Sometimes he blamed all the hours he'd been made to spend in the ice room, training to withstand near-freezing temperatures. Sometimes he blamed Dr. Hyde and the years and years the doctor had fed him tinctures. Maybe one day he'd feed the doctor some of his own medicine.

Modo was squinting at the space above the blanket. "Trying to find my eyes, are you?" Griff said.

"Why didn't you announce yourself earlier?" Modo demanded.

"I was told to operate alone. Does Mr. Socrates allow

166

others in the Association to know he has a shape-shifting monster in his employ?"

"I am not a monster!" Modo cried, and in a heartbeat, he was across the room, his hands around Griff's throat. "Who is your master? Tell me! Don't lie!"

"M-Modo." Griff spat the word out. The hunchback's grip was strong. "We're partners. And—and you know I can't tell you. We're not allowed to know the names of the other members of the Association."

"No, we aren't."

"Then her name would mean little, wouldn't it?"

"Ha!" said Modo, releasing him. "It's Lady Artemis Burton!"

Griff sucked in a breath. And another, stroking his throat. I'll flay you alive for touching me, he thought. "You said you didn't know their names."

"I lied. I met her and several others a few months ago. I believe she is the only female in the Association."

"Yes, and don't think that doesn't anger her." Griff continued to massage his throat. "Always complaining about those stupid, know-it-all men! She's the one who had the great idea to send me to the doctor. To be changed."

"Which doctor?"

"Doctor . . ." Griff paused. "Kilvore. His lordship was a brilliant chemist. I was—I was an orphan from Liverpool." Griff knew it was best to stick as close to the truth as possible. "My parents drowned at sea and Lady Artemis took pity on me. She brought me to Kilvore. A crotchety collection of bones, that one! But I learned! And as I grew older, they placed a concoction in my food every day. Yes, the illustrious creation of the invisible man. Me! Well, first I turned yellow, then paler and paler each year. 'You're to become a god,' Kilvore told me. 'It's your great destiny.' "

"But how can such an alteration be possible?"

"How can a cog as small as myself explain the brilliant doctor's plans? He drained me of all color, pink to yellow to white. All my organs, all my cells. My hair no longer grows. Not even whiskers. Do you understand how your eyes work? What allows them to see?"

"I—I believe so. They absorb the light."

"Yes! Yes! It's light that reflects off objects and gives us color. Color reflects light. See, it's so simple. I'm colorless. I do not reflect light, therefore I am invisible. Bone. Flesh. Blood, nails, nerves. All invisible as hydrogen. Of course, I can't float." Another giggle squeaked out of him. Oh, this is so much fun! he thought. I should have revealed myself earlier.

"It does make a certain amount of sense," Modo said.

"Of course it does, old boy. The joke is—I'm naked. The price I pay for invisibility."

"Naked?"

"People can see clothing. I tell you, that ship, the *Hugo*, it was freezing. But Ol' Sawbones adapted me to the cold. He would place me in his ice room until my blood slowed and I became impervious to cold. Well, almost. I still need some heat." Griff ran his hand over his face. "I haven't seen myself for over five years. I forget what I look like. Isn't that funny? Oh . . ." He paused. "I suppose you'd like to forget your looks."

The anger and shame that flashed over Modo's visage was an exquisite sight. "I could never forget my appearance."

"With a mug like that, who could? Ah, don't be offended, Modo. Perhaps I once looked as horrid as you. Who knows?"

A knock at the door. "Mr. Warkin." It was Colette. "I've brought you some food. How do you feel now?"

"I—I am much better."

"I heard you talking."

"I was reciting poetry, a habit when I am ill. My governess taught me."

"Ta-hee!" Griff whispered. "Good thinking!"

"What was that?" Colette asked.

"Oh, just my throat." Modo cleared his throat for effect. "Will you open the door?"

"I can't. Please leave the food outside the door."

"She'll slit your throat while you sleep, that one," Griff hissed.

"All right, Mr. Warkin, but"—and this she whispered— "I wish you would explain this ailment to me, Modo."

"I will. I need my rest, Colette. Thank you for coming."

Griff heard her footsteps fade away. He opened the door—the hall was deserted. "She really is gone, sneaky cat." Griff lifted the plate, knowing it would look to Modo as if it were floating. He took a huge bite of the bread and laughed at Modo's shocked look as the bread appeared and disappeared behind invisible lips. Griff enjoyed performing that trick!

He pushed the plate at Modo. "You can have the seaweed. It's worse than fish!"

Modo took the plate and set it on the dresser. "What did you mean about Colette?"

"Oh, don't trust her. She's quick with a knife, that one. I tracked her in New York and caught her sticking a knife into one of our agents, a man named Matthew Wyle. She watched him die. She's got a frosty heart, believe me."

"You saw this?"

"With my very own peepers." He's the puppet and I pull the strings, thought Griff.

"I—I don't believe it."

"She's very well trained. Do you think she climbed to the top of the list of French agents by being nice? You're a lovesick oaf."

"I'm not! Why didn't you stop her?"

"It happened too fast. A stiletto right between the ribs into the heart. A perfect blow. I saw it from a distance and tried to save Wyle, but I had no clothing to staunch the wound. He died in my arms, not even knowing who was holding him. I don't imagine it was her first kill."

"But that's terrible!"

"It's the nature of our business, eh, Modo? She's a stunner, she is. But being invisible, I can see right into people's minds." He let that sink in. Was the fool actually buying it? "Anyway, Modo, our masters must learn about this submarine ship. What did you see on your little perambulation?"

"I saw . . ." He paused.

Griff rubbed his hands together. This was the real test. Would Modo give him secrets?

"Out with it! What would Mr. Socrates want to know?"

"I saw the beginning of a city under the sea. They call it New Barcelona. It was—it was truly amazing."

"A city. So the grumpy captain isn't mad. Well, well, well. Our masters must know of this." Griff picked up the pieces of the wireless telegraph. "You'll fix this. I'm sorry. I was mad. I get angry when things don't go my way."

"And if our message fails to reach them?"

"It's obvious, Modo. We'll kill Captain Monturiol and take control of the ship."

25

Invisible Plans

Modo couldn't hide his shock. "Kill her?"

"Gut her like a fish. She won't see it coming. Well, won't see *me* coming. Ta-hee!" Griff chuckled, trailing off into another high-pitched giggle. It still seemed impossible to Modo that this man—this invisible man—was sitting right in front of him. "I'm jesting! I don't believe it'll come to that. Besides, how do you pilot this damned contraption? No, we would do better to force her to beach the metal beast in Liverpool."

"I doubt she'll submit to force," Modo said.

"Everyone will submit to force, Modo. It's just a matter of applying enough of it." He emitted a clicking cricket sound from deep in his throat. Modo feared that Griff had spent far too much time alone; he had several odd tics. "Anyway, we will find a way off this barrel. Then the Permanent Association can return in force to capture it and the city."

"Capture it?" asked Modo, wondering if Mr. Socrates and his colleagues would actually try to take the submarine ship. The thought of stealing it from Captain Monturiol made him sick to his stomach. Yet wouldn't it be better if a ship such as this was on Britain's side?

"Of course they'll want it. Or at least the plans to build one of our own. It's a staggeringly ingenious design."

"What have you learned about the *Ictíneo*?"

"I sneaked into the crow's nest, at the front. There are observation portholes there and a massive ram on the prow that'll tickle the underbellies of any military ships. Ha, get that? Tickle the underbellies. Ta-hee!" The sheet moved as Griff laughed. "They also have retractable bronze claws for cutting and pinching! I haven't been able to get into the engine room, at the aft. It's cleverly locked. I can only guess what she's hidden there." He gave a phlegmy cough. "Well, that's that. We wait for our moment, then we strike. I'll tell you when. We should shake on it." The blanket moved. "I'm holding out my hand, Modo."

"Oh, sorry." Modo put out his hand and it was grabbed by a cold, small hand that squeezed tightly.

"Long live the Permanent Association! I'll be the eyes and the ears, Modo. And you"—the sheet fell to the floor— "the ugly brawn. Toodle-oo!" The cabin door opened and closed.

"Griff?" Modo said quietly, looking around. He was pretty sure his visitor had left, but how could he know for certain? "Griff?" Modo held his arms out wide, touching either side of his cabin. He walked its length, arms spread. Griff was gone.

Modo's thoughts swirled about. Had he really been talking with an invisible man? But Griff had been on the *Hugo*, had followed them down the streets of New York, had heard private conversations. All that time Griff had been spying on him and Octavia, prying into their lives. He knew so much about them.

And he's seen my face! Modo touched the rough outline of his cheeks, the pockmarked skin and sunken nose. Griff's words still stung. Modo tried to keep his emotions at a distance—he couldn't get upset about such things. Yes, he was ugly. That was a fact. Another fact was that Mr. Socrates had told him never to show his real face to anyone. That way he couldn't be identified. But here he'd had no choice! It was impossible to hide from an invisible man.

Then he remembered that many others had seen his face. Mr. Socrates had saved him from a traveling freak show. He had no memory of that period of his life, for he had been only a year old. He imagined that hundreds had paid to see his ugliness. The idea made him tremble with anger.

He was still hungry. All that was left was the dulse and some other green seaweed. It was cold and salty, but at least it stopped his stomach from growling.

As he chewed he thought about Griff. Modo didn't completely trust him. There was a sense of madness and deep anger in him. Where did he sleep? As for what he'd said about the Association, it wasn't beyond reason that Lady Burton would have her own agents following a similar assignment. From the little Modo knew of the Permanent Association, it was a cohesive group, but its members sometimes operated independently.

He had to get a message to Mr. Socrates. Modo fiddled with the telegraph; the key was broken, but using a pin, he managed to click the machine on and off. That idiot Griff had broken the electric cell! It was doubtful there'd be replacement electric cells anywhere on board. Otherwise it seemed the device might work. He hid it under the mattress again.

Could Colette have killed Wyle? If what Griff had said was true, she was a consummate actor. She was a trained agent, just like him. She would know hundreds of ways to quietly kill an opponent, and had threatened to kill Monturiol, after all. Will she kill me when I'm no longer needed? Modo wondered. She might do so to keep the secret of the *Ictíneo* all to herself and to France.

He lay down on the cot. It took a long time to fall asleep.

26

A Glimmer of Hope

Mr. Socrates was very aware of the ticking of the grandfather clock in his study. It chimed eight times and his mind automatically calculated: thirty-six hours. That was how long it had been since Modo had fallen from the ship. He would most certainly have frozen to death by now.

Mr. Socrates hadn't heard from Octavia yet, but that didn't surprise him. She would have been out on the water until sundown, then would need at least three hours to return to Reykjavik.

The door chimes rang and his heart quickened. Would this be the message? Had she found Modo? It was all he could do not to get up and answer the door himself. He maintained his composure. The news would come to him.

Soon Tharpa came into the room with an envelope. Without a word, Mr. Socrates opened it. There were two telegrams inside. He translated the first one, which was from Octavia.

No luck. Stop. Permission to search tomorrow. Stop. Bring his body home. Stop.

Mr. Socrates inhaled, his breath catching in his throat. "The news isn't good. Even Octavia has finally come to the only logical conclusion."

Tharpa nodded, his eyes moist. Mr. Socrates looked away so his servant wouldn't see the grief beginning to well up inside him. . . .

They were silent for several moments. But why do I still feel hope? Mr. Socrates asked himself. The chance of another ship finding Modo was infinitesimal. Few ships crossed that area anymore; he'd recently learned that from the Admiralty.

His fingers found the second telegram. A note was attached that read: *This partial message was received yesterday at 6 p.m. GMT. Since it was insufficiently addressed, our delivery was delayed. We remind you that all communications must have a full address.*

Mr. Socrates unfolded the telegram. Some twenty letters spotted the page. He wrote them down, applying his code, and came up with:

A odo ard ubmar shi

He stared and stared at it, but it made no sense. Too many letters were missing. It could be from any one of his agents. Afghanistan? India? Australia?

"I can't make head or tail of this," he said to Tharpa, and handed the paper to him.

Tharpa tipped his head this way and that. "I see no words." He held the paper closer. "This *odo*. That word could be 'Modo.' "

"You may be right." Tharpa set the telegram on the table and they both looked at it. If it was received at six p.m. yesterday Modo would have already been in the water for eight or nine hours. How could he have sent it? Perhaps he had found safety.

Mr. Socrates chastised himself for not being rational enough. Was he letting his hope that Modo was still alive affect his thoughts? But, if this *was* a message from Modo, then he had still been alive only twenty-four hours ago.

"Can you guess at any other words, Tharpa?"

"I cannot make head or tail either, sahib."

"Well, send a telegram to Octavia. Tell her to assume Modo is alive and to keep looking."

It wasn't until later in bed that the answer came to him: *ubmar*. Submarine. Modo was under the ocean. The *Ictíneo* wasn't a trained whale. It was a submarine ship!

Good lord! Could it actually be? He pulled on his dressing robe and ran down to his study and examined the note again. "Yes, submarine ship." He rang the servant bell.

Tharpa arrived a minute later. "Send another message," Mr. Socrates commanded. "Tell the Admiralty that we need a fast, well-armed frigate ready by tomorrow morning. We have important cargo to pick up."

27

To Sing a Song of Madness

odo awoke several hours later. The lights were slowly
growing brighter, so the sleep cycle was over. The *Ictíneo* was thrumming. He now understood that this meant
they were traveling at a good clip through the ocean. He
rubbed his eyes and sat up. Assuming they kept the same
hours as the outside world, he'd spent two nights on the *Ictíneo*. On impulse, he felt around to be sure Griff was not in
the room.

The light flickered. He looked up at it and an idea occurred to him. He retrieved the telegraph; by standing on
his cot he was able to reach the glass and push it aside.
There were two bulbs inside, so he uncovered the electric
filaments that led to one of them. He knew not to touch the
bare wires with his hand. He grabbed the rubber around
them and cut one with his knife. The bulb went black, but
the other bulb kept burning. He used a wooden soup spoon

to guide the wire onto the telegraph. The device made a clicking noise. It worked!

He let out a triumphant laugh. "Modo, you've done it! Brilliant! Brilliant!"

There was no guarantee that the *Ictíneo* would be anywhere near the transatlantic cable lines, but he typed out a message, addressing it to Mr. Socrates and encoding it. He chose two-word sentences, hoping that if it was cut off they'd get at least part of the meaning.

Modo alive stop in submarine ship stop underwater city stop near Iceland stop agent Griff stop assisting me stop must

"Mr. Warkin, are you awake?" Modo jumped. It was Colette. He nearly dropped the telegraph. A spark shot from the wires. The one working bulb flickered, then grew brighter.

"Yes, I'm awake!" he answered. "I'm dressing."

He slid the glass plate into place. He heard a cough. Griff? "Are you well enough to join us for breakfast?"

"Yes, yes," he said, stepping down from the cot. He spread out his arms and searched for Griff, then hid the telegraph under his pillow. He'd take it with him, but none of the pockets in the Icarian clothing were large enough. He assumed people who didn't own anything didn't need pockets.

"Well, we'll see you there. But hurry, my friend! They'll be singing the song. You don't want to miss this."

Song? He changed into the Knight as quickly as possible, wiped the sweat from his brow, and finished dressing.

He opened the door and looked back into the room, realizing that he was becoming paranoid. If Griff had been there, he would have said something. They were on the same side, after all. Modo closed the cabin door, wishing he could lock it.

On his way to the dining room he heard the first odd notes of an organ echoing around him. The music was coming from all directions at once—perhaps it was traveling through the pipes that ran everywhere around the ship.

He passed an open door and discovered Captain Monturiol sitting at a pipe organ, pressing down keys to play the mournful song. Several Icarians were around her, and others had stopped in the hall. They began to sing all at once across the ship, and Modo was surprised by the timbre and emotion of their voices, as beautiful as any choir he'd heard the few times Mr. Socrates had taken him to church. He saw Colette, moved closer to her. "Are they singing in Spanish?" he whispered.

"No. Catalan. And it's their anthem. Once a week they do this. I'll translate, since you English agents don't know Catalan:

> "*Fiery are my cares,*
> *Toilsome is my cause,*
> *To know what hides unseen,*
> *In the mysterious sea.*
> *Icaria, be strong.*
> *Poor heart that trembles,*
> *Desist not from your cause!*
> *Conquer the fear,*
> *For glory is yours.*"

"It's a stirring song," Modo whispered.

"It's no 'La Marseillaise,' but it has its moments." Hearing so many voices as one, Modo had been surprised how the song had moved him. No sour notes. The joy and dedication it expressed. The pleasure at being part of an accepting group—something he rarely felt. They were one. They had a common cause. They belonged together. The music slowly faded.

Captain Monturiol stood. "Ah, Mr. Warkin, I see you are well today."

"The singing was absolutely lovely!"

"All sung from the heart, though we miss Cerdà's baritone. Now return to your stations, my comrades, for we have work, as always. I, too, have tasks to complete, my guests. Excuse me." She strode into the corridor.

"Let's fetch breakfast," Colette said. The galley of the ship was just past the dining room. Modo and Colette lined up for bread, hotcakes, and a mug of white liquid. They ate at one of the mess tables. The drink was not unlike milk.

"It's dolphin milk," Colette said as Modo took a gulp.

He nearly spat it out. "Really?"

She laughed. "No. I don't know what it is. It's probably better that way. After my first week I stopped asking. They don't die from drinking it, but I would kill for a croissant with real cow's butter and jam."

The word *kill* echoed in his ears, and he wondered if she really could have done what Griff had said.

"So, you'll explain to me what happened yesterday?" she asked.

"I felt trapped in the suit. That is all."

"But you weren't frightened on the way to New Barcelona."

"It came over me suddenly."

"And this mysterious rash?"

"It's a nervous reaction." She didn't seem to believe him, so he added, "My doctor says so."

"Really, Modo, you must work on your acting. I'm sure you'll tell me when you're ready. I have been forthright with you."

"It really is a reaction to—"

"Don't lie." She held up her hand. "We haven't discussed what we saw yesterday. This New Barcelona was . . . well, I must admit I was stunned beyond words."

"That mustn't happen very often."

"Are you insinuating that I'm verbose, Mr. Warkin?" She patted his hand. "A city under the ocean! The *Ictíneo* is just a bauble compared with that."

"It was beyond anything I had ever imagined too. The captain's father had a brilliant mind!"

"Yes. Imagine a new Paris spreading out below the water. A new Arc de Triomphe and a Palais du Louvre, all under the sea!"

"Yes, imagine that," he said. "Baking croissants at full fathom five."

"Oh, I'm sure you English would be starting your own colonies too. After all, you've had so much practice failing so far. Perhaps you've learned from it."

"Hmmph! Enough of these dreams. I have news: the telegraph was returned to me."

Her eyes widened. "That's odd."

"It was broken. I don't know what to make of it."

"Were you able to fix it?"

"Uh, no."

She tapped a finger on her chin. "I see. You seem secretive, Modo."

"That's my job," he said with a nervous chuckle.

"We shook hands, Modo. I gave you my word; do you doubt mine?"

"No, no," he said. Out of the corner of his eye he saw a cup rise a few inches in the air and the milklike liquid drain from it. Griff was brazenly sitting right next to them! All the Icarians were gone. "I'm not being secretive. It's only that I've been unwell."

"Oh, that's just all the tea you British drink. You need coffee, my friend. Coffee. Something we don't find on the *Ictíneo*, I might add." She paused. "Did you notice that we're moving at about fifteen knots?"

"You can tell the speed?"

Her smile was both gentle and mocking. "No, Modo. Monturiol told me that the top speed of the *Ictíneo* is twenty-four knots."

"Twenty-four knots! But the fastest warship only goes fourteen!"

"Yes, the *Ictíneo* is much faster. No waves to slow her down. Believe me, you'll know when we hit top speed." She felt the wall. "It was vibrating like this when we speared the *Hugo*. We are hunting, Modo. I fear the crew is preparing for another attack."

28

The Quandary

Octavia clutched the telegram to her chest. Modo was alive! Alive! She whirled around her room, dancing, holding out the piece of paper as though it were her prince, dancing with her at a royal ball. He lives! My little Modo lives!

She'd spent most of the previous day on the ocean with Captain Arngrímur and his small crew of drunkards, on a creaking, cracking fishing boat he'd named *Hallgerda*. It was a paddle steamer with a motor that, barking and coughing, drove the spinning paddles. But it stayed afloat, and for a man whose blood must be half rum, the captain could sail, Octavia admitted. But they had found nothing, and had to return at dark.

That night she'd come to the only conclusion that had seemed possible: she was searching for a body. She'd bring him back to England and bury him in British soil, at least.

Now, all those dark thoughts, that sadness, had been for nothing! Mr. Socrates had received a message directly from Modo. And from a submarine ship, at that! What else could have clipped the anchor from the *Hugo* or smashed holes in ships? She and Modo had talked about there being a slim chance that such a ship could exist. Modo had somehow stolen his way onto one?

Clever Modo! She shook her head in wonderment, then closed her eyes. Modo was alive. She wiped tears from her cheeks.

Mr. Socrates had instructed her to stay in the boardinghouse at Reykjavik and wait for him. He'd promised to be there with a frigate within the next two days.

And so she climbed to her room on the top floor of the lodging house and sipped her tea as she stared out the window at the darkened ocean. Ships moved in and out of port, their lights glimmering in the distance.

This waiting will drive me batty! she thought. Absolutely batty!

But Mr. Socrates had told her to wait. She drummed her fingers on the windowsill and hummed softly to herself.

29

The Wreck

After Colette left to read in her room, Modo spent part of the morning in the library, examining the books. He saw no further signs of Griff, but couldn't escape the feeling that invisible eyes were watching him. The lights outside the porthole were turned off; obviously they were traveling as stealthily as possible. Comrades strode through the library on the way to various destinations, but their faces, as always, were unreadable. He noted that most seemed to be European, but there were one or two Cubans, and for the first time, he saw a Chinese comrade. Was there some underground movement drawing people from across the globe to Icaria? He added this to his list of things he would tell Mr. Socrates. If that day ever arrived.

As the vibrations of the *Ictíneo* grew stronger, Modo became more concerned. Was Colette correct about the ship's hunting for victims? Occasionally, the *Ictíneo* turned in the water and Modo would grab the reading table, bracing for impact. Were they circling back? He had no sense of the direction they were taking, nothing to mark his compass by.

He found himself wanting to talk more with Colette, but she had made it clear she didn't want to watch the sinking of another ship. Modo felt guilty about having lied to her, but it had been necessary. He didn't know anymore if she was trustworthy, and it was frustrating how easily she could read him. He had studied how to play different roles all his life. Was his education failing him? Mrs. Finchley had taught him so much about acting; he'd spent most of his life pretending he was someone else. Perhaps, if he lived through all this, he would ask Mr. Socrates to send him to Mrs. Finchley for more lessons.

After skimming through *On the Origin of Species*, Modo felt a sudden fatigue and decided it would be best to save his energy. It had only been two days since he'd plunged into the freezing ocean, and so much had happened since then. Being exhausted wouldn't help his acting, that was for sure.

He climbed the spiral staircase that cut through the bridge. Captain Monturiol didn't acknowledge him, she was so busy making notations in her log. Several comrades were working alongside her, adjusting levers and speaking through the voice tube to the crow's nest.

He suddenly missed Cerdà. Though the man spoke little, his presence had a calming effect on the crew and on the captain, even on Modo himself. What was Cerdà doing in New Barcelona? There must be so many things to construct and plans to engineer when building an underwater city.

Back in his room, Modo first felt around to see if Griff was somewhere; then he lay down on the cot, letting his features sag. Every muscle ached. He pulled the net mask over his face in case someone entered while he slept.

Hours later a Klaxon sounded and Modo shot out of bed, clutching at the air. The light above him flashed a warning. He almost stumbled out of his cabin without shifting his features, but then he remembered to remove the mask and, with his back leaning against the door, stared into the small circular mirror. It was always harder to transform himself when he was sleepy. He pictured the Knight face.

Concentrate! he told himself, still seeing Mr. Socrates' judgmental glare. Modo gritted his teeth, feeling his features changing. His tongue grew smaller, smoother, and more able to curl around words than the tongue he'd been born with. When he was finished, he wiped the usual film of sweat from his forehead. The Klaxons hurt his ears.

"Oh, so that's how that works," Griff said from a few feet away. "I nearly barked up my breakfast."

Modo grimaced in annoyance. "You're here!"

"Obviously! Slipped in when your back was turned. I came to inform you that we're going to battle stations."

"I'm aware of that." Modo slipped his net mask into his pocket. He didn't know where to look and had the sense that Griff was everywhere. He wanted to hit him. Griff had stood there silently and watched Modo change his shape. It was a private act. No one, especially not someone as creepy as Griff, should see him do it.

"You seem pensive, old boy."

"Why are we going to battle stations?" Modo asked.

"Some poor vessel has strayed into Captain Monturiol's imaginary Icarian boundaries. This woman must be stopped, Modo! Everyone is her enemy, believe me. But this will be a good chance for us to gather information and plan tactics. We may have an opportunity to strike."

"Strike?" Modo scratched nervously at his arm. "How would we operate the ship?"

"Don't panic! Ol' Griffy will look after you. We strike only if we're on the surface. You watch how she operates and who her subcommanders are. Since Cerdà's in the city, I wonder who's her second-in-command. They all look the same to me. I'm going to try to bypass the door into the aft chamber again. I want a good look at that engine. Toodle-oo!" Modo felt himself being pushed aside; then the door opened and closed.

Modo glanced around the room. Was Griff really gone? And would he really attempt to take over the ship? If they were on the surface, they'd have to be right next to land or another vessel. Otherwise the comrades would capture them. Or rather, they'd capture Modo. No one would even see Griff.

He shrugged. There was nothing he could do about it now. He opened the door. The Klaxons were overpoweringly loud as he ran down the passage and the stairs onto the bridge.

A female Icarian immediately intercepted him. "Mr. Warkin, return to your room."

Without turning from her station, Captain Monturiol said, "Mr. Warkin can stay and observe how one defends a country. By now these trespassers should be well aware of our borders."

"But you've given them no warning," Modo said.

She continued to stare out the periscope. "They have had fair warning. The Icelanders no longer fish our waters. Nor do the Finns, the Faeroese, or the Irish. Anyone who now enters does so with the knowledge that they are trespassers. It's an act of war to cross into Icaria's territory." She twisted a brass knob, no doubt to magnify the outside world through her periscope. She spoke in Catalan, and a comrade at a bank of levers lifted two of them. Immediately Modo felt the *Ictíneo* rising. They must have been pushing water out of the ballast tanks.

Modo went to the porthole. It was black outside the glass, though he thought he saw a glimmer of light on what might be the surface of the water.

"*Objectiu a la vista,*" Captain Monturiol said. "*Abast vuitanta-cinc metres. Sentanta-cinc metres. Seixanta-cinc metres. Quaranta-cinc metres.*" Modo realized she was counting down the distance. He bit his lower lip and imagined the people on the other ship, moving on the water, with no idea that this shark was charging toward them.

His heart skipped a beat. What if Octavia was on that ship? Or Mr. Socrates? What if they were looking for him? "*Preparació per a l'impacte.* Mr. Warkin, brace yourself."

Modo grabbed a railing just before the *Ictíneo* struck.

The impact threw him forward. The logbook fell to the floor. The captain gave orders and the *Ictíneo* reversed its engines, moving slowly backward.

"Diana!" the captain announced. A small cheer rose from the Icarians. Captain Monturiol adjusted another knob on the periscope, then turned and looked directly at Modo, her eyes gleaming in satisfaction. "We have breached the hull of a fishing ship, slightly above the waterline, Mr. Warkin. It will not sink, but the crew will limp back to port to warn others about these waters."

"If your calculations had been off, you could have sent that ship to the bottom," Modo scolded.

She stepped closer to him, her hand on her cutlass. His neck felt hot and he searched his pocket for a handkerchief.

"Mr. Warkin"—her voice was a harsh whisper—"soft men and women do not forge countries; that is what I learned from my father's death. Did his peaceful protestations get him any closer to the Icaria he dreamed of? No. We must be hard. Every other country is out to undermine us. Being vigilant is the price we pay to keep our land safe. You are in Icaria now, and you would do well to remember that."

"I will, Captain Monturiol," he replied, but his mind was on the *Hugo*. Monturiol had never apologized for almost killing him.

30

Getting a Message Through

Modo returned to his cabin, still thinking of how the collision could have easily sent those fishermen down to the bottom of the ocean, all because they had crossed an invisible line known only to a few Icarians underwater. It was madness.

And yet, what frightened him more was the look of absolute determination in Monturiol's eyes. She would be ruthless if she believed it would serve Icaria. The sooner he could get off the *Ictíneo*, the better.

He knelt down beside the cot. The wireless was several inches from where he had left it.

"Hello?" he whispered. "Are you there, Griff?"

No answer. Modo moved the glass plate and sent out a message, keeping it short.

Ictíneo struck fishing ship stop 14:54 GMT stop that is my latest position stop

If they had not received his message by now, they would assume he was dead. He pictured Octavia in a black dress, mourning. And what would Mr. Socrates feel? Tharpa? He liked to think that they were missing him. However, the Permanent Association would no doubt carry on quite effectively without him.

"Stop being a dawdler, Modo," he whispered.

He felt lighter; the *Ictíneo* was ascending. He put the telegraph away, this time placing it in the darkest corner below the cot.

When he arrived at the bridge, Captain Monturiol and several Icarians were standing next to Colette. The captain smiled at him, a surprise after their last conversation. Perhaps this was how she apologized. "You are growing accustomed to the *Ictíneo*'s ways, are you not, Mr. Warkin? You sensed that something had changed. I am sure Colette would be pleased to tell you what we will be doing next."

"We're getting some fresh air," Colette said. She seemed to glow a little. "Imagine that, Mr. Warkin. We're actually going to see the sun again!"

Monturiol clapped her hands. "Yes, we are surfacing. Our oxygen tanks are low. I fear we have a leak, as we are still using more air than I had calculated. We will fill our tanks, sniff the rotten carcass that is the world, and retreat to the womb of Mother Earth again."

It finally dawned on Modo: the lost oxygen had gone into Griff.

"Doesn't she have a wonderfully poetic way of putting things?" Colette said. "Are you certain you're not part French, Captain?"

"I can assure you I have no French blood." Monturiol grinned. She could be quite beautiful. "No English blood, either."

"Well, one can't have everything," Modo said, and was surprised by an even bigger smile from the captain. For a moment he could see why the Icarians followed her.

"To the surface, then." She signaled and one of the comrades climbed the spiral staircase to open the hatch. Pure, bright, glorious sunlight shone down into the ship. Modo moved into it, letting the rays fall on his head, his shoulders. He had missed the sun!

"Come, my friends," Captain Monturiol said, "let us go topside." She began climbing the ladder.

Modo felt like a mole popping out of the dirt. At the top of the ladder, he stepped onto the deck of the *Ictíneo*, his hand shadowing his eyes. Nothing but ocean in all directions. He breathed deeply. He'd almost grown used to the clammy atmosphere of the submarine ship.

Now he could see the length of the *Ictíneo* clearly, and its size was staggering. At least seventy-five yards from stem to stern, glistening with copper bolts. Each plate slid over the next, layered like fish scales. Guide wires were strung so that it was possible to walk from stem to stern without the danger of ocean waves washing a seaman away.

"She is a beauty, is she not?" Captain Monturiol said. "We are standing on my father's dream. Have you noticed the overlapping plated hull? He plucked the idea from Nature herself."

Modo heard Griff's now too-familiar cough and looked around. Even in the bright sunlight the boy was invisible.

Griff had spoken about taking control of the ship while they were topside. Was the cough a signal? It would be pointless to try—they were nowhere near land.

They strolled to the bow of the *Ictíneo* and Modo continued to breathe deeply, finding the air even sweeter. "Your father must have been quite the man," he said.

"He was, Mr. Warkin. He was a man of *seny i rauxa*—sense and passion. He believed men and women should be equal. He had to hide from the Spanish police, all because he had a free mind. He wrote to my sisters and me every day when he was in exile in France. His first love was his family. Building a submarine ship was his second."

"I would have liked to meet him," Colette said softly. Was she acting? Modo wondered. Her words seemed genuine enough.

"The Spanish government killed him."

"He was murdered?" Modo grabbed the guide wire.

"By bureaucrats! By paper pushers and weak-kneed, small-minded generals from Madrid. They raised his first submarine ship out of the water, declared it useless. In their jealousy of us Catalans, they smashed it up for scrap wood. Then they put my father in prison, just for printing political pamphlets. Seeing his submarine ship destroyed broke his heart and he died."

Ah, Modo thought, it wasn't exactly murder. But sad all the same. "Then who built this?"

"I did, following my father's plans and with Cerdà's brilliant eye for engineering and finances. He had amassed a fortune in Cuba. It has all gone into the *Ictíneo* and Icaria."

Modo remembered that she'd mentioned a second

submarine ship. He was about to ask where it had gone, when someone shouted from the tower. One of the men was pointing west. Captain Monturiol lifted her spyglass from her belt and looked through it. "A balloon! Who would be foolish enough to cross the Atlantic in such a frail vessel?"

Modo squinted at the sky and soon could see a gray oval shape. Could Octavia and Mr. Socrates be in that balloon searching for him? Octavia!

"It may have blown off course," Colette said to Modo, excitement in her eyes. Ah, she imagined it could be a French balloon. But there was no balloon capable of crossing the Atlantic, let alone one with a navigation system sophisticated enough to find them. But what if it was tethered to a ship? No sooner had Modo entertained that thought than Monturiol said, "There is a rope extending down into the ocean, though I cannot yet see what exactly it's connected to. The balloon is close enough to read her markings now; it's called the *Etna*."

"The *Etna*?" Colette said. "Is it a Greek vessel?"

Monturiol adjusted her spyglass. "I cannot say, but now I can see a ship on the horizon." She lowered the spyglass. "I have never seen such a beast!" She gave it another look. "It has been painted to match the water. Their flag is black; they do not want anyone to know their country of origin."

A black flag? Would Mr. Socrates sail under a black flag?

Modo could now make out the ship. Though it was not much more than a square in the distance, he counted five funnels. By that measure alone it was massive! The whole ship faded from his vision. Modo wanted to rub his eyes in disbelief.

"Did you see that?" Colette whispered.

The ship reappeared, and a great puff of smoke was followed by a boom. Something shot toward them, whistling and screaming, and exploded twenty yards to the port side of the submarine ship. Waves washed over the *Ictíneo*.

Captain Monturiol had stood tall through the volley. "Comrades," she said evenly, "return to your stations. We are under attack."

31

The Forever Enemy

Within minutes they were all down the ladder, and an Icarian closed the hatch. If it was Mr. Socrates out there, why would they fire first? A warning shot? It had been a tad too close. Modo looked around for some sign of Griff. If he was still out there, he was as good as dead.

"Guests! Return to your cabins," Captain Monturiol commanded. "You are not trained for battle!"

"Go back to my cabin?" Colette exclaimed. "What do you expect me to do? Read a book?"

"I'd prefer to remain on the bridge too," Modo insisted.

"Fine, but if you become a nuisance you will be forcibly escorted to your cabins." Then Monturiol hollered in Catalan and the Klaxon sounded. A moment later the ship dove so sharply that Modo and Colette had to grab the handrail along the wall. Colette stood close to Modo, her knuckles white.

A dull thud sounded, as though a large hammer had struck the side of the *Ictíneo*. Modo covered his ears and tried to maintain his balance. If a big enough hole was blown in the side, they'd be trapped in a sinking sardine can. "It can't be the British," he whispered. "They wouldn't do this."

"Don't be so sure," Colette replied, also in a whisper. "You Brits tend to shoot first, then ask questions."

He was about to disagree, then remembered Mr. Socrates' words: *We must either have that technology or destroy it*. Was that the goal now? He'd have no idea that Modo was on board. Would he stop if he did know?

Another thud. A third. A fourth. But they were fading.

The *Ictíneo* dove farther, its engine working so hard that the whole ship shook. The comrades calmly adjusted the levers, following Monturiol's every command. Whoever was in the crow's nest would be staring straight at the bottom of the ocean.

Colette nudged his hand. "What sort of ship was that?" she whispered. "Not a corsair. And it was *camouflé*! Disguised with paint so that it appeared and disappeared. It wasn't a nationality I recognized."

"And judging by its size, it's heavily armed," Modo replied. "If we try to ram it, its metal hull may be so thick that the *Ictíneo*'s ram will be torn off. Then we'll sink."

Modo thought he'd been speaking quietly, so he was surprised to hear the captain say, "That will not happen. Cerdà built the ram to cut through any metal known to man. I trust his design. I am curious how you two know so much about warships, but we will discuss that at an appropriate time."

She said something in Catalan to one of the Icarians, and the ship began to level out. "We shall approach with caution. That balloon can spot us from a distance and can see a good depth into the ocean. They cannot strike while we are this deep. They'll be surprised when we stab their underbelly."

She gave another command and Modo felt the ship turning. They sped through the water for three or four minutes, then turned so sharply he was forced to hang on tight. They ascended, then slowed as Captain Monturiol stared through her periscope.

Modo glanced out the porthole. He could see the surface above them. The ship sat still as Monturiol watched her enemy. The Icarians waited silently for her next command.

There was a sudden bubbling in the ocean.

"What's that?" Colette asked. As they stared, several metallic barrels dropped in the water nearby and drifted down, lit by the sunlight. They curved toward the *Ictíneo* as though attracted to the submarine ship. More splashes; ten or fifteen other barrels plunged into the water.

"*Immersió! Immersió! Immersió!*" shouted the captain, a hint of panic in her voice. The Klaxon sounded, and the *Ictíneo* began to descend. Modo gripped the handrail. They hadn't gone very far when the first container hit the side of the submarine ship with a *clang*.

Colette grabbed Modo's hand and squeezed. She looked as terrified as he felt. He braced, expecting an explosion. They dove deeper and faster, but every half-minute or so there was another *clang* of a barrel hitting the *Ictíneo*.

"They aren't detonating," Colette said, perplexed.

"Maybe there's a timed fuse." Modo moved along the

railing, hand over hand, to peer out the porthole. One barrel had somehow attached itself just below the glass. "I wonder if they're magnetic." It was studded with bolts. It wouldn't take much of an explosion to shatter the glass. Just as he motioned to Colette to come and see, the bolts shot out of the barrel and something that looked like a large red jellyfish burst out, unraveled, and fluttered to life, dispersing a cloud of bubbles. It grew into a billowing giant bladder, its cables still attached to the submarine ship. Another barrel burst, another huge jellyfish appeared.

"Balloons!" Modo cried, suddenly realizing what they were.

"They mean to drag us to the surface!" Colette shouted, and Captain Monturiol ran to the porthole to see for herself.

"They won't be strong enough to defeat our engine," she said. The *Ictíneo* shuddered as the propeller worked to drive them deeper into the ocean. More clanging could be heard; the enemy was relentless in sending down the barrels. The balloons pulled the *Ictíneo* higher and higher.

Modo turned to the captain. "We could go out in the aquasuits and cut the lines!" He was surprised at his own offer of help.

"Thank you, but there's no time." She shouted several commands and the ship swerved left and right. "Look! A barrel has detached!" The crew let out a cheer. But a moment later the helmsmen cried out, "We've lost our steering!"

Monturiol dashed to the wheel to find that it spun uselessly. The ship made a grinding, groaning noise and rose with such speed that Modo's stomach lurched.

"Knock out the captain, Modo," Griff whispered. "I cut the maneuvering cable. It's Mr. Socrates on that ship. He expects you to act! Put her out of commission!"

"Who spoke?" demanded Colette. "Who said your name?"

Before Modo could answer, the *Ictíneo* hit the surface and Monturiol shouted more orders, now clearly panicked. Icarians armed with spearguns shoved their way past Modo and Colette, running up the stairs toward the hatch. Captain Monturiol paused to hit several levers above the helm, to no effect that Modo could see. Then Monturiol charged up the spiral stairs after her comrades, leaving her helmsman and a few other Icarians at the ship's controls.

Modo and Colette hurried after her, the last of the passengers to climb out of the hatch.

Outside, the sky was a kaleidoscope of balloons, red, green and blue, each about twenty feet tall. The balloons blocked the sun and most of the view. Modo heard popping and hissing everywhere. As the comrades cut and slashed at the balloons with knives, Modo smelled gas. A single spark and they'd all be blown to kingdom come.

One balloon sagged. Behind it, just yards away from them, was the deck of the attacking ship. On its side was painted *Wyvern*. Men in gray uniforms stood in position all along the rail, rifles aimed at the submarine ship.

Two dogs with metal jaws glared down at them. Standing between the beasts, her metallic hand glittering in the sunlight, was an enemy Modo knew far too well.

32

Force Will Be Applied

"Who is she?" Colette asked.

"You don't want to know." Modo remembered how Miss Hakkandottir had pressed one of her metal fingers into his eye until it nearly popped. "She's a member of the Clockwork Guild. Her name is Miss Hakkandottir."

"You're speaking in riddles, Modo."

"The Guild is powerful, secret and evil. We don't know who controls it, but their objective is to bring down the British Empire."

"A lofty goal," Colette said, laughing. Modo was impressed that she could joke, considering the circumstances.

"Put down your weapons, hold up your hands and surrender," Hakkandottir said through a speaking trumpet.

"Never!" Captain Monturiol shot back. A few Icarians raised their spearguns while others brandished knives; they all looked rather pitiful to Modo. The soldiers who stared down the rifle sights from the *Wyvern* didn't blink. Every man and woman on the deck of the *Ictíneo* was a heartbeat away from a bullet.

"I assume you are Captain Delfina Monturiol," Hakkandottir called. "Surely you recognize that it's useless to resist." She pointed at a soldier aiming a flare gun. "With one flare you will all be incinerated by exploding hydrogen. Don't tempt me; I enjoy a good blaze."

Just hearing her voice sent a shiver down Modo's spine. The hounds' jaws snapped menacingly. No barking, Modo remembered. They were silent killers.

"The crew at the helm have orders to dive if the balloons go up in flames," Monturiol answered.

"And leave you behind?"

"As you have pointed out, we would be incinerated."

"Then we have a stalemate. I see, though, that twenty-five of your crew members are on deck. Are the few who remain below enough to pilot your *Ictíneo*? Ah, but it is all too much work to even discuss this. Force will have to be applied. Now!"

Modo prepared to duck. The Icarians brandished their weapons. Hakkandottir went on smiling. Nothing happened, and her smile slowly turned to a grimace.

"I said now. You must act now!" she screamed through the speaking trumpet. Whom was she talking to?

Modo expected soldiers to climb up out of the water or to swing down from the warship, but no one moved. It was as though she were talking to someone . . . invisible. He gasped, realizing with gut-wrenching clarity exactly who was receiving those orders. You fool, Modo!

At that moment one of the Icarians had his speargun wrenched from his hands and was pushed into the sea. The gun floated in the air and Modo yelled, "Captain!" but before he could jump to Monturiol's defense, the butt of the gun slammed into her skull and she collapsed. The gun clattered across the deck.

Griff could be anywhere! Modo pushed his way to where Monturiol lay. The Icarians gawked down at her, panic in their eyes. *Cut off the head of an organization and the body will die*, Mr. Socrates had told him many times. It appeared there was no second-in-command. They held their weapons bravely.

A shot from above struck the deck. "Enough! Surrender or die," Miss Hakkandottir commanded. The Icarians looked at one another. In unison, they dropped their weapons and raised their arms.

Grappling hooks flew across the deck, and seconds later Guild soldiers rappelled down ropes onto the *Ictíneo*. Modo knelt and lifted Monturiol's limp body.

A ramp was lowered from the ship to the submarine deck, and Modo, Colette, and the crew were prodded, shoved, and pushed onto the *Wyvern* and brought before Hakkandottir. Modo's throat grew dry. Even though he had been wearing a different face the last time they'd met—his Peterkin face—he feared Hakkandottir might recognize him all the same.

"Who are you two?" she asked.

"That one is a British spy." Griff's voice was close to her shoulder.

"Which one?"

"That one!"

"I can't see your finger, Griff. I assume you mean him." She pointed a metal digit at Modo.

"Yes, he's Modo. One of Mr. Socrates' special projects. He can change his shape and his features. He looks fine now, but when his disguise fades he's an ugly sot."

Modo stiffened but said nothing.

Hakkandottir's left eyebrow rose. "I'd heard such rumors. Extremely interesting! I want a detailed report later, Griff. And the woman?"

"Colette Brunet. A witch. A shrew. And a French spy."

Colette was looking around at all the soldiers with their mouths closed. "Who is speaking? Show yourself!"

Griff let out a long high-pitched giggle.

"Colette, I should have told you," Modo said slowly, knowing how ludicrous it sounded. "There has been an invisible man on board the *Ictíneo*. An invisible boy, really."

Modo felt a burning slap across his face. He almost dropped Captain Monturiol.

"I'm not a boy! You take that back! I am Griff, Invisible Man the First!"

"Griff, Griff," Miss Hakkandottir said quietly. "Now is not the time or place." She stroked the metal skull of one of the hounds. "And was the lovely captain aware of your employer, Modo?"

"No," Modo said. Hearing his name from Hakkandottir's lips made him sick. He glanced down at Captain Monturiol. "She rescued me from a ship the *Ictíneo* had struck. She believes I'm a photographer."

"So she is not as heartless as rumored. A pity. Well,

Modo, Colette, I am not one to conduct interrogations in the open." She turned to her men. "Take them to the hold."

With Griff's cackle following them, Colette and Modo were led by Guild soldiers across the deck. Monturiol was growing heavy in Modo's arms, so he held her tighter. They passed thick-barreled breech-loading guns, and arrays of other weapons and towers. At the top of one tower was a huge black flag, and on it, the face of a clock. The Clockwork Guild was brazen enough to openly sail the high seas.

33

For Want of a Nail

Mr. Socrates stood in the office of the Admiralty. He was personally acquainted with First Naval Lord Milne, but the man was in India, and his second-in-command demanded that forms be filled out before he released a ship.

Mr. Socrates filled out the requisition forms as quickly as possible, Tharpa standing silently behind him. His frustration built with each stroke of his pen. He no longer cared whether his writing was legible.

"How many more forms?" he barked at the secretary, a thin man who had probably never been to sea.

"There are several more, sir," the secretary said, delivering a large stack. "In triplicate."

"Triplicate? Time is of the essence here! I told you that! I demand to see Second Sea Lord Hornby at once."

"Sir, he is engaged until this evening. He will sign off on the papers then."

Bureaucracy! Mr. Socrates wanted to shout. "For want of a piece of paper the kingdom was lost," he hissed.

The secretary stared at him blankly.

Ah, it was pointless! He had hours of paperwork ahead of him. All this paper would one day be the downfall of the Empire. "Come, Tharpa," he said. "We shall have to hire our own ship."

34

Down in the Hold

Colette breathed through her mouth. The hold smelled of coal dust, smoke, and carcasses, though there weren't any bodies she could see. Perhaps those on board had used the room to slaughter animals for their meals.

One Guild soldier remained standing silently at the door. If her hands hadn't been tied behind her back and then tethered to her ankles, she would have grabbed something and bashed Modo's head in.

"Colette? Colette?" Modo whispered. He too was tied up, and Captain Monturiol was bound and unconscious next to them.

"You kept a vital secret from me!" she snarled.

"I—I did. I'm sorry. Griff approached me yesterday and convinced me that he was a member of—of a British organization. He had followed us from New York. He knew things only a British agent would know."

"He's invisible and could've overheard any of your private conversations, or our conversations, for that matter."

"He said you murdered Wyle."

"Who?"

"One of our agents."

"That sounds more like something he would do. What was his name again?"

"Griff."

"Griff? What sort of name is that?" Colette tried to twist her wrists out of the ropes. "I shook your hand, Modo. I gave you my word."

"We're agents from different countries, Colette. We're actors; you know that."

"You should have trusted me." She drew in a deep breath, seeking calm. "How did they find us?"

"He was the one who stole my telegraph. He must have somehow used it."

"So you *were* able to get messages out?"

"I sent them, but I have no idea whether they were received."

"You've hidden much from me. I believed we were partners."

"We are."

"We were!" Colette huffed. Don't get angry, she told herself. Collect information. Reassess the situation. Then act. "How does this Griff stay invisible?"

"His body has been chemically altered so that every cell bends light. It makes him invisible to human eyes." Modo coughed and Colette looked over. His face was a little red. And distorted. "I—I think the drugs may have affected his mind," Modo continued. "He seems a little off, if you know what I mean. And he's got a temper."

Out of the corner of her eye, Colette saw Modo's head snap back as if forced. He groaned.

"Yes, I'm easily angered by lower creatures," a voice said. "I'm the only one—Invisible Man the First. You don't know what that's like."

Colette scanned the hold. Where was the voice coming from?

"Griff," Modo said, "we shook hands."

"Yes, you foolish beast, we did. Are you a child?" A rope flew up from the floor and looped around Modo's neck. It began to tighten.

"Stop that! Stop!" Colette cried.

"Shut your gob," Griff ordered. "Modo, your strength is something—I saw you rip open that door to the submarine ship." He gave the rope another good yank. "And I've watched you change the actual shape and size of your bones. My guess is that you can easily slither out of these ropes. So I'm going to tie this particular one around your neck, nice and tight. If you move too much, you'll choke." The end of the rope floated up and knotted around a steel girder, forcing Modo to stand on the tips of his toes.

"He'll choke," Colette shouted. "Stop!"

She was slapped so hard her teeth felt loose.

"You don't know how long I've wanted to slap you!" Griff said.

She spat toward the voice. Her spittle stopped in midair, then dripped to the floor.

"You'll pay for that," Griff said. "I'll have my hands around your lily-white throat soon enough."

"You don't frighten me," she said, straining at her ropes.

"Ta-hee! I'll drag you over to the hold with the other Icarians. They're standing in four feet of ice water." His laugh was grating on her nerves. "I can do it! I can. I'll be your worst nightmare, I promise you." The rope around Modo's neck tightened—Griff had given it another pull. "Now, Modo, if I had the time I'd sit and wait while you choke. What will your pretty little coquette think when she sees your real face?"

The door opened and slammed shut, cutting off Griff's laughter. The Guild soldier stood motionless with his hand on his pistol.

"Is—is he gone?" Colette said.

"Who knows," Modo rasped.

"Well, we must behave as though he is here," she said. "Are you going to be able to stay upright?"

"Yes. For now."

Captain Monturiol moaned and slowly opened her eyes.

"Where are we?" she asked. "Where is the *Ictíneo*?"

"We are imprisoned on the *Wyvern*," Colette replied. "An organization called the Clockwork Guild is in control of your submarine ship."

Monturiol pulled fiercely against her ropes. "They cannot have my ship!"

"Calm down, Captain," Colette said. "Struggling won't do any good."

"Yes, save your energy," Modo said, and Monturiol turned to look at him. Her eyes widened.

"They've hanged you!"

"Yes," he said. "It seems they have."

The door opened and Miss Hakkandottir entered, two soldiers on either side of her. A mechanical-jawed hound slouched along behind her. "Ah, I see Griff has been busy," she said. She patted the dog and it raised its head. "Find Griff. Bring him to my quarters." The dog sniffed and bounded out of the room. "I am interested in you two. I want to discuss your operations, but first my men will take the good captain out for some fresh air and a pleasant discussion about submarine science."

The four soldiers grabbed the screaming Captain Monturiol and lifted her easily. She spat and fought as hard as her bound body allowed her, but it was no use. They carried her out the door.

"We'll be back soon enough," Miss Hakkandottir said playfully as she followed her catch.

The door slammed. Modo hacked and sputtered. "I appear . . . to be . . . losing my breath." Before Colette could speak, he'd fallen forward, tightening the rope.

35

Blood and Flowers

Griff stood silently on the tiger-skin rug in the captain's quarters. Miss Hakkandottir sat with her back to him. She tapped with a metal finger on the golden key of her wireless telegraph, sending a message, he assumed, to the Guild Master. Griff trembled with joy. It was so wonderful to be with her again. He'd grown up under her tutelage and he loved her fervently. *Why isn't she talking to me?* he wondered. *Can't the telegram wait? I haven't seen her for six months. Six months!*

The longer the message grew, the more Griff rubbed his hands and fidgeted. The movement kept him from shivering. The *Wyvern* was an icebox—all ships were cold. He actually missed the cramped, humid quarters of the *Ictíneo*. At least he had been warm there.

He began twirling a nearby globe on its pedestal, first slowly, then faster, watching all the countries spin. *Turn,* he thought. *Turn! Turn! Turn!*

The world turned, but Miss Hakkandottir didn't. He jammed his finger on the globe and let out a squeak of pain. He put his finger in his mouth, then pulled it out and looked at it. It was, of course, invisible, but a bead of blood appeared in the air and slowly rolled down his finger, revealing some of its shape. He watched the blood drip, then stuck his finger in his mouth again. It was comforting, and he liked the brassy taste of blood. Dr. Hyde had never been able to explain why his blood still appeared red when he cut himself. It was the only color he had.

"I remember when you used to bring me flowers," Miss Hakkandottir said, abruptly standing to face him. "Do you remember that, Griff?"

"Yes! Yes! I was a boy then. I would watch you arrive in your airship. It was such a lovely vessel."

"Well, today you brought me something much better than flowers. You have exceeded all my expectations. I am so proud of you."

His invisible heart began to beat faster. "Oh, it was nothing, Miss Hakkandottir."

"You are not normally modest, Griff. Nor should you be. Dr. Hyde would be proud too."

"How is the old genius?" he asked.

"Busy. There is always work for him to do and places for his mind to go. He misses you."

"He misses my help, you mean."

"Perhaps, but he has other helpers now. Not as colorful as you, of course. He sends his best."

Griff had been prodded and poked so many times by the old sot, he didn't think of the doctor with much fondness.

But Hyde had made Griff who he was, Invisible Man the First. For that, he was extremely thankful.

"The Guild Master sends his greetings as well."

That made Griff swallow. The man who led the Clockwork Guild, who had no name but the Guild Master. Griff had never even glimpsed him. He had tried once to sneak into the glass and iron fortress on the far end of the island, but the dogs had prevented him.

"Then I've done well!" Griff said. "I will bring you many more flowers."

"I hope you didn't find New York too cold. The information you gathered there and from the submarine ship was crucial. And figuring out how to use that agent's wireless telegraph was brilliant! The Guild Master relied on your reports to design the balloons, and he provided us with much more equipment. Is there anything else you have yet to tell us?"

"There's a city, Miss Hakkandottir. Mad Monturiol created a city beneath the waters that she calls New Barcelona. I've not seen it with my own eyes, but Modo and Colette visited it."

"Ah! I am certain we will learn more about it from the captain. She was not talkative a few minutes ago, but the guards are 'encouraging' her as we speak." She paused. "I am especially curious about this Modo."

"There's not much to him," Griff snapped.

"Now, now, no jealousy, Griff. You are better than that. You say he can change his appearance?"

"Yes, and his actual shape. He can disguise himself as anyone. Well, not as me, of course."

"A very interesting skill."

"He's a bore, though. Unimaginative, strong, and dumb as an ox."

"And his loyalties. Are they deep?"

"He's loyal as a mongrel to his master."

"Well, we shall have to study him. The Guild Master will want to know details. Dr. Hyde, too. Perhaps we can learn how he performs his tricks."

The thought of them being thrilled with Modo made Griff grind his teeth. "But he's not invisible."

"No, my sweet, dear Griff—he is not you. No one is. I assume the knot you tied will not choke him. I would be disappointed if it did."

Griff bit his invisible lip. "No. No. He's safe."

"Good. Again, I am so very proud of you." She had an unerring ability to stare directly into his eyes. He didn't understand how she sensed where he was standing. "I *am* disappointed in just one thing, though. We have talked about your slowness to take action. Sometimes you hesitate too long. You could have brought that submarine ship to the surface much earlier."

"I—I will do better. I promise."

"I know you will, Griff. That is all. The coxswain's cabin has been prepared for you. Please relax. You deserve it."

She patted his shoulder, but what he wanted most of all was for her to wrap her arms around him. To be held, that metal hand clasped tightly around his back.

"Thank you, Miss Hakkandottir. Thank you."

36

The Hanging Man

Modo forced himself back into a half crouch, struggling for breath. He'd nearly blacked out—the suffering was too intense. His body was changing, sending painful ripples through the muscles in his arms, legs, shoulders, neck, and face. He was unable to hold the tall, slender shape of the handsome Knight. He felt his bones creak as his back hunched inch by inch, shortening his torso and tightening the noose around his neck. How long had he been standing like this? Minutes? Hours?

"Modo, are you well? You keep gurgling," Colette said.

He was thankful that there was very little light. He kept his face turned away so that she couldn't see the monster he was becoming.

"My shape is—is changing. That is my affliction."

"I don't understand."

"It's hard to explain. You see, I can change my appearance.

My body is contracting into a—a different shape. I'm not strong enough to stop it. The knot is growing tighter."

He was surprised at how calm he sounded. His calves were cramping, his feet, each toe. Waves of agony that came and went, and he had to concentrate on staying still and stretching himself against the weight of his own body.

The rope tightened around his throat again, so he whispered desperately, "Griff, Griff, are you here? Can you loosen it?"

He waited, but nothing happened. Griff must have been watching Monturiol being interrogated. Modo shuddered. He knew Miss Hakkandottir's methods. She had likely refined them further.

"Oh, Modo, I wish I could do something."

"Just don't watch me die," he said.

"Oh, don't be *si mélodramatique!*" Colette huffed.

He tried to picture a way out. What would Tharpa do? But it was like a Chinese finger trap—the harder he pulled, the tighter the knot became. Griff had known what he was doing. If only Modo could make his hands smaller and slip out of the ropes . . . but they were too tight and wrapped around in several loops. His only hope was to convince the guard to untie him.

"Sir! Sir! Miss Hakkandottir will be angry with you if I die," Modo said.

The guard remained impassive, though his eyes flicked toward Modo.

"Yes, release him," Colette pleaded.

"The prisoners shall not speak to me." The soldier's voice was dull; there was something wooden in his tone.

Modo swayed on his feet, his thoughts caught in a black vortex. He heard voices. Faces floated in front of him. Mrs. Finchley, was she here? And Mr. Socrates? And Octavia? He tried to reach for her, but his hands were tied behind his back.

"Modo! Modo!" Colette shrieked, waking him from his trance. He gulped, his lungs empty, and thrust himself a little farther forward.

"You stopped breathing," she said.

"I—I didn't mean to."

"Keep breathing!"

Maybe there was a way, he realized: if he let his whole weight pull the rope. It was tied tightly, but it was old and thin and there were ragged strands here and there.

"I have a plan," he rasped.

"A plan?"

"I'm going to pull the noose tighter."

"What!"

"It's the only way. Look, the rope is frayed." Even as he said that, he saw that the worn portions weren't that weak. "I'll pull as hard as possible."

"But if you fail, you'll die!"

"I don't have a choice."

He took a deep breath. Was all this madness induced by lack of air? His thoughts were already slower, his back hunching. Here goes! He let himself fall backward so that the rope tightened around his neck, crushing his windpipe. His face, he knew, was going purple. The rope was now a perfectly taut straight line. He stared, willing it to break. His eyes bulged as he blinked back sweat. He couldn't even swallow. He needed so badly to breathe, but his windpipe was closed. Dark spots pooled in his vision.

Now he was floating and felt light as smoke. He saw a young man hanging below him. *That's me!* The world was fading. *No!* He wanted to shout. His blood was rushing in his ears, a sound like the raven wings of death. Somewhere Colette screamed his name.

He let out a gurgled cry. He was frothing, maybe even bleeding, he didn't know. He pictured Octavia in her green dress and tried to step toward her.

The rope snapped and he fell to the floor. The noose remained tight around his neck. He still couldn't breathe!

Then he was jostled by something near his neck, and he worried that rats were at his throat. His lungs expanded like a bellows, pulling in air as he faded in and out of consciousness. He sucked in a breath. Another.

"I used my teeth to loosen the knot," Colette said. "I nearly dislocated my ankles bending over. Be thankful I've got good teeth. You look sick, Modo. Your face, it's hard to see in the dark, but you seem to have bumps. . . ."

Modo used his last bit of strength to turn away from her. "It's nothing. Nothing."

Someone began clapping.

"Griff," Modo said, almost spitting the name.

"You two have given a very exciting display. Very much so. You are not so great, though, Modo, remember that!"

"You are a . . ." Colette's voice trailed off.

"I know what I am. Well, your good captain has been very uncooperative. She keeps her secrets well."

Modo felt the knots around his wrists and ankles tighten again.

"That'll hold you," Griff said. "Well, it has been a busy day. I'll be dining with my captain. Venison, I am told. And after that I'll sleep the sleep of the just. Ta-hee!" The door opened for several seconds and then closed with a resounding thud.

37

Honor Among Spies

Modo lay on his side, his back to Colette. He breathed deeply and felt his spine curling in on itself. The hump was slowly rising: she would be able to see it soon enough, but better that than his face. Never his twisted, grotesque face. His wrists ached where the rope was biting into his flesh. Was the blood supply to his hands and feet being cut off? They tingled as though needles were poking them.

The door swung open and two soldiers dragged Captain Monturiol into the corner, where they tied her in a sitting position. Modo pressed his face against his shoulder, hiding most of it. Monturiol's jaw was set, her hair bedraggled, and her eyes red-rimmed, but she shed no tears.

"Captain!" he said. "Are you well?"

She stared vacantly for a few moments, then ever so slowly turned to look at him. "Spies!" she hissed.

"That's not true," Colette said.

"It was the only bit of truth they told me."

"Yes, it is true," Modo admitted. He was glad he couldn't see Colette's reaction to his words. "We were only investigating. We meant no harm."

"No harm?" she spat. "Infiltrators with golden tongues. I see your rash has returned, Mr. Warkin. Is that even your real name?"

"No." He paused for only a moment before saying, "My name is Modo."

"And am I to believe that the British, your masters, would not have acted in the same manner as these barbarians? You're all cut from the same cloth."

"We are honorable," he said, knowing as he spoke the words that this was untrue. What *would* Mr. Socrates have done to get the secrets of the *Ictíneo*? The plans for New Barcelona? These were two gems that would shine bright in the crown of Britannia. He might very well have come here with several warships.

"There is no honor among thieves or secret agents," Captain Monturiol said. "I should've left both of you to watery graves."

They were silent for several minutes. Modo did not want to imagine what sort of torture Hakkandottir had put the captain through. She didn't appear to be bleeding or terribly bruised, but they could have done anything to her. Tharpa had told him once that the Chinese methods involved the feet, since that part of the body experienced a deep, lasting pain. If anyone knew those sorts of tricks, it was the Clockwork Guild.

"Modo," Colette whispered. "Can't you turn over? Why do you have your back to me?"

"I am becoming deformed," he said simply. "I don't want you to see my face."

"Ah, don't be foolish. I won't be alarmed."

"I can't," he said. "Please leave me be. I must rest and catch my breath."

"Fine," Colette said. "Be stubborn."

"There are no deformities in Icaria," Captain Monturiol whispered. Then she closed her eyes.

Modo stole the occasional glance at her. She was sitting up ramrod straight, her breath a little labored, trying to hide her pain. She had a backbone of steel. This woman was, almost single-handedly, trying to create a new country. And she believed in it with such fervor she would sacrifice anything, even her own body. He doubted that the Guild had gotten a single word from her.

As he slowly shifted into his natural state, he wondered about this Icaria. Monturiol had said that everyone was welcome there, even cripples. And if anyone was crippled, he was. A hunchback! Forever! Mr. Socrates had told him many times, "You are deformed. You are ugly. Your unsightly countenance may seem unbearable now, but because of it the world will always underestimate you." But what if Modo didn't have to be underestimated? What if there was a place he could live without changing his shape? Where people wouldn't lock him in a cage and charge a fee for others to stare at him? Could Icaria really be like that? He would never walk the streets of London as himself.

The room grew darker as the sun set and the moon lit the dirty glass of the porthole. It was likely only dinnertime, Modo realized. The sun set so much earlier this far north. He shivered. The hold was becoming a giant icebox.

Someone tapped on the door, which then swung slowly open. The soldier on guard gasped and pulled his pistol, but before he could fire or let out a cry, a fist shot out of the darkness and smashed him in the jaw. He crumpled to the ground. His assailant took a step into the room, squinting. He was bearded, dressed in an India rubber suit, and holding a speargun. The wan moonlight lit his craggy features.

"Cerdà!" Modo and Captain Monturiol whispered in unison.

"Ever-faithful, ever-ingenious Cerdà," said the captain. "The pillar on which Icaria stands."

"Don't use such words." A knife flashed and the captain's bonds fell away. Cerdà helped her stand. "I received your SOS transmission. The *Filomena* brought us here. But we had to pedal the last kilometer, in order to approach silently."

"Where is the *Ictíneo?*" Monturiol asked, rubbing her wrists.

"She is grappled to starboard, several meters below the surface. They now understand enough of her operation to move her back and forth. I fear one of our comrades must have broken under interrogation."

"It is only to be expected—we are still flesh and blood."

"What of these two?" He pointed his knife at Modo and Colette.

"They are spies," Captain Monturiol said harshly. "Better to cut their throats as they would have done ours while we slept."

"But we didn't, did we?" Colette said.

"Only because you lacked the opportunity."

"No," Modo said. "You misjudge us. We are not your enemies. Take us with you. I—and Colette—have intimate knowledge of the Clockwork Guild."

"We don't need your knowledge."

Modo stirred, moving into the moonlight so that part of his face was revealed. Monturiol and Cerdà recoiled. Good! He wanted to shock them, to test their Icarian principles. "You are dooming us to torture and death at the hands of that evil woman. I thought compassion was at the heart of your Icaria."

Monturiol raised a fist. "You are not pure enough to speak the name Icaria. I offered you a place in a perfect society. My reward was to lose my most precious possession."

"*Quel drame!*" Colette said. "But how many people have you sacrificed? Are we two more to be left behind?"

"You knew the risk of being spies."

"Would your father leave us here?" Modo asked.

"Don't speak of him!" she snapped. "Don't!" She grabbed the knife from Cerdà and swung it toward Modo. He closed his eyes, was surprised when he felt the ropes fall from his arms and ankles. She had nicked his skin in several places. She stepped over him and he heard Colette give a few small pained grunts. Monturiol was obviously careless with the blade.

While she worked at Colette's bonds, Modo jammed his numb fingers into his pockets and fumbled to retrieve his mask. He felt a hand helping him. Cerdà was bent over him.

"It is secure now," he said. He lifted Modo up onto wobbly legs. There was nothing Modo could do about his hair, which would soon be falling out in clumps. Maybe the netting would hold it in place. Colette was beside him, looking as drained as he felt, but standing steady.

"We shall see what your words are worth," Monturiol said. She still gripped the knife tightly, as if she might at any second plunge it into either of their hearts. "Do you swear to help us free the *Ictíneo*?"

"What do we receive in return?" Colette shot back.

"Your lives," Monturiol answered.

"We need more than that," Modo said. "Where will you take us once we've helped you?"

"I shall deposit you on Iceland. I cannot promise anything beyond that. So do you swear?"

"I swear," Modo and Colette said together.

"What of our comrades?" Monturiol asked Cerdà. "They are locked up amidships."

"We have a hard decision," Cerdà said. "Only luck brought me to you—if we attempt to free them, we will wake up this hornets' nest of soldiers and accomplish nothing. We do not have room on the *Filomena* for more than a few."

She nodded. "The decision is clear. We must protect New Barcelona first and strive to release them later. We all swore oaths to defend Icaria. They will understand."

Modo felt a tightening in his guts. All those comrades,

deserted on this ship. He didn't want to imagine how Hakkandottir would treat them.

Cerdà opened the door and looked about. Modo's heart pounded—at any moment he expected Griff to laugh and their chance of escape to vanish. But Cerdà motioned them forward and soon they were climbing a set of stairs to the deck of the *Wyvern*.

Cerdà had left a grappling hook in a dark corner on the port side, only a few feet from the stairs. They silently climbed down the rope. Modo's grip was weak and he feared he'd fall into the water below. When he set his feet on the deck of the *Filomena* the ship sank a little deeper. It was much smaller than the *Ictíneo*, more like a cutter than a ship. He followed Colette, squeezing himself down through the hatch and into the aft, each motion making the submarine ship rock in the water. The interior smelled moist. Comrade Garay was at the helm, one hand on the wheel, as he peered at the dials and switches. He nodded at Modo.

"Take a seat," Cerdà whispered. "Both of you. Place your feet upon the pedals."

They did as instructed.

"Comrade Garay," Monturiol said, putting her hand on his shoulder, "please take us down ten meters." The vessel submerged and they began pedaling away.

38

An Underwater Assault

The cramped quarters stank of sweat. After his recent escape, Modo was worried there wasn't enough air, but he gulped in what he could. The *Filomena* was so small, the hull thin; all it would take was one sharp knock to crush it like an egg.

The ship creaked and Modo squinted at the shell. "This is made of wood!"

"Keep your voice down," Monturiol whispered. "Sound travels underwater. Yes, it is olive wood, reinforced with rings of oak and sheathed in copper. My father was a cooper's son, through and through. He learned to make barrels for wine and oil at his father's side."

"Is our intention to regroup at New Barcelona?" Cerdà asked.

"No," Captain Monturiol said. "We strike now. Before they discover we are missing."

"I brought four suits," Cerdà said. "And helmets."

"Then we will retake our ship," Monturiol said.

"How do you propose to do that?" Modo asked.

"Just pedal, comrades."

They maneuvered through the water as the captain stared out the front portholes.

"She must have the eyes of a cat if she can see through that murk," Colette whispered to Modo.

Monturiol motioned to Comrade Garay. "To the surface," she said. He pulled a lever and the ship rose slowly, but Modo could hear the scraping of gears, and he couldn't shake the sensation that at any moment the *Filomena* might be blown to bits by cannon fire.

"I'll help you get your ship back," Modo said.

"No. I don't trust you," Monturiol said.

"How will you get into the *Ictíneo*? I assume you'll want to open the hatch—either at the top or bottom. Cerdà is big, but you know I am the strongest one here."

"He is correct," Cerdà said. "He was able to tear open the *Ictíneo*'s top hatch. He is certainly stronger than I am. He'll easily be able to open the ballast portal."

"Modo won't go without me," Colette said.

Monturiol looked dubious but said, "Into your suits. You will not need the armor, only the India rubber; we'll be riding on the back of the *Filomena*." She patted Garay's shoulder. "Comrade Garay, it will be your task to pilot the *Filomena*. I have faith in your skill."

"I shall do my best," Garay said.

"We shall come up underneath the *Ictíneo*," said Monturiol. "There we will access the hatch, close the subhatches, and enter the pump room. Next we will overpower whoever is inside."

They climbed onto the top of the *Filomena*. The *Wyvern* loomed a hundred yards away, soldiers patrolling its decks. The moon was just bright enough to light their outlines. Taut ropes ran from the starboard side of the ship into the water. The *Ictíneo* had to be attached at the other end, yards below the surface. Modo pulled on his rubber suit while balancing on one leg, aware that one misstep would send him plunging into the water. He had to work hard to get the rubber over his hump.

"We will only have the oxygen that is trapped in our helmets," Cerdà explained quietly. "It will last about five minutes, if you breathe slowly. The magnetic palms in the gloves of our suits will allow us to cling to the *Ictíneo*'s side. Please put your helmets on now."

The aquahelm was too tight, so Modo turned away from his companions and removed his mask. Because the rubber suit had no pockets, he stuffed the mask into his collar and pulled down the helmet, covering his face. He felt as though he were suffocating. After all he'd been through, would he really have the strength to open anything?

The four of them clung to the railing of the little submarine ship, their leaden boots holding them down. Monturiol tapped lightly on the hull and the *Filomena* sank slowly into the water, piloted by Garay.

Modo held on, trying not to breathe too hard as they entered the water. At first they moved through darkness, but eventually Modo saw a light under the water that could only be the *Ictíneo*. They descended until they were underneath the larger submarine ship. How much time had passed? Two minutes? Four?

The massive hull of the *Ictíneo* loomed above them. As Modo watched, a crack appeared in the glass of his mask and slowly widened. If the glass shattered, would he reach the surface in time?

Finally they rose, until the bottom of the *Ictíneo* was directly above them. They would be crushed against it! But again Monturiol knocked on the *Filomena*'s hull and the small submarine ship came to a stop.

Cerdà reached up and used the magnetic palms of his gloves to cling to the side of the *Ictíneo*. The rest of them followed his lead, climbing like underwater insects. Soon they arrived at the ballast portal. Modo judged that it opened into the forward ballast tank that ran along the bottom of the submarine ship.

Once there, they all moved aside for Modo. It was up to him. Barely taking the time to consider what would happen when he opened the hatch underwater, he took a deep breath, twisted the handle, and pulled on the hatch, fighting the pressure until it opened a crack. He pulled harder and the water rushed into the chamber, nearly sucking him in. He struggled to keep the hatch open. The submarine ship, suddenly heavier, slipped a few yards deeper into the ocean. First Cerdà, then Monturiol, and finally Colette pulled themselves inside. Modo climbed in behind them and hauled the hatch shut.

39

Skeleton Crew

The forward ballast tank ran half the length of the *Ictíneo*, along the bottom, and was full of ocean water. With each crawling movement, with each aching breath, Modo wondered how much time had passed. Was he almost out of air? His lungs complained as he pulled himself ahead, periodically bumping into Colette's feet, all the while trying to prevent the magnets on his hands from clicking on the walls. He knew how that sound would travel through the ship. The light in his helmet revealed several fish trapped in the tank along with them.

They came to a stop. In front of him he glimpsed Cerdà turning a circular wheel on the side of the tank. Cerdà gave it a final crank and water splashed onto the floor, sweeping all four of them along with it. Modo banged his head on the way out. Once he had regained his footing, he removed the aquahelm but couldn't find his mask in the neck of his suit.

It must have fallen out! The water was up to his knees and sluicing out the door and down the hallway toward the bow of the ship. His mask was somewhere in that mess! At least in this darkness they wouldn't see his face clearly. He did find an oily rag, which he tied over his nose and mouth.

"We have entered undetected," Cerdà whispered. Captain Monturiol flung her hair out of her eyes. She unlatched the shoes and magnets quietly. Modo did the same.

Cerdà began walking down the hallway, but Modo grabbed his shoulder. "I should go first," he whispered.

"Why?"

"I'm trained for combat."

"I'll be your second-in-command, then, comrade," Cerdà said lightly as he stepped aside.

Modo led them down the slick hallway; most of the water had already drained away. He was unfamiliar with this section of the craft but knew they were heading in the direction of the library. The hallway lights flickered—maybe the Guild soldiers didn't understand the electrical system well enough to control the lights properly. The hardwood floor was relatively quiet, though occasionally their footsteps squeaked.

He paused at the open doorway of a cabin: the hallway light revealed a cot with the impression of someone's body on the sheets. Griff! Modo leapt into the room and grabbed at what he believed would be the man's neck.

His hand closed on nothing but sheets. He tossed the pillow onto the floor, patted at the foot of the bed. No, it must have been his imagination. He felt eyes on him, looked at the door to see Cerdà staring at him as if he thought Modo had gone mad. Modo shrugged and took the lead again.

The hall led them to a wider chamber. At the entrance, Modo pulled up short, signaling to the others behind him to stop. A Guild soldier was leaning over an instrument cluster, adjusting knobs and writing notes in a journal. He wore a gray cap, a holstered pistol at his side. Likely an engineer, Modo guessed. The man was intent on his work, so Modo crept toward him.

The soldier turned and yelped. Modo chopped him on the temple, knocking him out and catching him before he fell. Modo squeezed against the wall and peered toward the library. Several moments passed and no one answered the man's cry. Modo lowered the man's limp body to the floor.

"We could have questioned him," Captain Monturiol whispered.

"He might have alerted others."

"His cry may have done that already," Colette remarked as she removed the six-barreled pistol from the man's belt. "At least we're properly armed now."

Captain Monturiol thrust out her hand. "I'll carry that!"

"Are you familiar with the pepperbox pistol?" Colette countered.

"No."

"I won't betray you, Captain. I know your word can be trusted. If we aid you, you'll take us to Iceland. If the Clockwork Guild catches us, I'll not live much past today."

Morturiol nodded. "Then keep the pistol."

"What do you suppose he was doing?" Modo asked.

"The excess water has set the *Ictíneo* off balance," Cerdà said. "He was probably attempting to fix that. They do not seem to understand even the basics of buoyancy."

"Should we continue?" Modo asked.

"Yes," Monturiol answered. "They are most likely in the bridge."

Modo pictured climbing the stairs and being spotted halfway up. The pepperbox pistol wouldn't be much help if there were several armed soldiers above them. Run through your options in your mind, Mr. Socrates had told him several times. Look for weaknesses.

"I have a plan," he said. "I go on alone."

"Alone?" Cerdà echoed.

"Yes. They may be armed. I'll walk right up to the enemy and disarm them. I'm able to change my appearance. I cannot explain how it works, but I must ask that you give me room. Please."

"Why?" Captain Monturiol asked.

"I'm like a magician. I don't want you to see my tricks."

Colette gave him an odd look, but all three of them stepped back. Modo slipped the rag off his face and pulled the soldier's cap over his patchwork of hair. Then he dragged the engineer into the light and stared down at his face. Modo shuddered and struggled, slowly forcing his face into the same shape as the man's. Nerves tingled with pain. He'd not had enough rest! His bones shifted, his muscles tightened. He felt as if he might collapse, but he drew a deep breath and concentrated until he was certain he looked enough like the man to fool the other soldiers in the dimly lit submarine ship. As a final touch he replicated the birthmark on the man's cheek. He then grabbed the soldier's jacket and trousers and slipped them over his rubber suit. When he glanced at his companions, they gasped and stared back in wonder.

"*Mon dieu!*" Colette exclaimed. "That's amazing." Modo enjoyed the shock and admiration in her eyes.

"How is this possible!" Captain Monturiol blurted.

"It would take too long to explain." Modo did up the buttons on the jacket. The lights flickered again. "I'll scout the bridge and send a signal when all is clear. If things go awry, please be so kind as to come to my aid."

"We will," Cerdà said.

Modo entered the empty library and heard voices at the top of the spiral staircase. Now or never, he thought, then climbed the steps into the bridge. There were three soldiers standing at the helm. One carried a shortened rifle—obviously a marine. The other two were engineers, one with three stripes on his shoulder—a sergeant. In a moment, Modo took in this information; then he stumbled toward them, holding his head. He didn't know which language they spoke, until the sergeant said in English, "Krippen! Why did you leave your post?"

"I . . . electrical shock . . . hit head," Modo rasped, hoping to disguise his voice. The marine with the rifle was the biggest danger, so Modo veered toward him. "I—"

"Did you discover the source of the leak?" the sergeant asked. "Answer me! That's an order!"

"No . . . broken dial . . . hurt." He lurched between the engineers and the marine until he was close enough to grab the man's gun. Just as he was about to do so, a hand snatched his collar and spun him around.

"I gave you an order!" the sergeant said, then stepped back. "You look ill, Krippen. Your face! It's misshapen! And why is your birthmark on the wrong side?"

Modo put a hand to his cheek. "You—you're mistaken."

The sergeant motioned to the marine and pain exploded in Modo's skull. The rifle butt! Modo turned, caught the marine's arm, and flipped him over his shoulder and into one of the engineers, sending them both flying. They both lay still.

Modo heard the click of a hammer being pulled back. He froze. The sergeant was pointing a pistol.

Modo turned slowly and offered his empty hands. "I won't struggle."

"You aren't Krippen—who are you?"

"I stowed away in the ship."

The man's hand was trembling, but he kept the barrel pointed directly at Modo. "Hans, contact the *Wyvern*." The engineer was trying to stand.

Something hissed past Modo's ear; then the pistol went off, the bullet ricocheting around the cabin. How did it miss? Modo wondered. Then he saw a spear stuck out of the sergeant's arm, pinning him to the wooden paneling near the wheel. The pistol had fallen to the floor. The sergeant stared at his arm, then screamed. Cerdà rushed from the stairwell, speargun in hand, and with one blow knocked down the other engineer. Monturiol and Colette were a step behind. Colette aimed her pistol at the sergeant.

"Are there others on my boat?" Captain Monturiol barked.

"No. Ahhh, it hurts!" The man grimaced, holding his arm and trying to stop the bleeding. "We, ahhh, were a skeleton crew."

"Get them off my ship!" Monturiol commanded, looking at Cerdà. "Modo, go with Cerdà. I'll take the *Ictíneo* to the surface. While you are up there, cast off the prisoners and the moorings."

"This will hurt," Cerdà said to the sergeant, then snapped off the protruding end of the spear. He yanked the man's arm from the shaft and the soldier only let out a small groan. A moment later Cerdà had torn a coat in two and tied up the engineer's wound. Then, pistol in hand, Cerdà directed the now-groggy soldier and the two engineers up the ladder to the top of the ship. Modo went below and found the third engineer, who was coming to. He carried him up to the hatch and set him on his wobbly feet.

They waited until Monturiol had brought the *Ictíneo* to the surface; then Cerdà opened the hatch, letting in a blast of cold air. He pointed upward and the prisoners climbed out one by one. Modo imagined that the pistol shot had alerted the *Wyvern*, but when he got topside and looked up at the warship, all appeared quiet. Cerdà herded the shivering men to the front of the *Ictíneo*.

Six ropes secured the *Wyvern* to the *Ictíneo*. Modo raced from one to the next, unlashing them. As he undid the knot on the third rope, Klaxons sounded on the *Wyvern*. Shouts echoed over the ship, and seconds later lights blazed upon them. Modo yanked the fourth and fifth ropes free before the first shot ricocheted off the deck.

A splash. Another and another. Cerdà had pushed the prisoners into the water. Modo pulled frantically on the last rope and it came undone. Then he raced for the hatch. A bullet sparked near his feet as he threw himself down the hole, grabbing the ladder halfway to the floor, flipping, and landing on his feet. Cerdà followed, closing the hatch and shouting, *"Submergir! Submergir! Submergir!"*

40

Sleeping Dogs

A noise had woken Griff, and he opened his eyes to see a hand snaking toward him. He threw himself silently to the corner of the room. The man reached for where his neck had been only a second before. The intruder's face was hidden behind a rag, but his shape was Modo's. It was that ugly beast!

Griff held his breath, slowing his heart and making himself small, exactly the way Miss Hakkandottir had taught him to do it. He was more than invisible. He became only eyes. Yes, it was working. He needed to cough but stifled the feeling.

After Modo had left the room, Cerdà, Monturiol, and Colette each passed the doorway. They had escaped and somehow gotten aboard the *Ictíneo*! He hung back for a few minutes. He heard a small noise—a cry for help—down the hall. They'd caught someone else by surprise.

He had slept on the submarine ship because the room Miss Hakkandottir had assigned him on the *Wyvern* was far too cold. Not a coal heater to be spared.

He'd left the door to his cabin closed, but somehow Modo had guessed he was inside. Now that he thought of it, the *Ictíneo* was listing. Something had happened to a ballast tank, making his door swing open. Stupid Icarians! Not one lock on this ship.

No, he realized, that couldn't be true. The engine room was locked.

Griff stole down the hallway and found the unconscious engineer. He jammed a thumb deep into his ribs, but the man only groaned. Useless.

Griff hadn't told the crew he was aboard—at least no one would rat him out. A gunshot echoed as he crept into the library. This made him stop for another minute and listen. Voices carried down the stairwell. They had seized the ship! Then a figure in uniform slouched down the stairs, but Griff recognized him at once as Modo. His body was still twisted in that odd shape, though his face had changed. He passed within inches of Griff.

Griff looked about for something to strike him with, but the library had only books and a few small statues. If he missed, the room was small enough that Modo could lash out and hit him with a lucky blow. Griff stepped back as Modo returned, carrying the engineer.

He waited, then climbed the stairs. He found himself alone on the bridge with Colette and Monturiol.

There was a speargun on the ground, unloaded. There

was a pistol in Colette's belt, but it was tucked in too well. He might have trouble getting it out.

Grab it! Grab it!

But he only stood there. No matter how much he imagined Miss Hakkandottir's disappointment, he couldn't act. He was so used to watching.

Bah! He retreated to a corner. His moment to strike would come.

41

Icaria, My Heart

The *Ictíneo* quaked under Modo's feet and began moving in fits and starts through the water, nearly throwing him down the stairs. Cerdà burst past him and dashed toward the bridge. Modo followed.

"No, the left lever!" Captain Monturiol snapped. "We must fill the forward ballasts to dive."

"Remember, dear Captain," Modo heard Colette say, "this is my first time with these controls."

Modo had taken two more steps when the *Ictíneo* suddenly struck something with force—the bottom of the *Wyvern*. He grabbed the railing and waited for the water to come pouring in, but the *Ictíneo* held. He jumped the rest of the way into the bridge.

Cerdà took the wheel from Monturiol, who immediately raised the periscope and put her eye to the lens. They'd been driving blind!

"Push the red lever down and that will fill the ballast tank," Cerdà said, patiently. "Each click you hear is an eighth of the chamber filling."

Colette followed his instructions and the submarine ship dove.

"Good work," Captain Monturiol said. "Now bring it halfway up." Colette moved the levers again and the *Ictíneo* leveled out. "We'll make an Icarian of you yet."

At that Colette laughed, but she seemed proud of herself.

"Full speed, Cerdà," Captain Monturiol said. "We must return to New Barcelona and warn our comrades to prepare for war. Our comrades imprisoned on the ship will have spoken of our city. It is safe now, but soon our enemy will find a way to reach us. We will defend our city with all our might." She looked at the instrument cluster. "Forty-five degrees to port," she said. Cerdà turned the wheel and the *Ictíneo* responded. "They seem to have repaired the steering apparatus. All systems are functioning properly."

The *Ictíneo* hummed along, now going at full speed. "Is there anything I can do?" Modo asked.

"Just have a seat," Monturiol answered. "You've worked hard enough today."

He sat at the small map table. He noticed that Colette kept glancing at him.

"What is it?" he asked.

"I am not used to your new face."

Modo had already forgotten. He wouldn't have enough strength to transform his face into a more familiar one; better to cover himself. He felt in the trouser pockets of the

Guild uniform and discovered a black silk neckerchief. It fit snugly over his nose. He adjusted his eyes, and kept the gray cap on. He looked out the porthole as they rose in the water, and saw the underwater plateau that led to New Barcelona. He watched the lights of the city grow closer. The *Ictíneo* turned straight toward the city and was traveling at such a clip that Modo feared they'd crash into it. He jumped up to warn them.

"Fill the forward ballasts," Captain Monturiol commanded; the *Ictíneo* dove and Modo braced himself, expecting to hit the ocean floor.

"Don't be alarmed," she said. "We constructed a wide tunnel into the plateau." Jagged rock walls were visible through the window, and several lights burned underwater, making the tunnel bright. Soon the *Ictíneo* was rising up into an underwater bay. It came to a stop.

"Why didn't you enter this way before?" Modo asked.

"Because I enjoy the walk and I wanted to visit my father." Monturiol paused. "And vanity, I must say. After two weeks of Miss Brunet's mocking, I wanted to see her dumbfounded by the sight of New Barcelona."

"I was *très* dumbfounded, I'll admit that," Colette said.

"Cerdà, prepare Icaria's mace."

"Are you certain, Captain?" Cerdà said. Modo hadn't heard him question her before. She nodded.

"What is this mace?" Modo asked.

"You shall see soon enough. Let us warn our comrades."

They all climbed out the hatch and Cerdà closed it. He then went to a storage locker.

"Does he need help?" Modo asked.

"Comrade Garay should arrive shortly," Monturiol said. "Once he had pedaled clear of the *Wyvern*, he could engage the motor. He will aid Cerdà."

They entered New Barcelona. The same three women in white robes greeted them halfway down a long hall, along with four boys, the oldest looking not much older than eight. There were two elderly men, both with peg legs, and beside them a sickly-looking man who was missing an arm. Modo remembered that they had been outside working on New Barcelona the first time he had visited. In all Modo counted twelve people, including a swaddled baby and young twin girls. Several people were holding fishing spears. Modo's heart sank. The children were mostly afraid; the women grim. This wasn't an army trained to defend an underwater country.

"Our comrades are imprisoned on an enemy ship," Monturiol said to the gathered Icarians. "Our enemy is an organization that calls itself the Clockwork Guild."

"Captain! What can we do?" one of the old men asked.

"You shall protect New Barcelona with every beat of your heart. Cerdà and I will strike them with the *Ictíneo*."

"What about the balloons?" Colette asked.

"We will go deep enough that the balloon devices cannot follow. We will spear them directly from below."

"But is the *Ictíneo* designed for those depths?" Modo asked.

"Yes, she is. Her collapse depth is one thousand meters. We will only go a quarter of that distance. The deeper we go, the more speed we will attain when we empty the ballast tanks."

"The pressure will be tremendous," Colette said. "It's madness to risk it all."

"No, not madness. It is the unexpected, and that is how one wins wars," Monturiol said. "Your debt has been paid. You two may remain here."

"You promised to deliver us to Iceland," Colette said.

"I will fulfill that promise after this battle."

"You don't have enough sailors to run the *Ictíneo*," Modo added.

"We shall manage."

Modo looked at the women and the children, and at the old men. They were determined, even the youngest, but none of them was trained for battle. Everything was moving too fast. His assignment was to bring the technology home to England, to Mr. Socrates, but that would be impossible if the technology was destroyed.

No, it was more than that. Modo's eyes rested on the men missing limbs. Monturiol had brought them here, had given them a home—a homeland—where they could contribute. Could be accepted.

"I'll go with you," he said.

"You are very brave." Monturiol put her hand on his shoulder. "It will not be an easy mission."

Colette let out a long sigh. "I shall go too. I won't be outdone by an Englishman. You may have insulted my country, Monturiol, and I could not live under the water like this; I enjoy the cafés and dress shops of Paris too much. But I do not want your city destroyed."

Monturiol put her other hand on Colette's shoulder. "You are heartily welcome. We shall go now."

When they returned to the *Ictíneo*, Modo noticed that the hatch was open. Hadn't Cerdà closed it earlier? His brain was too addled to recall clearly. Observe! Remember! The *Filomena* was also in the dock now, and Comrade Garay was helping Cerdà bolt a large spiked metal ball near the tip of the *Ictíneo*'s sharpened ram.

Cerdà and Garay marched over. "The mace is attached, Captain," Cerdà said.

"Good, good."

"What is it?" Modo asked.

"Icaria's mace," Cerdà said.

"Yes," the captain continued, "the ram will tear a hole in the hull and the mace will detonate within a minute, ripping more wounds in the enemy's ship. That is the theory. We have not tested it before."

"Oh," Modo uttered. "I see."

"Comrade Garay," Monturiol said, "you shall be in charge of the defense of New Barcelona. You need to arm the citizens and patrol."

Garay's eyes were wide. "But Captain, I want to come with you!"

"No, Garay. Only you can pilot the *Filomena*. If all is lost, you must take your fellow Icarians to safety."

He saluted with a trembling hand. "Yes, Captain."

"Now we shall strike," Captain Monturiol said, "like a spear thrown by Poseidon."

42

The Dark Deeps

Once they had boarded, Modo closed the hatch on the *Ictíneo*, spinning it into locked position. "Quickly!" Captain Monturiol said. "Cerdà, take Modo to the crow's nest—he'll be our navigator." She patted Modo's shoulder. "You'll be watching for obstacles. There is a speaking tube, which you will use to communicate with the bridge."

"And me?" Colette asked.

"You were good with the ballast tanks—you are officially a control officer now."

Cerdà led Modo to the bow of the ship. "The crow's nest is normally at the top of ship, isn't it?" Modo asked.

"Yes, but on the *Ictíneo* it's the nose. Its purpose is the same as on any ship. You will have a view above, below, and to either side. You will be able to see much more than the captain can through her periscope."

Cerdà opened a hatch door and led Modo into the tight

little crow's nest. There were several large portholes, as though Modo were standing in the eye of an insect. A light shone from the bow of the ship, illuminating the underwater wall of the bay. Suspended over the portholes was a chair with multiple belts. It looked like something a clever spider might have designed.

"Be seated," Cerdà said. Modo sat and Cerdà began strapping him in. "These are to prevent you from being thrown around when we smash into our enemy."

Modo didn't like the feeling of being tied down.

"From here you can see above and below the *Ictíneo*, through the viewports. When you spot an obstacle, lift this shutoff valve and report through the speaking tube."

The tube was hanging to Modo's left and ended in a bell-shaped mouthpiece. "I understand."

"It is important that you flip the valve closed at the end of communication. Especially important if we are about to ram a vessel."

"Why is that?"

"If this chamber is flooded, we don't want the water to penetrate the remainder of the *Ictíneo* through the tubing."

"Oh, that makes sense." Modo tried to say this as calmly as possible, but his voice cracked.

"Don't worry, my friend," Cerdà said, "she is a sturdy ship. Remember, you are the *Ictíneo*'s eyes." He went to the door and, as he was shutting it, said, "I am sorry. I must keep this closed. You are very brave."

"Thank you," Modo said, but the door was already closed.

Modo hadn't thought about what might happen to the

viewports when the *Ictíneo* bashed into the *Wyvern.* And what damage would that exploding mace do?

"Uh, all clear," he muttered into the speaking tube. He pulled back on the valve. "Modo here, saying the crow's nest is all clear."

"Thank you, Navigator." Captain Monturiol's voice came back to him through another tube that dangled above. "Please inform me only of an obstruction. I know this area well."

They left the bay and accelerated over the plateau. Modo opened his eyes wide. No matter how hard he stared upward, he couldn't see the *Wyvern*'s hull.

"Shouldn't we shut off the exterior lamps?" he asked.

"We want them to follow us," Monturiol said. "We will reach the edge of the plateau soon, Modo. Please inform me once we have passed it."

Modo watched as the ground dropped away into an underwater canyon of unimaginable depth. "We are over the top of it now."

"You are looking at the Valley of Clavé." She sounded very calm.

Modo glanced up and saw a dark shape far above them. He couldn't even be sure it was real. "I believe the *Wyvern* is forty-five degrees to starboard."

"Good eyes!"

She had adjusted something, because now one of the *Ictíneo*'s lights lit the hull of the other ship. Which began to move.

"They're following us!" Modo shouted.

"Thank you, Modo," Monturiol said. Apparently she had

left her speaking tube open, because Modo heard her orders for Colette. "Fill the forward ballasts to twenty percent. We begin our descent."

The *Ictíneo* shifted. They were pointing down now, the screw propeller pushing them ahead as the ballast tanks took on water. The hydrogen light illuminated the darkness, showing him the *Ictíneo*'s battering ram. The red substance on it was probably barnacles, but it looked like blood. Icaria's mace was a fist clamped to the end of it.

He stared past the ram. There was no sign of rock or sandy soil. Occasionally he saw fish with large, bulging eyes and flat bodies as though the pressure of the ocean had shaped them, but mostly it was just a great empty blackness. He glanced at the pressure gauge: they were at twenty-eight atmospheres of pressure. He calculated that they were near three hundred yards below the ocean's surface. He didn't know how many meters that was, but guessed it was near the same amount. How deep had the captain said the ship was designed to go? A thousand meters? That was collapse depth. But it would all be theoretical. He examined the glass porthole; how much further could they go before it cracked?

Monturiol and Cerdà had built this ship well, he reassured himself, and had likely been much deeper than this.

The deeper they went, the more the pressure began to squeeze the *Ictíneo*. The ship began to groan as though it were trying to warn its occupants of the danger.

"We are at about three hundred meters," Modo said into the speaking tube.

"I am aware of our exact depth, Modo," Captain Monturiol said. "The *Ictíneo* will hold, if that is your worry."

Modo clicked his speaking tube closed. "That is exactly my worry," he whispered. He removed the handkerchief and wiped at his eyes. Just as he was replacing it, a dark, rocky form loomed in the central viewport, sticking out of the ocean floor.

"Hard right. Hard right!" he bellowed, but he hadn't flicked the switch on the speaking tube. He snapped the switch up. "Hard right! To starboard. Impact dead ahead!"

At once the *Ictíneo* veered to the right. Cerdà was responding. The ram missed the jutting rocks by feet, but the bottom of the submarine ship was not so lucky. With a sudden impact that sent Modo banging against his straps, the *Ictíneo* scraped the underwater mountain spire and began to spiral downward.

Modo looked out the main window. The outer light swept back and forth as they attempted to gain control of the ship. "All clear! All clear!" he said, wanting to contribute something. He glanced at the pressure gauge: fifty-one atmospheres. He calculated from five hundred fifty yards to six hundred yards. The hull of the *Ictíneo* moaned like a live thing, as though a giant were squeezing it with two hands.

Where was the bottom? he wondered. Where was it? How far? Any moment he expected to see it come rushing up. The *Ictíneo* rotated a half turn clockwise, then spun back the other way.

The glass would go first. He was certain of it. And then what? Could he flee to the other chamber in time? Or would the force of the water crush him? He looked down hopelessly at all the straps. A bolt, loose or rusted, suddenly shot across the room, and water began to spout through the hole.

He thought of Octavia. Found himself wishing, oddly, that he hadn't argued about Shakespeare with her. And then he had a second thought: I should have shown her my face.

"Ballasts are empty." Colette's voice drifted above Modo.

"A leak in the crow's nest! It's leaking here!" Modo said.

"Calm down!" Captain Monturiol commanded. "How bad is it?"

"Uh . . . uh, a few gallons a minute, I'd guess."

"Inform us if it worsens." Another mass was approaching. "Obstacle dead ahead," Modo shouted. "It . . . I think it's the bottom of the canyon!"

"Brace for impact, then," Captain Monturiol said. "I'm going to switch the center of gravity."

There was a loud thunk; the submarine ship straightened as though all its weight had shifted aft. It flipped further so that its nose angled upward. Modo thought a miracle had occurred until he realized the ship was continuing to plunge at the same speed.

A moment later he felt the impact.

43

A Game of Cat and Fish

Two hours had passed since the prisoners had escaped. Miss Hakkandottir strode along the upper deck. Already she had punished the Guild soldier responsible for guarding them by throwing him in the hold with the remaining Icarians. They could tear him to pieces. Her security lieutenant had also suffered her wrath, but he had sustained little more than a broken arm. All of the soldiers received a tincture that made them more obedient, but it dulled their minds. Automatons, she thought. She missed the days when she was a pirate with real men under her control.

The conclusion was obvious. The enemy had another submarine ship. Likely a smaller one that they had used to rescue the prisoners and reclaim the *Ictíneo*. Clever little water rats!

She had marveled at the *Ictíneo*, had walked through the

empty hallways, touched the thick hull. She sensed a mind behind it that equaled the imagination of the Guild Master.

Her men had not been able to break down the door to the engine room. That was where the real secrets lay. But the Guild Master would have rewarded her greatly for bringing this technology home. And now it was gone.

"A light! A light!" the lookout bellowed from the crow's nest. The call was passed along, and Miss Hakkandottir herself saw a brightness below the ocean as though a comet were speeding through the depths.

"Prepare the balloon guns!" she shouted.

Then, suddenly, the comet was diving down, down, until it disappeared into darkness. The speed of the submarine ship was beyond belief.

She was confident that Monturiol was not fleeing. The captain wouldn't abandon her underground city or her comrades still in the hold. She would strike but it would be useless; the hull of the *Wyvern* could withstand any blow. Would Monturiol risk the lives of the Icarians on board? Hakkandottir couldn't decide. Then she laughed. It was a game of cat and fish. She liked this sort of game.

44

The Bottom of a Well

Modo felt his chest, but nothing seemed to be broken. The straps had bruised him in several places. He stared at the pressure gauge. They were nine hundred yards below the sea, right near the edge of collapse depth. Would it happen all at once? Or would the ship slowly crumple in on itself?

The *Ictíneo* had settled at an angle, leaving Modo looking up toward the water's surface. It might as well be a million miles away, he thought. "Turn out the hydrogen light," the captain commanded through the speaking tube.

Modo found the switch and flicked it, and the outside world went black. He saw that the spout of water into the ship had slowed—perhaps something had shifted in the crash.

The door clanked open and Cerdà entered, glancing at the crack. "That is a manageable leak," he said. "Not good news, though. It means the forward ballast tank is more damaged than I thought. Come with me to the ballast station."

Modo unstrapped himself and followed Cerdà down the stairs, to a narrow hallway. The angle of the *Ictíneo* was awkward and the metal floor was slippery. He was glad that there were several handholds along the wall. "There are four forward ballast tanks," Cerdà explained. "I am certain that two of them were damaged and flooded after we struck that ridge—that is why we descended so quickly. We need to empty them and achieve positive buoyancy—we must go up!" He sounded almost jolly. "The *Ictíneo* will rise again, my comrade. And we will rise with her."

"I wish I'd seen the ridge sooner!"

"You reacted as well as any *Ictíneo* navigator. Our luck did not hold, that is all. There is no blame. Ah, here we are." They opened another door and stepped into the same room they had entered when they'd sneaked aboard the *Ictíneo*.

"The pressure will make it difficult to empty the ballasts—the sea pushes in, we must push her out. The motors will have to be started manually." Cerdà led Modo to a wall covered with gauges, switches, and a large crank. "The question is, will they engage? And if they do, can they force the water out? It depends on where the breach is." Cerdà flicked a switch near the panel and lights came on. All of the needles on the gauges were at zero. "Again our luck is bad—the batteries are dead. We must crank the motor." He struggled with the crank without success.

"Please let me try," Modo said. He wedged his feet into a corner, balancing himself so that he could grab the crank with both hands. It wouldn't budge. He gritted his teeth, pulled harder. At last it began to screech and turn and the dials jumped along with it.

"Ah, good, good, Modo!"

The turning gradually became easier and the pump motor awakened. "The faster you go, the more you help the motors," Cerdà said.

Modo heard a scraping sound and it felt as though his arms would fall off, but he kept working.

"That should push the water out of the tanks. There is a safety system which Delfina—Captain Monturiol—added for emergencies." Cerdà pulled another lever. A thunk echoed in the chamber and several of the gauges shot to the center. "Success!"

The *Ictíneo* shifted as though nodding in agreement.

"We are rising off the floor. Assuming the propeller is not damaged, we will be able to ascend. Let's return to the others."

They joined Captain Monturiol and Colette on the bridge. Both women were clutching handholds to keep from sliding away from their stations. Cerdà explained the situation to the captain. "Your backup system worked perfectly," he added.

"You designed it," Monturiol said. "We shall fill the aft ballasts to keep us pointing toward the surface. Please do so now, Miss Brunet."

Colette pulled a lever and the ship slowly vibrated and shifted again; they were at a forty-five-degree angle from the ocean floor. The captain peered through her periscope. "We have left the seabed. Engage the propeller."

The *Ictíneo* shook with the force of the propeller and began to move forward.

"Return to your stations," Monturiol said. "Strap yourselves in. We will be making our ascent as fast as possible. We need a massive amount of momentum to penetrate the *Wyvern*'s steel hull. The trick will be to find them."

Modo glanced over at Colette, who turned to look at him. Her hair was out of place, and there was determination in her eyes. And excitement, Modo realized. She's loving this! "Keep your eyes peeled, Modo," she said. "You're the bravest of us all."

"You're brave, too," he replied. He climbed up the sloping hallway to the crow's nest, swallowing a lump of fear as he closed the door and strapped himself into the chair. Thankfully, the leak wasn't any worse. The higher they climbed, the lower the pressure would be on the hull.

"Leave the light off, Modo," Monturiol said through the speaking tube. "We travel blindly for a few more minutes."

He stared out the portholes above him, into darkness blacker than the night sky.

45

Into the Underbelly

Modo looked from the pressure gauge to the blackness beyond the glass. He couldn't see more than a few inches out the viewports of the *Ictíneo*. According to the needle on the pressure gauge, they were slowly rising, the angle of the ship growing sharper and sharper, until Modo felt as though they were traveling straight up. The *Ictíneo* shook violently. The buoyancy was pulling her toward the surface, and the screw propeller was at full speed. How many knots? He had never traveled this fast before!

Monturiol's voice sounded clearly through the speaking tube: "Modo, in a moment I will command you to turn on the hydrogen light. It will illuminate a wide area. If my guess is right, the *Wyvern* will be circling above where they last spotted us. You will guide us toward the hull. Aim for the center aft of the ship so that we disrupt its engines as much as possible. Icaria's mace will do the rest. Do you understand?"

"Yes, Captain."

"Please, Navigator, turn on the light now."

He reached up and pushed the switch. The light burst into life, filling the ocean as fish darted out of the ship's way.

"I don't see anything," he said at first. Then he spotted a large hull, glittering with bronze rivets. "I have sighted the *Wyvern*, Captain. She's at a forty-five-degree angle to starboard."

"Good! Keep calling out, Navigator."

"Thirty-five degrees," he said after a few moments. "Twenty-five degrees."

The hull was growing larger and only now did *Ictíneo's* actual speed come home to him.

"Fifteen degrees."

At this rate they would plow right through the ship!

"Five degrees. We're now in line."

"Thank you, Modo. I have her in my sights," Captain Monturiol said. The *Ictíneo* picked up speed as it approached the surface. What am I doing here? Modo wondered. I'm at the front end of an exploding spear. He stared at the massive metal ram that had skewered so many ships without even bending. But how would it penetrate something with such a thick hull? The bottom of the *Wyvern* filled his vision.

The sailors and soldiers above them could probably see the light coming from below their ship, but there would be no time for them to escape. Nothing could stop the impact now.

"May I say," Captain Monturiol announced through the speaking tube, "that it has been a pleasure working alongside all of you. What you do today for Icaria shall always be remembered."

She was saying goodbye. Modo shut the valve to the speaking tube as the *Ictíneo* struck the *Wyvern*.

46

An Act of Charity

Miss Hakkandottir felt an ache in the palm of her metal hand. She chuckled. How many years had it been since Mr. Socrates had sliced off her real hand with a cutlass? Fifteen? Sixteen? He'd been called Alan Reeve then. None of these fancy code names.

No matter how much time passed, the ghost of her old hand still had feeling. Cold. Itchiness. Pain. And, sometimes, it even felt the future. It had ached in Egypt a few years earlier, so she had stepped out of her tent, only to have a cannon shell destroy the tent a moment later. Dr. Hyde would laugh and say it was illogical to connect the two events. The hand had ached many other times for no reason at all.

She acted on this ache now, though, walking from her cabin onto the deck. The sky was dark around her, stars glistening, a hunter's moon glaring in the sky. It was well after midnight. They had spotted the *Ictíneo* over an hour ago and lost her to the depths. Now the *Wyvern* circled. Guild engineers were in cutters next to the warship, scanning for signs of the enemy.

Something was amiss. She looked down at Hecuba, one of her hounds, and whispered, "Find Griff. If he is anywhere on this ship, find him!" Grace, the other hound, waited. She had been sent to search the ship earlier and had failed; perhaps Hecuba had a better nose. Where was that boy?

A shout went up. Miss Hakkandottir leaned over the railing to see an engineer on the deck of a cutter, waving a warning. A moment later, Klaxons sounded and soldiers ran out of their bunks, rifles in hand.

"What is it?" she yelled. The engineer staggered back, shouting, but his words were lost. The other engineers were already scrambling up the ropes to the *Wyvern*.

Then Miss Hakkandottir saw a light coming at them from deep below, like a comet. "Engines, full speed ahead!" she shouted toward the helm, though she knew it was too late. The *Wyvern* rose momentarily as if a giant hand were pushing up from under the hull. Miss Hakkandottir was tossed into the air, then fell against the deck, bracing her fall with her metal hand.

"Fool!" she hissed at herself. "You didn't dream of this!" She was confident of the warship taking any blow from the side, but had not expected them to risk their very lives and their submarine ship by attacking directly from below.

She ran in to the helm, knocking officers out of her way. All the speaking tubes whistled and she flipped one open. "Hakkandottir here. Report."

"The engine room is flooded, Admiral. We—we were unable to seal the compartment."

"Then seal the next one. Now!"

"Sir, the damage, it's . . ." He was breathing heavily. The sound of water splashing echoed up the tube. ". . . massive. I'm afraid the water . . . We . . ." She heard gurgling.

"I need to know how many compartments are flooded!" she shouted at the officers in the helm.

No one answered. The speaking tubes fell silent. She pointed at a lieutenant. "Go down there. Now! Report!"

He saluted and ran from the room. The ship rocked violently again and a sonic scream lifted all the lids on the speaking tubes. An explosion! The engine?

"The rest of you had better dream up a plan to rescue this ship."

"We will, sir," Commodore Truro said.

The *Wyvern* suddenly shifted and gave a metallic moan. Miss Hakkandottir recognized the sound. They had been struck to the core. She grabbed the balloon pilot. "Prepare the *Etna*. If any unauthorized person attempts to board her, shoot them." She pushed the pilot out the door, then pointed at the surgeon and the commodore. "You two go with him." They ran after the pilot. "The rest of you keep this ship afloat as long as you can."

She kicked open the door, causing one hinge to fly off. Then she strode down the deck. The ship had become a quickly tilting fortress. In the darkness, Guild soldiers ran to and fro. There were only a few lifeboats, she knew that. A warship such as this, perfectly designed by the Guild Master, would never need a lifeboat. Who would have dreamed that anything could penetrate its hull deeply enough to sink her?

Miss Hakkandottir hurried toward her balloon. The Guild Master would be unhappy, perhaps murderously so.

Grace loped along at her heels. Hecuba had not yet returned. As Miss Hakkandottir arrived amidships, she rounded a gun emplacement and then froze, her hand clenching Grace's collar.

The Icarians, eyes wide, a few holding metal bars and makeshift weapons, stood in a clump before her. They had broken free!

"It's their captain!" shouted a broad-shouldered female. She raised a jagged piece of metal. "Where is Monturiol?"

Miss Hakkandottir held tight as Grace strained against her collar, wanting to strike. "You are a very persistent group."

"Where is she?" a man rumbled. "Release her!"

"Your captain escaped several hours ago. She struck the bottom of the *Wyvern* with your submarine ship. Surely you recognize her handiwork."

"That's not true!" the woman cried. "That's a lie!"

"Your captain abandoned you," Miss Hakkandottir said. Several Icarians glanced fearfully from side to side, and Miss Hakkandottir realized that they weren't actually soldiers. In the absence of their captain, they had no system of command.

"Our captain chose to do what is best for Icaria," the hulking woman said. "We swore our oaths."

"Perhaps. But now *you* have a choice. Some of you may live if you can get off this ship. There are lifeboats behind me." There were twenty-four prisoners. There would be nowhere near enough boats. "If you pause to join battle

270

with me, you will not make it. Grace here will tear your throats out."

They were silent.

"So," she continued, "you will let me walk through you. Then you will run to the lifeboats. That is my act of charity for the day. You can fight over which of you will survive."

She took a step forward and the large woman backed up. Grace snapped her jaws and a few more Icarians edged away. Hakkandottir strode through them, not giving so much as a backward glance.

The *Etna* was waiting at the bow of the ship, the basket straining to be freed from the ropes that bound it to the *Wyvern*. The pilot, wearing goggles, was adding coal to the steam engine. Both the commodore and the surgeon held the ropes.

Griff had not shown up, nor had Hecuba returned. The boy would die—a wasted investment. And she would miss him: over the years she had grown attached to him.

"Up, Grace," Miss Hakkandottir commanded, and the dog leapt into the basket. With all her metal parts the hound was so heavy that the basket sank closer to the deck. Then Hakkandottir climbed in. She motioned to the other men, but the pilot said, "We can only carry one of them, Admiral, as long as we're taking the hound. Otherwise we'll be too heavy."

She nodded and pointed at the surgeon. A commodore could be easily replaced.

"I understand, sir," Commodore Truro said as the surgeon climbed aboard.

"The Guild Master thanks you for your service," she

intoned. Then they threw off the sandbags and the *Etna* began to rise.

She watched the lights of the *Wyvern* below her, the ship shifting, heard the groaning of metal and the sounds of panic. It had been such a beautiful vessel.

They would build another. And she would one day strike a blow to the very heart of the empire.

The *Etna's* steam engine fired, the propeller spun, and the great winds carried them south.

47

The *Ictíneo* Is My Heart

The impact had been worse than Colette had imagined it would be. She had centered herself in the way her father had taught her and made peace with the fact that she might die in defense of a country made up of fewer than a hundred people. But when the *Ictíneo* sliced into the *Wyvern*, Colette was thrown so hard against her straps that one broke and she bashed her head on the levers. For a few moments all she saw were stars, and she fought to keep her thoughts from turning to black. When her vision returned, all the lights on the *Ictíneo* were flickering.

A stream of water fell through the grate of the walkway above the bridge and hit her. The hull had been breached! She tried to stay calm; she wanted to undo her straps, but knew she'd only fall backward with the ship at such a sharp angle.

"I believe we have penetrated the hull," said Monturiol,

who was bleeding from a blow to her cheek. "Crow's nest, report! Report!" she shouted into the speaking tube.

"Modo!" Colette yelled. "Report!" There was no sound from the crow's nest.

"Report, Navigator!" Monturiol commanded. "Modo, report! Colette, go check on the condition of Comrade Modo!"

"I will!" Colette said. She let go of her handholds and slid down the floor to the stairwell.

"Be quick," Monturiol added. "The mace is about to detonate!"

The *Ictíneo* had settled at a sixty-five-degree angle. Colette grabbed the railing and pulled herself along the stairs, until she was in the corridor leading to the crow's nest. She latched on to doorknobs to help her climb, pulling herself past the captain's quarters. It took a full minute, thanks to her feet sliding with every step on the wet floor. With each second, she expected to feel the blast.

When she got to the door of the crow's nest, she peered through the porthole, fearing the room would be filled with water. It was lit by one dim, fitful light, enough to see Modo, his head bowed, in his straps. She spun the wheel that opened the door, and water washed across her shoes and down the hallway. Two of the observation ports were cracked; one was leaking water. The others wouldn't last much longer.

"Wake up!" she said when she'd crawled up to Modo. She grabbed his wrist. It was cold, but there was a pulse. He must have hit his head or something must have struck him—she saw several broken pipes on the floor, any of

274

which could have taken his head clean off. Through the portholes she could see that the submarine was right up against the hull of the *Wyvern*. They would never extricate themselves.

Not knowing what else to do, she slapped him. "Wake up, Modo. Wake up, you English dog!"

Modo blinked and looked at her, stunned. "Stop yelling!" he slurred. "What's happening?"

"We pierced a hole in the ship. Get out of those straps! The mace is about to explode."

She helped him undo his clasps, then grabbed his arm to prevent him from tumbling down the hall.

"Quickly! Quickly! Help with the door!" she shouted. This seemed to rouse him finally, and they worked together to close it, fighting against the draining water.

The door closed, and a heartbeat later the mace exploded, the sudden jolting shock knocking them backward. Colette skidded halfway down the hall before grabbing a handle. Modo was clinging to one several feet farther along. She stared up at the door into the crow's nest. The door had held.

"Let's go," she said. They slowly climbed down to the bridge.

"Ah, you are alive! Report," Monturiol said.

"We fully penetrated the hull," Modo said.

Colette added, "We were lucky to get out of there before the mace exploded."

Monturiol nodded. Her eyes had an empty look. "Good work. While you were gone, Cerdà and I tried to extricate the *Ictíneo*."

Cerdà was moving the wheel, grunting. "The engine no longer has enough power to loosen us. We are lodged in the ship."

"Well then, we will drag them down to the bottom with us," Monturiol said emphatically.

"I'd prefer not to go to the bottom," Colette huffed. "If it's all the same to you."

There was a long silence.

"It's done," said Monturiol finally. "The *Ictíneo* has struck the last blow for Icaria. I shall go down with my ship." She paused. "Cerdà, return to New Barcelona with our companions. You are released from your duties."

Cerdà set his jaw. "No."

Monturiol's eyes widened. "No?"

"My duty demands I stay by your side."

"But what of Icaria?"

"New Barcelona cannot survive without the *Ictíneo* to re-supply the city. Those who remain will have to return to the old world, to dream of another Icaria, another day."

"Very well." Monturiol held out her hand and Cerdà took it, moving closer to her. Colette was surprised to find tears in her eyes. Such love and loyalty between the two of them. They were insane, but admirable.

Monturiol saluted. "Comrade Modo and Comrade Brunet, you are officially relieved of your duties. There are four pods in the engine room, designed for escape. You have my permission to pilot one. Cerdà, give them the key to the engine room."

He reached into his pocket and produced a silver-colored key, which he handed to Modo.

"I appreciate your contributions," Cerdà said softly. "You have both been extremely brave."

"It was an honor serving on the *Ictíneo*," Colette replied, surprised by her own sincerity.

"But Captain!" Modo exclaimed. "You don't have to sacrifice yourself. The *Ictíneo*'s secrets will be safe at the bottom of the ocean."

"You do not understand," Monturiol said. "The *Ictíneo* is my heart. Without it, I am a ghost. Icaria is dead. I cannot live in a world without my ship or my country, so I will join my father. It is not the right time for me. For Cerdà." Her voice caught in her throat. "The obscurity of the deep; my father used to speak about it all the time. Now it waits for us. Farewell." She turned her back to them and began flicking switches and dials. "Go! Now! Both of you!"

Colette pulled Modo to the stairs. They made their way aft, slipping and sliding down the hall.

"They are quite mad," Colette whispered. "Incurably, idealistically mad."

"Yes," Modo agreed, then looked her in the eye. "Or, perhaps, they're the sanest of us all?"

They crawled past rows of cabins, the *Ictíneo* trembling like a live thing. There was hammering on the hull and a creaking like metal bones bending and breaking.

They pulled up short when they reached the end of the hall. The door to the engine room was now at the bottom of a deep pool of water.

48

The Pod

Oil and other substances glistened on the surface of the water. Modo cursed and said, "I wonder how deep it is."

"It can't be more than a few meters," Colette said, holding a doorknob to keep from sliding into the pool. "I can easily swim down."

"No," Modo said. "I will. Cerdà gave me the key."

"Only because you were standing closer to him. I grew up on the water. I'm a better swimmer."

She was as exasperating as Octavia! "I'm going!" He withdrew the key, then splashed awkwardly into the water. He took a deep breath, opened his eyes, and pushed, kicked, and pulled his way down by grabbing on to door handles. A bit of light from above penetrated the water—the door was so far away. Finally he reached it, and grabbed hold of a pipe so he wouldn't float back up. His lungs were burning. He felt around for the wheel and found it. But where to put the key?

Already he desperately needed to take a breath. Then his hand touched a small panel that slid back. He inserted the key, turned it in the lock, felt it click. He turned the wheel, pulled on the door, and struggled against the weight of the water.

He opened it an inch; water poured into the engine room. Another heave; the door opened, water flushing down the hole. He latched on to the pipe while holding the door. In a few seconds his head was out of the water and he gulped in air.

"Marvelous, Modo! Simply marvelous!" Colette said, climbing down along the wall. "We might live after all."

She was the first into the engine room, Modo right behind her. The engine filled the center of the chamber—a collection of giant gears, tubes, and wires that ran into the ceiling and floor of the ship, all powered by two six-foot-wide glowing glass batteries. They looked extremely delicate to Modo.

"No wonder they kept this locked up," he said. "One blow to these batteries and no engine."

Modo felt as though he were looking at a dying heart. Sparks flew here and there; he knew that water and electricity were a deadly mix, but they had to risk it.

Beyond the engine, set into either side of the chamber, were four round pods. Modo opened the door to one. Two people could just fit, sitting side by side on the bench. He and Colette squeezed together and set their feet on the pedals in front of them.

The *Ictíneo* lurched. Was it breaking away from the *Wyvern*? "Go! Go!" Modo shouted as he closed the door, sealing them in. "There must be a way to release the pod." He spotted switches, several small levers and a long cord.

"I'm pulling this!" Colette yanked on the cord. They heard something clink outside the chamber, followed by whirring, as though a giant clock had begun ticking. The pod moved slowly backward.

A metal door clanged shut outside the pod. Modo peered through the porthole and saw that the pod had moved into a circular room slightly larger than the pod itself. It quickly filled with water up to the porthole. Nothing else happened. Long seconds ticked by. Were they trapped?

"What else can we press?" he asked.

Colette flipped one of the switches. Music began to play from some hidden phonograph—the national anthem of Icaria. "What madness!" She hit more switches until the music stopped.

The pod rolled like a ball out of the *Ictíneo* and into the ocean. Modo spotted a switch with a sunlike symbol above it and flicked it. A light burst into life on the exterior of the pod. Through the front porthole, he saw the *Ictíneo* dropping past them like a sinking whale. Much larger and sinking equally fast was the *Wyvern*. Heavy bubbles burst out of its side.

"We're going to collide!" Modo yelled. They pedaled madly while he pushed and pulled the levers, which didn't seem to do anything.

"You turned us toward it!" Colette cried. Modo desperately shoved the levers in the opposite direction and the pod went toward the open ocean.

A section of the *Wyvern* smashed them aside, and the Icarian anthem blared again, playing at double speed as they spiraled uncontrollably. Their lone hydrogen light showed them they were going down farther. It took a lot of pedaling and maneuvering to slow their spinning. The *Wyvern* was below them now, its wounds oozing air, oil and several bodies.

Swiveling away from the horrific sight, they took a few moments to right the craft. Neither Modo nor Colette spoke, but Modo was certain Colette had seen the same dreadful sight.

After trying every combination of switches and levers, it became clear that they couldn't straighten the pod entirely. They were rising, though, according to the needle on the pressure meter.

"We're close to the surface," Colette said happily. But it was getting harder to pedal, and the gauge now seemed to be stuck. Modo could actually see a dim light staring down at them through the water—the moon! They sank a few feet, and another few, despite all their rapid pedaling.

"I can't empty one of the ballast tanks," Colette said.

"So we have negative buoyancy."

"Ah, you listened to the captain."

"And Cerdà," Modo added. "The bottom line is that we're sinking."

"Yes, very slowly. We can fight against it with our pedaling, but reaching the surface will be impossible."

"Can we swim for it?" he asked.

"We're already at thirty meters' depth. The moment we opened the door we'd drop like a stone. Plus, we'd have to stop pedaling, which would make us fall even faster."

"We could ride the oxygen bubble to the surface."

"We're too deep. It would rise too fast and the pressure would knock us out. Plus there's diver's sickness to worry about."

Modo knew the deepest anyone could dive from the surface was only about twenty yards.

"We must find New Barcelona, then," he said.

"*Oui! Oui!* It's our only choice! But where is it? We traveled quite a distance by electric motor."

The pod's air was oppressively humid. Sweat glistened on Modo's palms, and he felt as though the room were squeezing in on them. With the pod's movements he kept bumping into Colette. "But we retraced part of that distance when we attacked the *Wyvern*."

"Yes, and the ship was anchored west of New Barcelona."

"Then we simply follow the compass east and we'll be there," he said, trying to sound cheery. "Unless we were knocked completely off course."

They pedaled, adjusting so that the compass always pointed east. They sank farther, but slowly enough that Modo didn't panic.

Colette let out a groan. "I've decided that you're *mon porte-malheur*, Modo—bad luck. Ever since I met you horrible things have happened."

"That's not fair! You were already a captive before you met me. You're the *porte-malheur*. Ever since I saw your picture, it's been nothing but murders, shipwrecks, and insanity."

She leaned forward, looking down through the bottom

porthole. "Take heart, Modo, we've passed the canyon and reached the plateau."

"Good!" Modo thought of Monturiol and Cerdà. Were they dead now? The pressure would eventually crush the *Ictíneo*. Maybe they'd come to their senses and taken another pod. Its spherical structure was the best design to withstand pressure. But how much could one of these endure?

"There! There!" Colette shouted hoarsely. "I see lights."

At first Modo thought she was seeing things. Their predicament was too much for her. There was nothing but darkness before them. Then he saw the distant glimmering. "You're right!"

New Barcelona was shining ahead of them. "We just might make it, Modo," Colette said. "I take back what I said about you being a *porte-malheur.*"

As they approached the underwater city, they also skimmed closer to the floor of the plateau. They pedaled as hard as they could. Modo aimed for the door they had entered on foot only a few short days ago. "We're almost there!" he yelled as they got closer and closer to the door. He held his breath.

The pod bounced down the steps, then skidded across the plateau bottom and slid to a stop little more than an arm's length from the undersea entrance.

49

Under Pressure

They stared out the porthole. Modo grabbed another set of levers, moving the arms on the pod, which he assumed were designed to open underwater doors or harvest seaweed. The arms were too short.

"Can we use them to push ourselves closer?" Colette asked.

"They can't reach the ocean floor. We are truly stuck," he said. "Perhaps someone in New Barcelona has spotted us."

"There were only the mothers, children, and old men left," Colette said.

"And Comrade Garay," Modo added.

"Yes, but they would need several comrades in aquasuits to drag us into that chamber."

"How much oxygen remains?"

"I would guess another hour's worth." She tapped the dial and the needle dropped further. "Or half an hour."

"Stop tapping it!" Modo said.

"Why? Should we pretend we have more oxygen than we do?"

"I felt better when I thought we had an hour's worth. How deep did Monturiol say New Barcelona was?"

"Fifty meters," Colette answered.

"We have to get through that door," he said.

"We have to battle the pressure." The air was clammy, her hair drenched. She ran her fingers through it. "I'm a mess, and it looks as though your rash is returning."

Modo knew the neckerchief still hid most of his features, but he was losing control of the area around his cheekbones and eyes. "That doesn't matter. How do we safeguard against the pressure?"

"Our rubber suits may keep it at bay for a few seconds. But our ears and eyes? I can only guess what damage would be done."

"Maybe they have some sort of emergency kit in the pod." They searched around the compartment, under the seat. "Aha!" Modo sat up, displaying his treasure victoriously. "Diving goggles! At least we'll be able to see."

"Yes, but are they fashionable?" Colette said as they slipped them on. The lenses enlarged their eyes like insects' and they both laughed so hard that Modo worried they were getting giddy from lack of oxygen.

He took a deep breath. "Once we are in the lock chamber, there won't be as much pressure, correct?"

"Yes. It will only be the pressure from the water in the chamber, not the ocean."

"So we only have to endure the deeps long enough to enter the chamber."

"Correct. And we must close the sea door, find the switch that empties the chamber, and somehow hold our breath until it drains. Assuming the draining mechanism will work."

"You sound doubtful."

"Oh, I'm not doubtful. We don't have a chance in Hades of making it," she said, laughing. "But it is our only option. I suggest we divide the duties. You, *Monsieur Musclé*, swim out there and open the door. I'll stay here, out of the pressure, until the door is open. Then I'll swim straight to the switch. Which, as I remember, is located at the opposite side of the chamber. You close the door behind me so we can drain the chamber."

"Good plan! Now let's take a few breaths."

"Oh, one more thing, Modo," Colette said. She lifted the bottom of his handkerchief and kissed him on the lips. If he hadn't been sitting down, he would have fallen over. As it was, he inadvertently spun the pedals a few times.

Modo had never been kissed on the lips. His thoughts were bouncing around in his head like mad. She kissed me! She kissed me! Her lips were so soft.

"Wh-what was that?" he asked.

"A kiss, silly. For *bonne chance*, Modo. I believe in luck. And I don't want to go down without a fight. Now open that door."

He leaned forward and turned the handle that opened

the pod door, then held on tight, prepared for all the water that would rush in. Nothing happened.

"Oh no, the pressure is holding it closed," Colette said.

Modo pushed until the door opened a crack and ice-cold water began seeping in, swirling around their shoes as it rose higher and higher.

"I'm so very tired of being wet," Colette whined, but before Modo could answer, the water was up to his neck. He took a deep breath, waited until he heard Colette take one of her own, and pushed.

Immediately his body felt as though several loads of frozen bricks were piled upon it. He launched himself the short distance and grabbed the wheel on the entrance to the lock chamber. He was floating too high, too fast! He needed leverage. He looked down, and spotting two loops set in the ground, he stuck his feet in them. It was like moving in stone, trying to turn the wheel. His lungs compressed. Yet he wasn't panicking. He could function in the pressure; it was as though his face, and his body, which had so often changed shape, were adapting to this environment. He'd felt this sort of pain before.

Finally the door clicked. He pushed it open and kicked until he was inside. He couldn't see clearly, but a blur of long, dark hair and then legs passed him. He pulled the door closed, planted his feet again in another set of footholds, and turned the wheel.

When the door was locked he kicked his way farther into the chamber, realizing he was seeing grayness through one eye. Was his brain affected? Even worse, he spotted Colette a few yards away, floating without moving, her hair like wild dark seaweed. He pushed off the floor toward her, shooting up so quickly that he nearly missed her. At the last second he grabbed her extended arm, but he didn't have the strength to swim down and pull her toward the lever that would drain the room.

We're doomed, he thought, as his head smashed the top of the chamber. He bobbed up a second time, his limbs going numb. His lungs screamed for oxygen. He bobbed a third time and broke into a pocket of air. He sucked in a breath. Air! He lifted Colette, and after sputtering for a bit, she breathed too. Slowly the bubble of air grew larger. The water was receding! Minutes later, Modo found himself on the floor, sopping wet but breathing normally. He flipped back his goggles. The interior chamber door had been opened. Fish were flopping around between him and Colette's still body. Footsteps splashed in the water, but no one was there.

"I couldn't let the ocean kill you," Griff said, chuckling harshly. "Not when it would be so much more satisfying to do it myself."

50

A Wound That Moves

Modo spat out seawater. He couldn't see Griff, of course, but was further alarmed because, through the door, flames were dancing across wooden furniture and up a set of curtains. How much of New Barcelona was burning? And closer to him, her body looking like a broken doll, was Colette. Before Modo could check to see if she was breathing, his head was driven into the floor.

"You're lucky I saw the light of your craft and recognized your predicament. Yes, lucky!" Griff cried. He smashed Modo's head again. "Where's the mad captain?"

"She went down with the *Ictíneo*," Modo grunted out in pain.

"Good! Good! Good!" With each exclamation Griff bashed Modo's head harder.

"She took the *Wyvern* and all her crew with her."

"You lie! That ship is unsinkable."

"Well, it's at the bottom of the ocean now."

"Liar!" Griff smashed Modo's head again.

With each blow lights sparked in Modo's darkened vision. But he was too tired to lift an arm to defend himself. "Both ships went down," he said. This seemed to silence Griff for a few seconds, and in that time Modo stole a glance at Colette. She hadn't stirred.

"Don't bring me bad tidings," Griff hissed. "I'm Invisible Man the First!" Modo felt himself dragged a few feet and then was thrown onto his back. Invisible hands grabbed his throat. "Take back your lies!" Modo lifted a hand, but Griff knocked it aside and continued to choke him. "Your face is growing uglier, Modo. Did you show it to that Colette? No? How she would squeal if she could see it, eh? But don't worry, when I'm done with you, I'll slit her throat. She won't see you again."

Modo tried to speak but only gurgled.

"You may have sunk the *Wyvern*," Griff said, "but Miss Hakkandottir had a balloon and she'll pick me up. I am Invisible Man the First. She wouldn't leave me! She wouldn't!" He slapped Modo. "If you could only see my face, you grotesque sot. Ta-hee! I'm smiling now. I am! I— Arrgh!"

Some clarity returned to Modo's vision. Griff's hands were no longer on his throat.

"French witch! Aghh!"

Modo found the strength to raise his head and saw Colette on all fours, one hand swinging a stiletto. Blood was squirting out of thin air onto the floor. It was a wound that moved. It darted here and there. Colette swung once more and stabbed Griff again.

"Achhh!" Griff shrieked. Two wounds jumped back. "You can't see me! You can't stab me!"

"I did!" Colette spat out, coughing with each word. "And now we see you."

Modo got to his feet. His head throbbed and he staggered to one side. He stretched out his arms and threw himself toward the place where the blood was spurting. His arms closed on nothing.

"I'll kill both of you!" The blood suddenly stopped and Modo heard running, splashing footsteps as Griff's voice grew more distant. "When you sleep I'll gut you like fish!"

Modo helped Colette to her feet. He was so happy to see her alive that he wanted to embrace her. Instead, he asked, "Where did you get the knife?"

" 'Always carry a blade.' My father taught me that."

"Griff will try to escape from New Barcelona," Modo said. "I wonder where all the Icarians have gone. I'm afraid he . . ."

"Let us hope they have somehow reached the surface," Colette said. "We must get to the docking bay. The *Filomena* is the only way out of this place."

They stumbled as quickly as they could through the adjoining room. Flames were burning in the far corner, catching paintings on the wall, chairs, and desks. The Icarian flag was in ashes. Modo could hear Griff shouting from some distant place, but the echoes made it hard to be sure of the direction.

"He's gone batty!" Modo said. "He's burning the place down."

They stumbled into the bay and discovered that

thankfully the *Filomena* was still there, its hatch open. The room appeared empty.

"No blood on the floor," Colette observed.

A muffled cry drew Modo's attention. Then several more voices could be heard behind a nearby door. Modo and Colette crept closer and knocked on the metal surface.

"Hello," Modo said. "Who's there?"

"Who's out there?" a young male voice asked.

"Colette Brunet," Colette answered. "And Modo."

"It's Comrade Garay," the young man said. "Let us out! Is Captain Monturiol with you?"

Modo lifted the lever and the door opened. Comrade Garay was bleeding from a cut above his eye, and his right arm was in a sling. Behind him stood the women and children and old men Modo had seen before.

"That—that thing drove us in here," Garay said. "We could not see it, but it broke my arm."

"You are safe for the moment," Modo said. "Come out. Come out."

Modo explained Captain Monturiol's orders for them to flee and what had happened to her and Cerdà as best he could. The Icarians stood stoically as they learned about the death of their captain and Cerdà, and that many of their fellow citizens had gone down with the *Wyvern*.

"There is no time to explain much more," Colette said urgently, taking a child's hand and leading the people to the *Filomena*. All the while, Modo kept his eyes and ears open for any sign of Griff. He and Colette helped the women, children, and elderly into the ship, urging them to press as hard as they could against the sides. Garay was the last to board, grimacing as he bumped his arm.

There was barely room for one more person. "You go," Modo said to Colette. "I'm too big. I'll find another way."

"And let you become the hero of Icaria? Never!"

Modo sighed, exasperated. "Go!" he said to Comrade Garay, not wanting to waste time arguing with Colette. "You know how to control this ship. Travel as swiftly as you can to Iceland."

"We have sympathizers there," Garay said. "They will resupply us."

"Then sail with all haste. If you must surface, do so as far from here as possible. Our enemy may have other ships."

"Thank you," Comrade Garay said. "Thank you both. We will not forget you!"

"Long live Icaria!" Modo exclaimed, a lump coming to his throat.

Comrade Garay saluted as Modo closed the hatch. The *Filomena* slowly moved away from the dock and submerged.

51

A Bell That Doesn't Ring

"Quickly!" Colette pointed down the hallway that led out of the bay. "The fire is getting worse, and I don't know whether we should be more worried about running out of oxygen, or whether this whole place will collapse around us."

They dashed into the main hallway and found water swishing across the marble floor and cascading down the steps. "The walls have been breached," Modo said.

"Not the walls." Griff's voice was jovial. He was in the hallway with them, but Modo saw no sign of his blood. "I let the sea in. I'm invisible, so I can't drown. The sea won't see me! But you two will drown. I'll have the pleasure of watching you bob and writhe and choke. Ta-hee!"

"You'll drown as easily as us."

"Will not! Will not!" His voice was farther away. If he was still bleeding, it was into the water, so they couldn't track it.

"Forget him," Colette said. "There must be another way out."

They splashed frantically down the hall, the water up to their knees. As they dashed through the kitchen, chairs and loaves of seaweed bread floated around them. Modo led them through another hallway and up the wide stairwell carved into bedrock that took them to Icaria's National Museum.

He glanced back. Behind him, down the hallway, he saw bubbling water; he heard only the shattering of glass and the groaning of metal girders. His heart beat with fear, but he also felt a momentary sadness. New Barcelona had been such a beautiful place. The Icarians had worked so hard to create it. And now the ocean was taking it back.

Modo and Colette stumbled into the large oval hall, and Modo remembered Monturiol saying it was the highest point in New Barcelona.

A rowboat hung above them, alongside a model of a trireme, and the miniature *Adelaida*. Modo went to it and opened the hatch. "Well, it's not a working model. Not that we could even fit our heads in there."

Colette pointed to the other side of the great hall. Hanging from the ceiling was the diving bell.

"Do you think it actually works?" he asked as they rushed over. The wood was thick, strengthened and water-proofed by India rubber. All around the circumference of its base, long tethers hung to the floor, a ten-pound weight at the end of each one.

"Monturiol told us it was a functioning model," Colette said. "But it wouldn't be designed for such depths."

The lights in the room flickered. Modo looked down the steps and along the hallway that led to New Barcelona. It was nearly full of water that now bubbled up into the museum. Already the exhibits were floating; a fleet of toy boats drifted by. "We don't have much time. It's the diving bell or death."

"But how do we get it into the ocean?"

Modo looked up at the large porthole in the center of the oval ceiling. "Through there!"

"But that glass is too thick to break."

"We won't have to break it. When the water reaches the ceiling, the pressure will be equal. It's the pressure of the ocean that is holding it in place. I bet I'll be able to push it open."

"We're going to bet our lives on it?"

"We'll have to." The water was up to their hips now and Modo felt himself being driven off his feet by the currents. The bell was already floating, the weights holding its bottom edge in the water, trapping a pocket of air. They stole under its lip and were suddenly in the dark. There was enough room for both of them and more—the bell being at least six feet across. Already his feet couldn't touch the floor, and Modo had to tread water to stay with the rising bell. He felt around above him and discovered several handles at the top. "Grab hold," he shouted.

"There! Got one!" Colette shouted back. "How much oxygen is in here?"

Before he could guess, Modo heard clicking above them as the bell butted up against the roof. "I'm going to see what I can do." He dove under the edge of the bell, kicking, amazed that a few of the lights of New Barcelona were still working.

The museum was now full of water and they were directly below the large porthole. Modo slammed the edge with his fist, the action forcing him down. He kicked his way back and hit it again and the glass moved! The top of the bell was knocking up against the porthole. It needed to float higher, faster. The glass began lifting away from the building.

Modo swam back under the bell. "Colette?" She didn't answer. His eyes were slow to adjust to the dark. "Colette?"

A barking cough. "I'd rather be back on the surface," Griff said, landing a blow right on the bridge of Modo's nose. It knocked him under the water. He sank enough to find Colette tangled on the tethers below, her eyes wide and her mouth gaping. He kicked his way to her, yanked at the ropes, and tugged her up into the bell. They gasped for air, splashing all about, and swinging their fists and yelling. Twice they hit each other, but they couldn't find Griff.

He heard the bell bang hard against the glass and felt it rising. "Quick! Grab the handles!" he yelled. She did so and all of a sudden Modo felt the pressure on his chest and legs. He unhooked several of the tethers, letting the weights fall away. The bell gained speed. Modo imagined that they looked like a jellyfish, their legs and the remaining tethers dangling as they rose.

Something grabbed his hand and slipped away, then latched on to his shirt.

Then Griff's voice bubbled nearby, "I can't hold on. The tethers are wrapped around my legs! The weights are pulling me down! Modo, help, I—"

Modo hesitated. Help him? He thought of Tharpa and all the hours of training and strategy. *Unless you have complete control of your enemy, do not release him. A dead enemy cannot strike back.* This was a battlefield, and Griff would murder both Modo and Colette in a heartbeat.

"Is Griff still here?" Colette shouted.

"Yes. But he's drowning. The weights are pulling him down."

"Good!"

A hand grasped at Modo's belt. He thought of kicking Griff away, but didn't. Face to face, fist to fist, he believed he could kill an opponent. But he couldn't do it like this! What would Mrs. Finchley think? He couldn't leave anyone—even an enemy—to die. Even though he nearly lost his grip, Modo grabbed for Griff with one hand. He caught only a fistful of water. He reached down for the arms that were now around his legs. Briefly he felt fingers, a hand in his; then it slipped away. He took a deep breath and stuck his head under the water. The lights of New Barcelona were already far below them.

He glimpsed an odd sinking shape perhaps thirty feet below them, caught in the tethers. It was yellow, twisting, writhing and expelling bubbles. It soon stopped moving as the bell shot upward.

52

On the Surface

The bell broke the surface with such speed that it flipped over and Modo and Colette were tossed into the air. Modo briefly saw the moon, then fell back into the water, fighting to breathe and stay afloat. It was several moments before, blinking hard, he was able to kick his way over to the upside-down bell. When he grabbed its side, he was relieved to find Colette already hanging on its edge.

They helped each other into the bell, then leaned back, breathing heavily. The moon looked down at them. They shivered and were silent for a time. Modo was just happy to let the air restore his body. Happy to be on the surface! He had more aches than he could count; he was cramping, especially his stomach muscles. Was this what they called diver's sickness? He pulled the sopping neckerchief over his lips, but left his nose uncovered. He could only see Colette's eyes and the slight outline of her nose and cheeks.

"Is Griff dead?" Colette said finally.

"He was caught up in the tethers and drowned."

"Bonnes nouvelles," she said, though she didn't sound smug.

Modo felt something like sorrow. Griff had been driven mad by being invisible. What might he have become if he'd been allowed to have a normal life?

Time passed. Modo slept, despite the cold. The sun was beginning to rise. Colette stirred, opened her eyes. "Any news from the crow's nest?" she asked.

He lifted himself high enough to look over the edge of the bell. "No rescue ships."

"Captain Monturiol's penchant for ramming ships has chased all the sea traffic away."

Thinking of Monturiol and Cerdà made Modo's heart ache. "At least the Clockwork Guild are gone."

"Yes, they won't pick us up again," Colette said. "That woman, what was her name?"

"Hakkandottir."

"I won't soon forget her. She would have torn our hearts out with that metal hand."

"Yes. She would have." Modo couldn't help hoping she had gone down with the *Wyvern.*

"You look hunched, are you in pain? And your rash is getting worse," Colette said.

"Yes, maybe." Modo felt his face shifting, his body elongating as he got warmer. He'd thought the burning sensation in his body was just exhaustion. He poked two holes in his neckerchief and pulled it up over his face.

"This rash, this sickness, what is it?" Colette asked.

"I've always had it."

"And yet you could manipulate your face so you looked like that soldier?"

"Yes."

"So the face you've been showing me is not your real face? The one that lies behind the neckerchief is the face you were born with."

"Yes."

She sat back and closed her eyes. He was happy for that; maybe she wouldn't see that he was growing more hunched, stretching his India rubber suit. It was constricting, but didn't seem to be cutting off his blood flow. If only there were something around large enough to cover his whole body.

An hour passed, or more. Modo had difficulty measuring time. The winter sun warmed them only slightly.

Colette still lay with her eyes closed, though he couldn't tell if she was asleep.

Without opening her eyes, she spoke. "They used to tease me at the academy. The other agents hated me. I am an *ainoko*—half Japanese and half French, accepted by neither. I felt like a monster at times."

You have no idea what it's like to be a monster, Modo wanted to say. But instead he said, "That must have been terrible."

"It was. But it made me stronger. I believe that I understand some of what you feel. We have lived and nearly died together, Modo. I consider you to be my friend. I don't know why you would be frightened to show me your face."

"I'm not frightened. It's a choice I've made."

"I kissed you, Modo. Now, reveal your true face. I dare you."

"It's not a game."

"I never play games."

Only a few short months ago he had refused Octavia this same request, and his heart still ached when he remembered her reaction. Colette had saved him, had fought side by side with him. What would it hurt? She wanted to see him. To know him.

He hadn't the strength to create another face.

"I—I am disfigured. Horribly. I warn you."

"Modo, I'm not a child."

He breathed in, the air whistling through his flattened nostrils. Slowly he pulled the neckerchief away.

Colette stared directly into Modo's eyes; then her eyes wandered over his face. He could see that she was fighting to keep her expression impassive. She was forged in fire, made of steel, yet he saw revulsion rising inside her. She grimaced and looked away, then squeezed her eyes shut. "Please cover your face," she whispered. "Please."

He did.

"I am sorry," she said after several minutes. "I thought I was stronger than that. I have let you down."

"It's the way I am, that's all."

They floated along and Modo slept on and off. The sun was too far away to warm them. Colette shivered, but he knew she would not want him to hold her.

Despite being cold, he wanted to drink from the ocean, but he knew that would only quicken his death. " 'Water,

water, everywhere,' " he whispered hoarsely. " 'Nor any drop to drink.' "

"I suppose that's one of your British poets," Colette said. They were the first words she had spoken since he'd revealed his face. "Poetry cannot be written in English."

Modo did not have the strength to defend Britain or its poetry. He looked to the horizon. The world became four things: the sky, the water, the sun, and the cold. Where would the currents take them? As he watched Colette close her eyes and drift off, he wondered how long they could last without water. His throat was a parched tunnel.

He slept. Awoke. Slept. He dreamed about sweet biscuits. In the distance someone called his name—Mrs. Finchley calling him to dinner. There was always a pitcher of lemonade.

But it wasn't her voice. Still, it was familiar. A shadow fell across the diving bell. "Ho there! Ho there!" a woman shouted.

Modo blinked. A fisherman's boat, sails flapping, sat a distance away. But right next to them was a rowboat with two bearded men at the oars. Standing at the stern, like a figurehead, was a young woman.

"Is that you behind that neckerchief, Modo?" Octavia said. "I've come to take you home."

53

A Fellow Agent

"Is Modo well?"

Octavia looked across the boardinghouse table at the woman who had spoken. When they'd found Modo she hadn't recognized the French agent, but on the return voyage to Reykjavik, Modo had said her name repeatedly and Octavia had drawn her own conclusions. Many conclusions.

"You mean Mr. Warkin?" Octavia said with a raised eyebrow.

"No. I mean Modo. He told me his real name. In confidence."

"Hmm. He's well. No thanks to you."

Colette calmly sipped her tea. Octavia remembered that Colette was three years older than her and had done much with her life. She had an intensity in her eyes that even Octavia found disconcerting.

"You are protective of Modo," Colette said. "I understand your hostility."

"He's a fellow agent."

"You English are such poor actors."

What was that supposed to mean? Octavia wondered. "If I were a doctor, I might say he is suffering from extreme exhaustion."

"He did many brave things," Colette replied casually. "He is a remarkable and gifted individual. And he spoke highly of you."

"Of me?"

"Yes, he said you two were married. A ruse, I know, but he often mentioned his wife. He worried about you. Did not want to be parted from you."

"He said that?" Why did Octavia feel a blush coming on? Her eyes were drawn to her wedding ring.

"Yes, he did."

Octavia looked up, steely. Whatever her thoughts toward Modo, this Frenchwoman wasn't going to know them. "We were acting. I am certain an expert agent like you has been 'married' numerous times."

Colette shook her head. "I've never gone that route, myself. I work better alone."

"No one wants to work with you?" Octavia asked.

"Ah, such naked hostility. I understand it."

Hostility? Octavia wanted to shout. I have spent every last waking moment searching the high seas, begging a one-legged drunken fisherman for passage, only to find Modo with *you* in a diving bell. Octavia cleared her throat. "I just don't trust the French."

"And I don't trust the English. Modo, though . . ." Colette paused. "I do trust him." She stood. "I do not think we can accomplish much more. This tête-à-tête has come to an end. Though I must ask a favor."

"Which is?"

"Would you give this to Modo?" Colette produced a folded note from a pocket in her dress. Octavia did not reach for it, let her hold it out in the air.

"You don't want to give it to him yourself?"

She was surprised that Colette seemed a little shaken. "Have you ever seen his face? His true face?"

"No. Have you?"

"Well, that is—how shall I put it?—a matter of confidentiality."

Did he show it to you willingly? Octavia wanted to ask, but she bit her tongue instead.

"Please take the note," Colette said. "I must go and find out when my ship leaves."

Octavia closed her fingers around the paper. "Good day, then," she said. "Good luck."

"Yes, *bonne chance* to you and to Modo." Colette gave her a slight smile. "*Adieu.*"

The Assignment Ends

FROM HIS BED ON THE THIRD FLOOR of the boardinghouse, Modo could watch the fishing and whaling ships and the occasional steamer come in, but mostly he spent his time reading, and recovering, wearing a mask he'd made from a pillowcase. The water brought back so many memories, and he couldn't yet come to terms with what had happened to Captain Monturiol, Cerdà, or Icaria. It was just too painful to think of their sacrifices for a country that no longer existed.

No, that wasn't quite true. There were the survivors on the *Filomena*. They would still have Icaria in their hearts. He hoped they had landed safely with their sympathizers. However, Garay had said they intended to resupply. Where would they go next?

There was a knock at the door. Before he could answer, it swung open. "I am eternally looking after you." Octavia entered the room, holding a lunch plate. She set it down next to him, and Modo sat up to see lamb, cabbage, and rye crêpes. "As per your request. Lamb is expensive here, but you deserve it."

"Ah, you are a dear soul," Modo said. He still felt as though he hadn't eaten for weeks. He took a moment to straighten his lips and teeth, then lifted the bottom portion of his mask and forked half of a crêpe into his mouth.

Octavia had seated herself across from him and poured them tea. She seemed smartly pleased with herself. In fact, if he hadn't known better, Modo would have said she was enjoying looking after him. She had explained that after the *Hugo* had been attacked, they had docked in Reykjavik, and she had been searching for him ever since.

"You're looking stronger."

"Only thanks to you," he said. "Who would have known that you could be such a nurse?"

"Ah, I play so many parts. And I do have new information. Fishermen found a few of the Icarians in lifeboats."

"How many?"

"Twelve."

His heart sank. "There were more than twenty locked up on the *Wyvern*. The rest must have perished."

Octavia nodded. "Apparently there weren't enough lifeboats and they drew lots for their places. A very organized and brave group." She sipped her tea. "But that's not all, Modo. The survivors have disappeared."

"Disappeared?"

"Yes, they were locked in one of the government buildings. The Icelanders weren't too happy about all the ships they'd sunk. But they vanished overnight. They must have sympathizers here. A secret cell."

"They were from every country," Modo said.

"Are they a group we should be wary of?"

Modo shrugged. "I believe they just want to be left in peace."

"Well, they're gone now. Mr. Socrates will not be pleased. I'm certain he would have wanted to interview them."

Modo was glad that the Icarians had escaped. From both the British and the French. "Any sign of the *Wyvern*?"

"Fishermen found only bodies of Guild soldiers. It's as if they preferred death over being captured."

Somehow that didn't surprise Modo. "And Mr. Socrates? Any orders from him?"

"He's coming to deliver his orders himself, though it'll be tomorrow before he arrives and his inquisition begins. My brief explanations of what you saw and what happened are not enough! He'll want his goods straight from the horse's mouth, so to speak. He did ask about your health. Since when has he been concerned about an agent's health?"

"Perhaps I am his favorite," Modo said, then laughed. When he was done laughing, he asked, "And what of Colette?"

"Why are you asking about her?"

"I only wonder how she is. Is she up and around?"

"Actually, she left for France this morning. I had tea with her last night, though. She gave me a few details about your adventures together. And this."

She handed a note to Modo, but he just held it.

"Aren't you going to open it?" she asked.

Modo shrugged, then unfolded the note carefully. It read:

> *Modo,*
>
> *I am weaker than I want to be, and that shames me. One day I will be strong enough to greet you as you deserve. Ignore my reaction. Remember, you are more than your appearance.*
>
> *With great admiration and gratitude,*
> *Colette*

He folded it up. She couldn't look at me again, he thought. Not even to say goodbye.

Octavia studied him. "Did she curse you and England?"

"No."

"Ah, we are better off without her," Octavia said. "She seemed a bit of a harpy. And her accent was so provincial."

"Provincial? It was Parisian."

"I know. I just wanted to see if you would defend her."

Modo chose that moment to eat a little more of the food she'd brought.

"And what now?" he asked finally.

"I'm hoping you'll be well enough this evening to walk about the town with me. Once You-Know-Who gets here we'll be drilled with questions, questions, questions. Perhaps we can go out to eat. They have scrumptious fish here."

Modo closed his eyes. "Tavia, I don't care if I ever, ever eat fish again."

ARTHUR SLADE has published several novels for young readers, including *The Hunchback Assignments*; *Jolted: Newton Starker's Rules for Survival*; *Megiddo's Shadow*; *Tribes*; and *Dust*, which won the Governor General's Literary Award for Children's Literature. He lives in Saskatoon, Saskatchewan, with his wife, Brenda Baker. Visit him on the Web at www.arthurslade.com.